BLAIR DENHOLM

TRICK SHOT

VINCI
BOOKS

By Blair Denholm

The Fighting Detective

Vinci Books

vinci-books.com

Published by Vinci Books Ltd in 2026

1

The publisher and the author have made every effort to obtain permissions for any third party material used in this book and to comply with copyright law. Any queries in this respect should be brought to the attention of the publisher and any omissions will be corrected in future editions.

A CIP catalogue record for this book is available from the British Library.

Paperback ISBN: 9781036708252

The EU GPSR authorised representative is Logos Europe, 9 rue Nicolas Poussion, 17000 La Rochelle, France

contact@logoseurope.eu

When you come to a fork in the road, take it.

Yogi Berra

Chapter One

HOW HAD he ended up here, sitting on the cold floor of his own kitchen, a throbbing neckache and legs splayed out in front of him? It was absurd.

Then came a flicker of memory. A tap on the door, a late-night visitor.

He remembered a conversation that rapidly descended into a slanging match. Insults, pushing, poking, prodding.

He must have lost his balance, slipped on the tiles. He blinked hard, the scene before him wobbled like a mirage. He reached behind his head, grabbed the handle of a drawer, tried to pull himself up. The effort was excruciating. He got halfway there, buckled at the knees. Heart pounding, he regripped with shaky fingers, pulled himself to an unsteady standing position.

He reached behind his head and rubbed the back of his neck. Had he collected the edge of the bench on the way down? He ratcheted his head up from his chest, click-click-click went his neck bones. He squinted, tried to focus, but the room swam before his eyes. Was that a table, a chair? And that…what the fuck is that?

Christ, the man's still here, breathing in and out like a bellows. Blazing red eyes glared. The figure shuffled forward until it was inches away. Spittle formed on his lips and the corners of his mouth. The man's fists hung low, clenched by his sides, his chest puffed out.

'Wait!' And then it came back, he remembered the cause of the argument. *Shit, shit, shit. This was bad, real bad.* 'I promised to do as you asked. Enough now, mate.'

'I'll say when it's enough. I'm not done with you yet, you son of a bitch.'

'Listen.' The man clearly wasn't planning to end the encounter with words. *Stall, negotiate a way out.* 'How about a drink?'

'Fuck you.' A hand darted out, squeezed a pressure point on the collarbone. Like the bite of a high-voltage taser, it sent him crumpling to his knees again.

'What else could you possibly want?' he whimpered.

'This for a start.' The man lunged at the silver chain. *No, you're not having that!* He parried with his left hand, grabbed the man's wrist as it made a second attempt to seize the necklace.

So much for defusing the situation. He'd only managed to infuriate the man. A forearm quickly reached behind his neck and deployed a crushing headlock. A bolt of pain arced along his spinal cord as the man hoisted him up. A vicious double knee to the groin followed. He let out a strangled wail, his mouth pressed tighter against the man's ribcage as the restraining hold intensified. *Do something now or he'll kill you!*

His hand flailed behind his back, patted the bench top. An object to use as a weapon, a knife would be perfect, but anything solid would do. Fingers twitching, he located the handle of the glass coffee pot. *Yes.* He grasped the handle tight, swung blindly over his right shoulder.

The man let go and screamed at the same time. 'You bastard, you've cut me!'

Escape, run to the basement, bolt the door. He had his mobile in his pocket, he'd call the police, file charges. *Fuck him and his threats.* Tiny shards of glass crunched under his flip-flops as he staggered out and headed down the corridor. The man was only two metres behind, lumbering and yelling. 'You cut me, you cut me!'

A wonder the dog hadn't started barking. Why did he put her outside? She could be defending him right now. *Get to the basement.*

'You coward!' the man screamed. 'Get back here.'

He flew down the stairs, heart beating out of his chest. The man was gaining ground with every step. At the bottom now, turn the handle, open and in. Shove with your shoulder, close the steel door and lock it.

No! The man's foot was wedged in the door. He shoved back, but the man was pushing too. Resistance was futile, the man was too strong. He fell backwards, sprawled on the ground as the man clanked the door shut, turned to face him.

'Listen!' he cried. 'I-I-I know we can work this out.'

The man said nothing, grabbed him by the collar and dragged him across the carpet tiles, past the pool table towards the bar. He kicked his feet wildly, tried to free himself from the man's grip, grabbed at the thick legs of the pool table. Useless, ineffectual efforts. It was like the visitor was possessed of some unearthly strength.

The man wasn't getting the locket, though. He tore it

from its chain and stashed the memento deep inside his pants pocket.

Looking down, the enraged man breathed like a steam-train, mumbled something under his breath.

Why are you doing this now? Is it drugs? he wanted to ask the man, but no words came out.

A boot crashed into his ribcage. Then another brutal kick. He tucked a hand deep into his pocket, curled fingers as tightly as he could around the locket. He closed his eyes tight and prayed to God. *Please make it stop. I promise to do what he told me.*

God wasn't listening. Then came the worst pain he'd ever felt, like a drill boring a hole through the top of his skull.

A dark fog descended and drew his eyelids closed. The pain was gone. God had come to the rescue.

Forever and ever.

Amen.

Chapter Two

'GOT ALL those files in order yet, Constable Wilson?' barked Detective Sergeant Jack Lisbon of the Yorkville Criminal Investigation Branch.

'Sorry, sir?' The uniformed officer straightened, his hands recoiling from the edge of his superior's desk.

'I said, have you sorted my case files into order?' Jack arched his back as he spoke, pushed a fist into the lower part of his spine. The boxing session at McGrath's gym last night proved much harder than he'd expected. His sparring partner was Jordan Batista, son of Yorkville Police's boss, Inspector Joe Batista. Now Jack was paying the price for taking the kid lightly. Jordan, newly signed swing forward for the Yorkville Scorpions Basketball franchise, had landed nearly as many punches as he'd worn during a fifteen-minute sparring session. The height difference meant Jack had to constantly look up at the taller man. Muscles in his shoulders and neck screamed for a vigorous massage, his ribs ached where Jordan had landed half a dozen telling rips.

'What kind of order?' Wilson stared at the jumble of folders and papers almost completely obscuring the desktop.

The lad was too literal. Couldn't tell when Jack was taking the mickey out of him. 'Any effing order you like, sunshine, I don't care. I'm off to London tomorrow to visit my daughter.' He hadn't seen Skye in four years, not counting online chats and telephone facetime. The only downside of the trip, he'd have to deal with Sarah, his volatile ex-wife. *Every silver lining has a cloud.*

'I don't want to be rude, DS Lisbon, but–'

'Listen, Wilson. I'm only going to be gone for three weeks. What you see here on my desk, well, it's a mess and I ain't too proud of it.' Jack tapped the constable smack in the middle of his name badge. 'But I know you've got this analytical mind. I've seen you smash out those Sudoku puzzles quicker than I can land a combination punch.' Jack shadow-boxed a jab-cross-hook-cross medley around the man's ears.

'Oi!' Wilson staggered backwards before recovering his balance. 'Careful, sir.'

'Keep your dukes up when someone comes at you.' Jack grinned, holstered his fists in his trouser pockets. 'A good cop's gotta be alert for trouble at all times.'

Detective Constable Claudia Taylor put down a psychological profile report she'd spent the entire morning trying to decipher. 'Stop it, Jack.' She failed to repress a smile. 'He's got his work cut out for him sorting your chaos. You cause a workplace injury on the eve of your trip and Batista won't let you go.'

'It's OK,' Wilson laughed. 'I'm getting used to DS Lisbon's antics.'

'Seriously though, sunshine,' said Jack. 'You'll be OK. There's not much happening in the old town at the moment. What you see before you,' an expansive wave of the hand, 'needs to be cross-referenced with the computer files. It's mainly minor stuff, complaints about noisy parties, unfenced dogs on the loose, traffic infringements, that kind of thing.'

'Detectives don't issue traffic notices.' Wilson's eyebrows bobbed up and down.

'Not as a rule, Ben, no' said Taylor. 'But if we see a car speeding we aren't just going to watch it disappear around the corner. We've got the same powers as uniformed police.''

'Yeah, I know that.' Wilson, chastened, dropped his gaze.

'See, Claudia. The lad's got this thing covered.' Jack walked towards the water cooler, fat bubbles rose and popped as he filled a plastic cup. 'With his grasp of the bleedin' obvious, I'm completely confident in his abilities to assist in my absence.'

'Don't listen to him, Ben,' said Taylor, shaking her head. 'With the DS out of the office for three weeks, we might even make a dent in the backlog. Jack prefers the limelight of sensational crimes. Humble burglary victims get pushed to the back of the queue.'

'Leave off, Claudia. I don't make those decisions. Batista tells us what cases to work.'

'Sure he does.' She readjusted her scrunchie with a deft twist, picked up the file and went back to studying its contents.

Jack knew he was being disingenuous. Batista had rewarded the DS's victories in recent high-profile cases with more autonomy. Yorkville's crime rates were low compared to the state average, so most detective work revolved around routine matters. Break and enters, car theft, drunk and disorderly, petty drug offences. Uniforms were quite capable of handling the bulk of that stuff. But when the occasional serious crime demanded a different skill set, only Lisbon and Taylor could get the job done. For Jack's brief sojourn back in the Old Dart, Batista decreed Wilson was now experienced enough to help Taylor with any investigations and, in the quieter moments, restore order to Jack's chaotic filing "system".

'Come on, DS Lisbon,' Wilson implored. 'Where do I start with this…stuff?'

Classic 80s punk music split the air. "London Calling" by the Clash was Jack's ring tone. The other officers at Yorkville CIB hated it. Jack didn't give a monkey's. Nevertheless, a vote was held and the majority pleaded he change it to something else. As someone who respects the democratic process, he did change it. To Rick Astley's "Never Gonna Give You Up". The officers quickly demanded he change it back again.

Jack held up an index finger to end the conversation in the office. 'Yeah, wot?'

'Ray Hook.' It was the Assistant Commissioner of Police for Far North Queensland. Another rung above Batista in the Queensland Police Service hierarchy. A framed certificate bearing Hook's signature hung on the wall beside Jack's corner desk. In recognition of the detective's sterling work in collaring the killer of an MMA trainer and two pro fighters. Unfortunately, the one and only meeting between Jack and Hook had ended acrimoniously. At the award ceremony in his honour, Jack made a flippant remark about a woman he saw in tatty jeans. *How could she wear that to an official function?* Then he commented unfavourably on her silicone-injected lips and dodgy facelift. The woman in question was Hook's wife Juanita, in her late fifties but trying desperately to appear younger. Jack tried to cover his tracks with a joke, but only managed to inflame the situation. The Assistant Commissioner's face turned florid as he told Jack he didn't give a toss about his heroic crime-busting feats and that he could "fuck off". Hook would be closely monitoring the detective's performance. One step out of line and Jack would be back in uniform pounding the pavement on permanent night shift.

'How can I help you, sir?' Remain professional. That last meeting was an eternity ago. The man has surely forgotten Jack's faux pas.

'Are you alone?'

Jack covered the mobile with his palm, glanced at Taylor and Wilson. 'Sorry, gotta take this one in private.' He placed his phone on his desk, plucked a packet of Nicorettes from the top drawer, regripped the phone and marched to the small landing where the smokers indulged their habit. Jack had long given up the lung busters, now he was addicted to nicotine gum instead. He'd tried vaping as an alternative but found the practice totally naff. On the landing, he chased away Constable Xavier "Breath" Jenkins, an inveterate smoker puffing away on a low-tar ciggie. Any other time he'd engage the uniform in a chat just to savour the free second-hand smoke. Not today. 'Piss off, Jenkins.' The officer dropped a third of a smouldering cigarette in a water-filled tin and slunk back into the cool interior of the police station. Jack glanced at the filthy orange slurry in the tin and shuddered. Gum. Mouth. Chew.

'I'm alone now. At your service.'

'I require your help with something.' Hook's voice was gravel in a cement mixer.

'Yes, sir.' Jack's brain spun like a kaleidoscope. *What does he want?*

'I need you to oversee a delicate matter. Something's happened a bit too close to home and I want you in charge.'

'I'd be delighted to assist, sir,' Jack lied. 'Only I'm flying out of Cairns International Airport tomorrow night. Heading home after all these years.'

'Cancel it.'

'Sorry, sir. No can do. All the paper work's approved.' *Who the fuck does this joker think he is?* 'It's a non-refundable ticket.'

'What do you mean? Who the hell buys non-refundable tickets?'

Jack scratched his head as a Qantas passenger jet soared into a cloudless azure sky about 25 kms distant. 'Ah, most people, actually. They're a shit-load cheaper.' He'd be enjoying an English summer when he got home, which would, strangely, be colder than winter in tropical Yorkville. But this moron wasn't going to spoil the party, no matter his rank.

There was a brief uncomfortable pause. The overweight Hook's laboured breathing made Jack wince. It sounded like the wet snuffling of one of those flat-faced dog breeds with a genetic respiratory ailment. 'This is very important,' Hook finally rasped.

'So is visiting my daughter 'n all.'

'Listen, Lisbon. I haven't forgotten what you said about my wife.'

'How about you say something nasty about my ex. Then we'll be even.' Jack waved at Constables Trevarthen and Semmens escorting a heavily tattooed, green-haired woman who could barely stand into the reception area. He glanced at his watch. A bit early in the day for getting wasted. If Hook continued in this vein Jack might renege on his pledge of sobriety and join the woman in the holding cell for a shot of brandy.

'That's not going to cut it. I heard you hate your ex.' Hook was well informed, you had to say that much for the obese bastard.

'Yeah. But I love my daughter. I'm afraid you'll have to get someone else to do your dirty work. Good-bye.' Jack ended the call and took a deep breath. His oversized suitcase was packed. One change of clothes for him, the rest – presents for Skye. The taxi was ordered, everything was done. Hook wasn't going to derail this trip. Jack pulled his phone out of his pocket, went to switch to vibrate, when The Clash's driving guitar intro burst forth. *Press the red button!* Against his better judgment, Jack pressed the green button. Call it professional curiosity.

'Listen to me, Lisbon.' Hook couldn't keep the worry out of his voice. *What on earth could he have done?* 'I'll personally make up the difference with any money you lose on rescheduling your flight.'

'I told you, I'm not delaying this trip.' Jack wanted to scream at the fool. Somehow, he controlled his temper, spoke at a conversational level. 'Sarah will have my guts for garters. She's already nominated me for worst father in the history of the world, fills Skye's head with bullshit about me. If I don't show, the kid'll hate me for the rest of my life.'

'If you can get this sorted for me in, say, five days, I'll upgrade your flight to business class.'

'First class. Whether I get it "sorted", as you put it, or not.' One of Jack's favourite mottos was: *You don't ask, you don't get.* The chances of "getting" were especially high when dealing with desperate policemen in the top brass. They had more to lose.

'All right, then. First class, fuck you, Lisbon.'

'Steady on, sir. No need for profanity.'

'I'm stressed.'

'You'll be even more stressed when I ask for something else.'

'What?'

'Tell Batista to grant me another week off because you need my help so badly. That'll round my holiday off to a month. Also, I want a signed letter I can show Sarah saying *you* held me back from travelling and that I had no choice in the matter. Speaking of which, you haven't mentioned what's going on, sunshine.'

The huffing and puffing on the other end of the line grew more ragged. The fat toad's going to have a coronary. Jack thought he heard the sound of a long, frantic inhalation on an asthma puffer. Gradually Hook brought his breathing under control. 'I want you as my man on the ground, so to speak. Here's what I need you to do...'

Chapter Three

'WHAT THE…?' The coffee cup stopped halfway to Taylor's mouth. 'You're still here in Yorkville? I thought you'd be 30,000 feet in the air by now. What the hell happened?'

'Don't ask.' Jack tossed his jacket over the back of his chair. 'Last-minute stuff up with the booking.' He hated lying to Taylor. Once the case was concluded, he'd tell her the truth.

'Isn't there anything you can do?'

'It was a double booking. Happens a lot, they tell me. The airlines anticipate a percentage of people are going to cancel and they don't wanna be left with empty seats flying all the way to Europe. So they sell tickets for more seats than there are on the plane.'

'Ridiculous. Imagine if restaurants did that. Is it even legal?'

Jack nodded. 'Apparently it is. It's got me stymied how they get away with it. Anyway, there were no effing cancellations for my flight. I'm not the only one who got bumped, either. Another ten people have to make different arrangements.' The mini head shakes from Taylor as he relayed his tale of woe proved the invented extra details were painting a credible picture.

'Didn't you tell them at the call centre you were a famous crime-fighting hero?'

'Very droll. Apparently they've never heard of me in India. Go figure.'

'You getting your money back?'

Jack flashed her a broad grin. 'I'm not just a heavy hitter in the ring, Claudia. I made them give me an upgrade. First class, if you please.'

'Now I'm confused. I thought you said you weren't going?'

'I never said that. I am. But not for another five days. There's no openings in the toffee-nose section until next week.'

'Won't your ex-wife Sarah be—'

'Don't mention her name, please. I'm only going back to see Skye.'

'My apologies.' Taylor switched her gaze to her computer monitor.

Jack glanced at his watch. The call would come soon. In the meantime, he chatted to Wilson on options for organising his old case files. The constable suddenly asked a reasonable question. 'I'm wondering, if you're stuck here for another week and things are quiet, why can't you do this yourself?'

As the cogs whirred in Jack's mind, he was saved by the bell. Literally. The landline phone delivered its old-fashioned ring.

'Excuse me while I get this, Wilson.' Jack removed the handset from its cradle. 'Good morning sir.' A long pause. 'What?' Feigned surprise. 'Are you sure? Right, we're on our way.' Jacket on, snatch car keys, stash Nicorettes in pocket. He'd need them later to mask the bitter flavour of duplicity he'd be tasting in the back of this throat.

———

JACK BIT a fingernail on his left hand as he set the cruise control button to 101 kms per hour with his right. The drive to Hook's office in Cairns would take a little over an hour. The last of the rampaging cyclones and torrential summer rain was behind them, clear autumn weather ahead for the next few months. Bliss. Pity he'd miss a good chunk of it in cold, rainy England.

'What's all this about then, sir?' said Wilson from the back seat. Batista insisted they take the constable along. *For the experience.* Jack would have preferred otherwise, but the lad might prove useful.

'We've been summoned to kneel before the Assistant Commissioner while he briefs us on an urgent matter.'

'Quite the honour. Cairns is a fair way off our patch, though.'

'Yeah, so enjoy the ride. I double-checked with Batista to make sure Hook's on the level. The Inspector has to assume he is. You two are coming along to help me…ah… keep the chap honest.'

'What did Hook say it was about?' said Taylor.

'Nothing. Just that it was important and he wanted me to oversee something.' Jack was finding it easy to deceive Taylor. Too easy. 'He didn't want to say anything to me over the phone and Batista doesn't know anything, or at least he claims not to. This is one of those directives light on the details. As they say in the classics, all will be revealed.'

'For God's sake, Jack. I'm starting to think you're bullshitting me. We don't get our cases assigned by the top brass, there's a chain of command to be observed. Everything gets passed on through Batista. In all my career I've never heard of anything like this.'

'No? Happened a lot back in the UK. I had one case that was two officials removed from Number 10 Downing Street.' Utter bollocks, but she couldn't refute it.

To stifle more questioning, he turned on the Ford Territory's radio. FM modern alternative. The female vocalist's voice sounded like a tone deaf cat being strangled with piano wire. Time to exercise his new love of classical music. A quick station change. He had no idea what it was emanating from the 750 watt speakers in the back, but the heavenly strains of a violin section worked wonders. Taylor and Wilson seemed content to stare out the window and watch fields dense with sugar cane whiz past.

The trio travelled without conversation until they reached the outskirts of a flyspeck town halfway to Cairns. Jack slowed to the mandated 60 kph, cruised by a lonely petrol station guarded by a chained-up blue heeler dog, dozing with one eye open. Then a handful of classic Queenslander timber homes on stumps with wide verandas, the deep green foliage of shrubs highlighted by the cheery pink, white and orange blooms of hibiscus and frangipani. The richness of the landscape's palette in northern Australia never ceased to gladden Jack's cold English heart. Must be his Portuguese genes appreciating the warm tones.

'DS Lisbon.' Wilson couldn't resist breaking the conversational silence. Either that or the music had stopped casting its spell.

'What?'

'Do you have any theories what this might be about?'

'None.'

'I have one. Want to hear it?'

Jack sighed. 'Keep it brief and to the point. I'm starting to get a migraine.'

'I think it might be something to do with the that pool hall owner who's been accused of suspect property deals.' Wilson spoke with confidence, as if he dealt with this subject on a daily basis.

'Let's just wait and see what the Big Kahuna has to say about it.' Jack gritted his teeth as they stopped at a T-junction to let a road train rumble past.

'Who?'

'Hook, you daft git.'

The landscape once again changed, this time to farmland. Another ten minutes of beef cattle grazing in pastures until they abruptly entered a lush, thick-trunked rainforest. The interior of the vehicle darkened as it traversed a section of ancient tall trees, their canopies touching like extended hands about 20 metres above the midpoint of the road. As the car neared the exit of the arboreal tunnel, Taylor looked up from her glowing iPhone. 'Don't be so quick to dismiss Ben's theory. He might be onto something.'

'That'd be a nice change.'

Taylor ignored the sarcasm. 'I found an article on the *Cairns Clarion* website. It's about a guy who's been trying to buy up expensive real estate near the waterfront.' She scrolled for a few seconds. 'He recently purchased the old Pilkington fish processing plant. He's got plans to turn it into a massive games centre.' Taylor looked up from her phone. 'The word "alleged" appears a lot in this article by the way, the paper covering its arse legally I reckon.' She looked back to the screen. 'Anyway, some disappointed developers are asserting there're dodgy dealings afoot. The fish plant is part of a deceased estate and should have gone through probate, but this bloke somehow bought it before it hit the market. Allegedly.'

'You said something about a pool hall?' said Jack, craning his neck towards Wilson.

'Correct.' Taylor blurted before Wilson could reply. 'The pool hall in Cairns is called Chalkies. The owner in question is…hang on…Cameron…'

'Snyder,' chimed in Wilson. 'Nickname "Cueball." On account of his bald head.'

The Ford slowed to a stop at a set of lights. Two more blocks and they'd be at Hook's office. 'And what makes you think us being summonsed to Far North Queensland HQ has anything to do with this Cueball character?' said Jack.

Through the rear vision mirror the DS saw Wilson shrug and smile. 'Because of a connection with Yorkville, maybe?'

Jack quirked an eyebrow. 'And what's that?' His colleagues had nearly hit the bull's eye. Hook told Jack he wanted the DS on board to ensure attention was deflected away from Snyder's affairs. The task somehow involved liaising with the media, but the details were still sketchy. Jack had no idea why Hook was so concerned about the fate of this particular man, and he didn't want to know. He could almost feel the first-class ticket in his hand.

'A relative of mine plays competition pool at a joint called Trick Shot Billiards and Snooker,' said Wilson. 'Oliphant Avenue, downtown Yorkville. The name's misleading, they play everything there, including pool.'

'I don't care if they play bloody croquet on horseback, what's your point?' Pulling the wool over his colleagues' eyes in a charade orchestrated by Hook didn't sit comfortably with Jack. A seat near the pointy end of the plane, however, now that *was* comfortable. *Just play dumb for now. Your colleagues will forgive you later.*

'Snyder owns it as well. My cousin Russell says he's a regular visitor and that Snyder's a right cunt…oh, sorry DC Taylor.' In the rear view mirror Jack watched the constable's face turn crimson.

Peals of laughter in the front seats drowned out the crashing canons of Tchaikovsky's 1812 Overture pouring through the back speakers. Taylor turned at the waist to face Wilson. 'How many times do you think I hear that word every day in the line of duty?'

'I dunno.'

'Plenty. But in this case, you're quoting your cousin, so I won't take offence. Not that I would anyway.'

'Thanks, DC Taylor.'

Jack smirked as he parked the car in a diagonal bay next to the blue-and-white police sign. Cairns District Police Headquarters in Sheridan Street was a three-story boxy construction lacking architectural merit. Functional if not pretty. An important facility painted exactly the same colour sat beside it. Cairns Courthouse.

'You worked in Cairns for a bit last year, didn't you Jack?' said Taylor. 'Know any good places for lunch?'

Taylor's memory was spot on. Jack had appeared before the magistrate ten months ago, testifying as an arresting officer in a joint task-force drugs bust with Cairns CIB. The trial lasted five days and in that time he'd managed to sniff out some reasonable eateries. 'Sure do. It's a bit early to be thinking about that, though, innit? Maybe Hook's gonna treat us to a slap-up feed at a five-star restaurant as a token of his appreciation.'

'You think?' Wilson's eyes sparkled in the rear-vision mirror.

'You never know. Be polite to him, say "yes sir" and "no sir" at the right times and we could be in luck.'

'Yes, sir.'

'Was that a practice run?'

'No, sir.'

Taylor burst out laughing as they slammed the car doors shut and proceeded to Hook's office on the second floor.

———

THE ROLE of Assistant Commissioner for Far North Queensland was a relatively new one, established just two years ago in the rapidly growing region. Hook had been rewarded with a posting to his home city of Cairns after working through the junior executive ranks around the state. His last position was a three-year stint in Brisbane, a special role, something to do with community liaison. In other words, a nice, cushy job. Looking at the man now, Jack could only think of Jabba the Hut in a uniform three sizes too small. How a senior police officer could let himself grow so obese, *and* secure a top executive role in the force, was a real head-scratcher. Old boys' network was the first thing that sprang to mind. Or maybe he was simply a good administrator. Yeah, right.

'Please, take a seat.' Despite the cool ambient temperature of his plush office, silver blobs of sweat beaded on Hook's bloodhound brow. He had a swarthy complexion tempered by the ruddy tones of a seasoned boozer. Nose broad and fleshy, an assortment of moles dotted a protruding chin that resembled an overripe plum.

The furnishings in the 25 square metre room wouldn't have been out of place in a Ritz hotel penthouse. A richly patterned carpet thicker than an unmowed lawn was the first thing that impressed as you entered the office. Then your eyes were drawn to the polished Tasmanian oak conference table that stretched out like a runway. Upon the table sat a pewter coffee set that sparkled under numerous downlights. Soft black leather swivel chairs caressed the body like a Thai masseuse looking for tips. A tall bookshelf loaded with copies of legal books and other weighty tomes rested against a far wall.

Jack shivered as he took it all in. The room was probably this cold to keep the occupant's core temperature at a safe level. Jack was tempted to take the jacket he'd draped over the spine of the chair he was sitting in, put it back on and do up all the buttons. Wilson sat with his arms wrapped around his body, Taylor kept her cotton blazer on.

'Excuse me for a second.' Jack gave in to the temptation, redonned his jacket. 'Seems to be a bit chillier here than Yorkville. Which is odd, considering it's closer to the equator 'n all.'

'Very humorous, Detective Sergeant Lisbon. If you want the aircon turned down, just ask.'

'Can I–'

'No!' Hook leered like a Bond villain. 'Just kidding, DS Lisbon.' He pushed a button and a fresh-faced constable appeared at the door, face flushed and eyes bulging.

'Yes, sir?' Her timorous voice was barely audible.

'Would you mind adjusting the air conditioning a tad? One of our guests is feeling cold.'

The woman grabbed a remote and with trembling hands pressed a button or two. 'Oh, sorry, I forgot to ask what temperature you'd like.'

'Maybe two or three degrees warmer.' Jack wished he'd kept his mouth closed and spared the poor woman the indignity of Jabba's bullying.

She offered a feeble smile, turned to leave, but she wasn't getting away that easily. 'Would you please pour us all a coffee before you go?' said Hook.

'I'm good,' said Jack. He could have murdered a nun for a strong Brazilian brew right now, but fuck Hook. Jack glared at his companions.

'Me too,' said Taylor and Wilson together. Subliminal message received.

Doing this prick a favour was starting to seem like a bad idea to Jack. *Never again.*

'OK, thank you Constable Tinsdale,' said Hook with condescending alacrity. 'Back to your desk now.'

The urge to belt Jabba a series of hefty blows was a hard one to resist. If not for his superior rank, Hook's blood would be spilling over the desk and onto the fancy carpet.

Hook tugged gently on his flappy bottom lip. 'I'm pleased you brought the other officers along, Lisbon. It'll make the job easier. Now,' he made a throat-clearing cough in his ham-sized fist, white and soft from a career of deskwork and, Jack surmised, little physical toil. 'Let me briefly explain what's going on. I'm not sure if you're aware of certain allegations against a Mr Cameron Snyder being made in the press.'

'Yes,' said Taylor. 'I've seen one story in the *Clarion*.'

'Good, good.' Hook rubbed his hands together. 'That'll save me explaining some of the background.'

'Not entirely,' said Wilson. 'I mean, you've got a bigger police presence in Cairns than we have in Yorkville. Plus this is away from our turf. With all due respect, what's it got to do with us?' He injected a tone of professional curiosity into his question before sinking his teeth into the black cap of a well-chewed ballpoint pen.

'Fair question, Constable' said Hook, nodding understandingly. 'There are two reasons. Indeed, as you rightly point out, resources in Cairns outstrip what you have in Yorkville. However, there's a big event coming up in two weeks' time, the Commonwealth Heads of Government Meeting, or CHOGM as it's better known. Leaders from around the world will be descending on our city and we have to make sure everything runs smoothly. We don't want any nasty…ah…assassinations or other scandals spoiling things for everyone. Most of our available manpower is tied up with that, so…'

'Even the detectives?' said Wilson. Jack wished the lad would keep his mouth shut.

'Yes, Constable. Even them. Basically all non-administrative staff will be on stand-by, many are already seconded to our dedicated CHOGM unit. There are so many…' Hook waved his hands about… 'security implications it's hard to know where to begin. We've had to enlist assistance from Brisbane and Canberra.' Hook dropped his voice to a whisper. 'Even MI6 from the UK.' He reclined into the spine of his creaking chair. 'So you see, the Snyder matter can't fit into our workplan.'

'And what exactly is the Snyder matter?' said Taylor.

'I'm sure the Assistant Commissioner was about to get to that, Claudia.' Jack looked at the ceiling as he spoke. *Lord, make these two shut up, please.*

A calm-down hand motion from Hook. 'It's OK, Detective Sergeant Lisbon. I don't mind them asking questions. Cops lacking curiosity are bad cops. Snyder's been the target of serious but entirely false claims, and it will be your job to fix things. We can't exactly make the allegations go away, what's done is done. But we must be primed to take action should certain parties move against him in a legal sense.'

Wilson shook his head. 'I acknowledge and respect your rank, sir, but why are you taking an interest in a civilian who, as far as I'm aware, is nothing but a dodgy pool hall operator. My cousin Russell called him a right cu– .... I mean a person of bad character.'

'Bear with me, Constable Wilson.' Hook gazed at Wilson like a benevolent uncle. 'I hadn't got to the second reason I asked for your help. Although Snyder's biggest enterprise is in Cairns, he also operates out of Yorkville. In fact, he lives in your fair city.' Hook stopped to drink half a litre of water in one gulp and wipe his dripping forehead. 'I can't go into the nitty-gritty because there are serious security implications involved. Despite what your cousin told you, Mr Snyder is of immense importance.' Hook tapped the side of his bulbous nose. 'All I can say is this. Homeland Security.'

'Aha,' said Wilson. 'That makes sense...but hang on. Isn't–'

'We understand certain situations must be handled on a need-to-know basis.' Jack realised he had to take control of the conversation. He cast a stern glare at Taylor and Wilson. 'And we are honoured that someone in your position would feel confident in entrusting us with this special task.'

'Only fitting, DS Lisbon. You and your team have cracked some serious cases and I rate your skill and professionalism.'

Jack thought the arse-kissing from Hook was a little over the top but nevertheless smiled politely. 'Please, tell us exactly what you want us to do.'

Chapter Four

'SO OUR *SPECIAL* job boils down to what, warning off the press?' Wilson clicked his safety belt into place, wiggled his backside into the seat. 'Big deal!'

'No,' said Jack. 'They are also being asked to print and broadcast retractions about Snyder if they've already published something. To apologise for making unfounded allegations based on rumour alone.'

'They do that every day against other people. How come that's not clamped down on?'

'I don't know, Wilson, do I! Don't get side-tracked from the task. Hook stressed we have to visit the media outlets personally because of the security implications, show 'em we mean business, like. Starting here in Cairns. Rinse and repeat in Yorkville.'

'It's pointless.' Wilson again. 'Media all over the country could be saying stuff about Snyder. Then there's the social networks. The genie's out of the bottle. How are we supposed to stop it all?'

'That's not our concern. We've been given the parameters

of what is, let's be honest, a pretty easy effing job. Plus you've had a day trip to beautiful Cairns. When we're done we can drive up to Kuranda and take pictures of the butterflies and have an ice-cream. So suck it up and let's get this shit over with.'

'Come off it, sir. Snyder's nothing but a small-time petty crook dabbling in some shady real estate deals.'

'Allegedly,' said Taylor.

'Yeah, allegedly, whatever,' said Wilson. 'He's a nobody. I don't get it.'

'Wilson, were you at the same meeting I was? Were you listening, or are your ears painted on?' said Jack, his blood pressure rising by the second. 'The CHOGM meeting is of paramount importance, innit? Somehow, Snyder's got something to do with it.'

'Then why didn't Hook tell us what it is?'

'Above our pay grade, obviously,' offered Taylor. 'We are but humble servants of the people.'

'I'm not arguing that. What I wanna know is, why are three of us required?' Wilson again.

'To get the job done quicker,' Jack snapped. 'There's two local papers, three TV networks and a bunch of radio stations. Claudia, make appointments for the lot of them while we drive around enjoying the sights of the northern capital.'

'How are we going to split it up?' said Claudia.

'Wilson takes the papers, I'll do the TV, you handle the radio.'

'What about lunch?' said Wilson. 'I'm starving. Hook never came good with the wining and dining like you said he would.'

'That's 'cos you wouldn't stop jabbering, you muppet. We'll stop for a bite on the way back to Yorkville. Now kindly refrain from interrupting while Claudia makes the calls.'

After Claudia finished confirming the appointments, Jack set the car's GPS for the *Cairns Clarion*. Drop Wilson off first, continue on to 99.8 FM. After that, Jack would visit TV station Channel 4 and read them the Riot Act. *Don't say anything about Cameron Snyder or you'll be shut down!* It was all bullshit. Hook mentioning "Homeland Security" should have rung alarm bells for Taylor and Wilson, because there was no such agency in Australia. Luckily it flew over their heads. Hook must have been watching too many American TV shows.

Twenty minutes later, they'd arrived at the first port of call. 'What's the plan for when we get back home?' Wilson stood on the pavement next to the three-storey glass-and-chrome *Clarion* headquarters. 'Rock-paper-scissors who gets Holly Maguire?' He smoothed back his hair and donned his police hat.

'Nice try, Wilson.' Jack noisily mashed a wad of nicotine gum between jaws tired from constant clenching during the meeting with Hook. 'You're getting her because we both outrank you.'

'C'mon, sir. She's a nightmare.'

'Listen, you handled Jabba pretty good back there. Maguire'll be a piece of cake.'

'But sir, she's—'

'Enough! Let's get this settled now so I don't have to listen to Wilson whining later. I'll take Maguire, you can have Peroni at Channel 5, and Taylor, you take the *Times*. Go straight to the editor, no one under her.'

'Roger that.' Taylor looked up from her mobile phone. 'This CHOGM meeting's actually a big deal, Jack. Thousands of delegates, top-notch security. They're focusing on climate change this year.'

Jack stifled a yawn. 'Reckon they could work out a way to turn down the furnace here over summer? I'd be eternally grateful.' He patted the envelope in his pocket. The printout of his upgraded status to first class and the even more valuable signed letter from Hook that he'd show Sarah. *See, I was forced to delay my trip!*

Just as Wilson turned to walk to the newspaper's front entrance, the Ford's dash monitor lit up to the accompaniment of a squawking beep. Batista. Jack took the call on loud speaker.

'Yes, boss?'

'Whatever it is you three amigos are up to in Cairns, stop it right away and return to Yorkville.'

'Just as soon as we finish this little job for Assistant Commissioner Hook.'

'Fuck Hook. There's a dead body in the morgue you need to get acquainted with. Lying perfectly still on the slab after losing all his blood.'

'Yeah, we know,' said Jack with a morbid chuckle. 'It was on the radio. A German tourist got too close to a saltwater crocodile. I heard the crocs prefer the taste of Europeans.'

'No, not that one. A bloke called Cameron Snyder.'

'Oi!' Jack stuck his head out the car window. 'Wilson, get back here. Change of plan.'

Chapter Five

THE ULTRA-MODERN MORGUE gleamed and sparkled under the bright lights. Detectives Lisbon and Taylor stood on one side of the long rectangular bench, Doctor Margaret Proctor, Head of the Yorkville Forensics Unit, on the other. The focus of attention, the laid-out corpse of freshly deceased pool hall owner Cameron Snyder. The lower half of his body was covered by a white sheet with the chest, neck and head exposed.

Out of the corner of his eye Jack observed Taylor's features twitching. Her gaze shifted from floor to ceiling, from deep wash sinks to shelving packed with bottles, instruments, hoses, all manner of apparatus. Anywhere but on the victim. Jack knew she hated the grim reality of death, but her presence was essential if she was to have a proper handle on the investigation.

'Is this height OK for you?' Proctor looked at Taylor's left ear. 'Are you with us, DC Taylor?'

'Uh huh.'

'You're not quite as tall as DS Lisbon or me. Shall I raise Mr Snyder?'

'Yes,' Taylor snapped, eyes fixed on the exit. 'Whatever, just get on with it.'

'I agree, a wee bit higher would be better,' said Jack.

Proctor pumped a foot pedal with her size 10 Wellington boots and elevated the slab, affixed to a steel cylinder about a metre in diameter. 'That good?'

Jack and Taylor nodded wordlessly.

'Look at this deep cut.' Proctor pointed at a gaping wound in the side of the victim's neck. The pathologist was a tall, gangly woman who strutted around in her mask, gown and rubber gloves like it was the latest word in fashion. It wouldn't have surprised Jack if she slept in a white Tyvek suit. A professional to the core, she was respected and admired by everyone at Yorkville CIB. The woman knew her stuff.

Jack craned his head to get a better angle. 'Bloody hell, you're not kidding. You could stick your hand in that.'

'I'd prefer you didn't, DS Lisbon.'

'What, and leave my DNA in there? You'd have me fitted up as the murderer 'n all, Margaret.'

The pathologist harrumphed under the blue surgical mask. 'Don't be ridiculous, why would I do that?'

Jack shrugged.

'Back to the wound,' Proctor continued. 'The killer's gone absolutely ballistic with this cut.' She drew her hand back, squinted and blew out her cheeks as she made a vicious stabbing motion.

'Ease up, Margaret,' said Jack. 'You look like Norman Bates's mum out of that movie *Psycho*.'

'My apologies. It's not often I see such deep cuts not

caused by industrial machinery accidents. And I hate to correct you, but it was Bates dressed as his mother.' She paused, regained her breath. Jack was sure Proctor got perverse pleasure out of aspects of her job that she probably shouldn't. 'There are other shallow cuts in the neck around the big gash. Also smaller wounds around the clavicle and upper ribs, but they haven't penetrated the flesh as much. The deep neck wound was the fatal one. I'd say the perpetrator got his eye in, so to speak, on the front of the body. With each successive cut he's gained in confidence until he's worked up the courage to go for the throat. Some hesitant stabs and then…BAM! A driving overhand thrust into the neck. The murderer severed both the internal jugular and carotids on the left side of the body, leading to massive blood loss.'

'Poor bastard,' whispered Taylor. She stared at the vent on the ceiling, her face drained of colour.

Jack tugged her sleeve. 'Don't be all squeamish. Margaret's done a great job cleaning him up, look.'

Taylor's eyes remained fixed on the vent.

'I thought you'd gotten over it,' Jack pressed. 'Didn't you try hypnotherapy or acupuncture or something?'

'Shut up, Jack. I'm doing my best.' She widened her eyes and gawped at the open wound. Her legs wobbled fractionally. 'Is that better?'

'Yeah, sorry.'

Proctor's blue-gloved hands rested on her hips. 'Have you two finished? There's something quite interesting about this case. Please, come around towards the back of the bench.' She pointed a scalpel at the top of the gleaming forehead. As Wilson had described, the man was bald as a billiard ball. Bushy black eyebrows and one of those slightly elevated-at-the-tip piggy noses. The smallish ears were tucked close to his skull, almost flat. Both lobes were adorned by hooped gold earrings about 2 cm in diameter. No facial hair. Jack was reminded of the actor, Yul Brynner, in his famous role playing the King of Siam. He assessed the man as being tantalizingly close to handsome without quite making the grade. Death bestowed an angelic quality on all humans, which made it impossible to make prejudgments about a person's temperament. Snyder was no exception. He could have been a lovely bloke, or, as Wilson's cousin Russell reckoned, a right Helen Hunt.

'Look,' said Proctor. Jack and Taylor studied the area the pathologist indicated. 'You see the extensive bruising and large indent? I'd wager the fellow was knocked unconscious by something heavy before the killer went about their handiwork with the blade.'

'Why do you think so?' said Jack, intrigued by the scenario.

Proctor walked around the left side, lifted up the arm and twisted the hand towards the detectives. 'No defensive wounds.' She leaned across the torso, lifted the other arm. 'Same here. Both arms and hands clean as a whistle. No cuts.'

Jack cupped his chin in his hand. Taylor stood a metre behind the stainless steel autopsy bench, clearly she'd seen enough of the close up details.

'So,' Proctor's voice slipped into summing-up mode. 'We've got blunt-force trauma to the head – a single, hard blow – almost immediately followed by lots of practice stabs before a vigorous knife thrust to the neck which caused the man to bleed out. It's almost impossible to say which action was the cause of death considering the killer carried them out with very little time in between. I'm leaning towards the latter, which I'd hazard a guess was a large kitchen knife with a wide 15 to 20 cm blade.' She pointed at the victim's ribcage. 'This bruising is also noteworthy. It suggests a severe kicking took place before the man was killed.'

'Blimey,' said Jack. 'Poor bastard's had the full menu.'

'Indeed. Quite a frenzy.'

'Time of death?' said Jack.

'I'd estimate between 22:00 and midnight last night.'

'How did we find out about it?'

'His neighbour called it in bright and early this morning. It's a good thing I'm an early riser. I like to take my beagle Watson for a walk in the park before the sun comes up and so—'

'Please. Will you get to the effing point!'

'Oh, my,' Proctor laughed, unflustered by the DS's outburst. 'You are in a tetchy mood today.'

'Yeah, I am 'n all. We've just spent half the day driving to Cairns and back for no good reason.' He stuck both thumbs under his belt and hiked up his trousers. The extra two kilometres he added to his daily run were paying dividends. He'd have to fork out for new pants or put another hole in his belt. 'But you know as well as I do, Margaret, most murders that get solved are…uh…solved in the first forty-eight hours. The way you're jabbering on, it'll be next week before Claudia and I get out of this bleedin' morgue. Hopefully alive.' Jack thrust a hand in a pocket, pulled out a pack of gum. 'Now, please, and keep it concise, what were the circumstances?' Batista had already briefed the detectives on the phone as the Yorkville cops drove back from Cairns, but the DS wanted to hear as much as possible first-hand from Proctor. She was among the first on the crime scene and was as observant as a hawk.

Proctor pulled the surgical mask away from her face,

tucked it under her chin and gestured for the detectives to follow her. 'Let's go into my office. There's nothing more to be gained by discussing the matter standing next to poor Mr Snyder here.'

Jack noticed instant relief flattening the lines on Taylor's moist brow. 'Yes, please,' she blurted. 'That makes sense.' She'd once confided in Jack that, for no explicable reason, certain types of men gave her the creeps. Comb-over enthusiasts, for one. There was no rhyme or reason to it, they just did. From his experiences with the Detective Constable in the morgue, all dead guys without exception had that unfortunate effect on her.

The interior of Proctor's office was immaculate. The chief forensics officer was known for having an ordered mind, blessed with an extra archiving compartment other humans missed out on at the design stage. As Jack and Taylor shuffled in behind Proctor, he observed the tightly packed metal bookshelf was arranged in strict alphabetical order by name of author. He spied *Fifty Shades of Gray* tucked in among all the scientific books. *You're a sly one, Proctor.*

'So, spill your guts, Margaret,' said Jack. 'What can you tell us about the crime scene.'

'Just a moment.' Proctor dropped her mask in a trash can, shed her white coat and hung it up on a steel hook. Underneath, she wore grey pants and a primrose blouse, which looked incongruous teamed with her agricultural gum boots. She sighed and dropped inelegantly into a swivel chair. The detectives had already nested on identical pieces of furniture. 'Tea?' Proctor pulled a thermos from a drawer by her knees and pointed at a scrum of mugs on a bench in the corner. The detectives declined with polite headshakes. The pathologist's brew was rumoured to be a concoction of dandelions and stinging nettles.

'Just the facts of this morning's sweep, thanks Margaret. Then we'll be grabbing a coffee.'

'Right. I'll stick to the salient points.'

'Promise?' said Jack. 'No detours down speculation lane?'

'No.'

'Right. This is what I know. The neighbour at number 2 Rogers Close of the inner-city suburb of Mortimer, Mr Raj Mallick, called the station at 6:15am to report that he could see the body of Cameron Snyder in a pool of blood through a lowset window that looks into Snyder's basement.'

'Why was he looking through the bloke's window early in the morning?' said Taylor, more relaxed now the deceased was an abstract concept and not a vampirish cadaver inches away from her face.

'I'm getting to that. I'm telling you the facts in order as requested by your partner, DS Lisbon.' She nodded at Jack with a sarcastic smirk.

'Go ahead,' said Taylor through gritted teeth. 'Sorry to interrupt.'

'As I was saying.' Proctor wriggled her backside into her chair, warming to the task. She spoke without referring to any documentation. 'Mr Mallick called the CIB hotline and Constables Trevarthen and Semmens were despatched immediately to secure the crime scene. Mallick told Constable Trevarthen he and his wife had heard loud talking coming from Snyder's house last night, thought nothing of it since he sometimes had friends over to play pool, and went to bed. Early this morning he was awoken by uncharacteristic howling by the deceased's Staffordshire terrier. Mallick knocked and rang the bell, no answer. He then walked down the side of the house to check the backyard. On the way his attention was drawn to light coming from the lowset windows looking into the basement. He bent down, saw the victim and called it in.'

'What about the dog?' said Taylor.

'Tied up outside beside two empty bowls.'

'It's not still there, surely?'

'No. I took her to my place to keep Watson company.'

'Very public-spirited of you, Margaret,' said Jack. 'So you arrived, when?'

'About 7:30am, together with other members of the forensics investigation unit. I've got a preliminary report prepared for you.' She passed a manila folder across the table. 'More details regarding DNA and other forensic evidence will be emailed to you when ready.'

'Summarise the preliminary report's contents for us, please, Margaret.'

She took a sip of tea, cleared her throat. 'Sure. After a brief examination of the kitchen area, hallway, bedrooms and bathroom, the forensics team and I headed to the basement to assess the cadaver. The body lay next to a full-sized snooker table, face down. There was ample blood around the body and small splatters from the practice stabs. I quickly established the blunt and sharp force trauma injuries I described to you earlier. No obvious weapon was found, although I recommend a more thorough examination of the crime scene as the poolroom is full of small, hard objects that may have been used to strike Mr Snyder and then wiped clean of prints and/or DNA. Same goes for the knife which may have been wiped clean and placed back in a kitchen drawer. Or the perpetrator could have taken it with them.'

'What kind of objects are in the poolroom?' said Taylor.

'You name it. Billiard, pool and snooker balls, cues, dozens of trophies, statuettes, ashtrays. Then there's the bar full of bottles and glasses and whatnot. We dusted as much as we could for prints and took a range of forensic samples. Rather a large undertaking, so I envisage a return visit tomorrow to continue examining the scene.'

Jack rubbed his chin. 'Very interesting. What else?'

'A broken glass coffee pot with a plastic handle and spots of blood in the kitchen would indicate a struggle took place there before the murder was committed. Tiny glass shards from the pot were found on the kitchen floor and also embedded in the soles of the victim's flip flops. DNA analysis will reveal whether that blood belongs to the victim, someone else or both.' Proctor leaned back, folded arms across her chest. 'Most likely the coffee pot was used by Snyder to hit another person. I think those small droplets are someone else's.'

'Why?' said Taylor.

'There's nothing on Snyder's body to indicate he was the one cut with shards of glass.'

'No,' said Jack. 'His cut was a doozy.'

'That's one way of putting it.' Proctor's face wore a self-satisfied expression as she held her cup to her lips. 'The tiny pieces of skin left behind on the tiny shards could point us directly to the killer.'

'I don't share your optimism, Margaret,' said Taylor.

'Me either,' said Jack. 'We look forward to your full report.'

'Two more things,' said Proctor. She leaned forward again and tapped a pen on a white desk blotter. 'The most interesting parts!'

'What?' Jack had thought she was done talking. He

already had one arm in the left sleeve of his jacket, the other aimed at slotting into the right.

'This.' Proctor placed a thin silver necklace on the table. On the end, a charm locket engraved with the name Lydia. 'We found it in the curled-up fingers of Snyder's right hand.'

'The ex-wife,' said Taylor. 'Uniforms have already informed her of what's happened.'

'We'll be chatting with her ASAP,' said Jack. 'Apparently she took the news rather badly, went into shock, like she still cared for the guy.'

'Hang on,' Taylor countered. 'Perhaps she's just a person with a sense of decency. You'd go into shock if your ex-wife was murdered wouldn't you, Jack?'

Silence.

'Jack?'

'I'm thinking…'

Proctor shook her head. 'Would you two mind discussing ex's and motives and so on somewhere else? I want to have another look over the body. I'm not satisfied I've discovered all there is to know yet.'

'Sorry, Margaret.' Jack stood, gestured to Taylor that they'd finished here for now. 'We'll get out of your hair in a minute. You said there were two things. What was the second? '

'I'll spare you a physical demonstration, but we also recovered a used condom. It was found in a small waste bin in the bathroom wrapped in toilet paper. I should have the results of the analysis tomorrow for you. If the wearer was Snyder, we'll know straight away. If not, it could take a bit of trawling through databases. As for the other participant – I'm guessing a female – we'll only know if they're on record, of course.'

'What?' Jack's eyebrows lifted. 'I thought you could only determine who the bloke was. You know, from his little deposit.'

'Not at all, DS Lisbon. We're able to retrieve cells shed by a female during sex from the external surface of a condom. Put simply, we use fluorescence to locate female cells and then employ polymerase chain reaction-based methods to positively identify the female.'

'That's simply put, is it?'

'Well, yes. This technique's been around for several decades.'

'Geez Louise,' said Taylor. 'This sounds like a helluva case.'

'Indeed.' Jack unwrapped a stick of spearmint gum and tossed it into his mouth.

'Not nicotine ones?' Taylor observed.

'Correct. Turns out all I'd done was switch from one type of nicotine addiction for another. I'm trying this sugarless variety for a change.' Jack executed a couple of exploratory chews and frowned.

'Won't you get addicted to those too?' said Proctor. 'I've been studying obsessive behaviour in an article by Lara Menzies et al published in 2010. Clinical psychology's a subject I've always been interested in. Did I mention the case of the–'

Jack held up a hand. Once on a roll, Proctor was hard to stop. 'There's one thing I'll never stop being addicted to, Margaret.'

'Oh? What's that?'

'Catching killers. Come on, Taylor. I just got a text. Wilson's waiting for us at the crime scene with Trevarthen and Semmens. I wanna talk to that neighbour.'

Jack saw Taylor shaking her head as they pushed their

way through the swinging plastic doors and exited into the main corridor. 'What?'

'*Addicted to catching killers?* I reckon that's the corniest line you've ever come up with.'

'Really? Stick around, kid. I promise you they'll only get worse.'

Chapter Six

LOCATED at the end of a cul-de-sac in a quiet neighbourhood of the middle to upper-class suburb of Mortimer, the late "Cueball" Cameron Snyder's house was a tidy, two-storey white-brick building. The unfenced front yard comprised a small patch of lawn dwarfed by an expansive concrete driveway. Between the couch grass and the house was a riotous bed of azalea bushes crying out for pruning. In the driveway stood Inspector Batista's sapphire blue Mazda CX-5 and two squad cars. In a double carport to the left of the house, screened by a high stand of densely packed bamboo – Snyder's black Toyota Rav 4, thick with squashed insects and road dust the colour of cocoa powder. Probably acquired on his frequent trips to Cairns and back. Along the bottom of the back windscreen ran a corny sticker of questionable taste: *Pool Players have Long Sticks and Hard Balls*. Jack stopped beside the Toyota as the detectives approached the front door of the house, wiped away a patch of dirt and cupped his hands up against the glass.

'See anything interesting in there? said Taylor.

'Nope.' He tried the handle, no luck.

Twin cane palms bookended the front portico, under which stood the ever-ebullient Constable Kylie Smith, hands behind her back. Bouncing up and down on her toes, she greeted the detectives with a toothy smile that illuminated a lightly freckled face. Not yet jaded by the job. Give her time. She'll soon lose that enthusiasm.

'Who's here, Kylie?' said Taylor.

'Who isn't would be a better question. I think Aden's in the kitchen, the rest are in the basement. Whoever heard of a basement in an Australian home?' She shook her head. 'I haven't.'

'No,' agreed Taylor. 'I've actually never even seen one. I think they have them in the southern states.'

'Very suss, if you ask me.' Smith wrinkled her nose like a bad smell just passed under it.

'Why?' said Jack. 'What's odd about it?'

Smith shrugged. 'I dunno. Seems kind of creepy, people lurking about underneath a house like cockroaches.'

'My place in London had a basement. Do you think I'm creepy, Smith?'

'I…ah…'

'Best you don't answer that, Kylie.' Taylor curbed a burgeoning smile. 'Keep up the good work, Constable. Don't let anyone in, OK?'

Smith nodded wordlessly, her face turning red after Jack's challenge.

Just inside the front door was a small chrome-and-glass table, on it a macrame doily and a carved wooden bowl containing pens, business cards and two sets of keys. Jack snatched the bunch with the Toyota keyring, pointed it at the car and pressed. A noise blipped, lights flashed. 'We'll check the interior of that car on the way out,' Jack grinned.

He side-eyed Taylor. 'I've never had a basement in my life, by the way. Always lived in apartments.'

'Yeah, I figured as much.'

'Why?'

'Because you're renting a small flat when you could easily afford a nice house on your salary.'

'Why would I need a rambling effing house when it's just me living in it? A modest flat's all I need. Makes no sense to me why people throw good money away on luxuries.'

'Like that Toyota Hilux you bought last year? Cost you about over sixty grand, didn't it?'

'That's different.'

'Why?'

'Never mind. Come on, let's have a look in here.' Jack and Taylor ducked under blue-and-white police tape across the frame of the doorway to the combined kitchen and dining room. Shards of glass and the plastic handle of a coffee percolator holder were marked off by a series of plastic yellow evidence markers on the tiled floor. Droplets of blood, decreasing in size as they trailed away from the floor under the sink, piled high with dishes, stopped at the threshold into the hallway. Jack recalled the discussion with Proctor. In his head, he visualised an argument and a scuffle in the kitchen, Snyder whacking his assailant over the head with the coffee pot and fleeing down below, with the enraged and bleeding killer on his tail. And, bizarrely, some pre-fight shagging in a location and with participants yet to be determined.

'Evening, detectives,' said Constable Trevarthen, rising to his feet from a kitchen chair. The screen of his iPhone glowed blue on the table. Trawling the Internet to kill time, Jack surmised. 'Glad you could make it.' Trevarthen glanced at his watch. 'Can I go now, sir? My son's got football training this evening and I'm late to pick him up.'

'Go over what you've seen since this morning,' Jack demanded.

'It's all in my notes, sir. Plus I've already told Proctor. Can't it wait until the morning?'

'No, it can't. I want your take on it. Everyone sees and reacts to things differently. You were first on the scene with Semmens. Tell me what you saw. Fifteen more minutes and you can go.'

'But my kid'll be—'

'Your kid will be fine. Need I remind you we're looking for a killer? From what Proctor's told us, a damned vicious one. The victim, until this morning, was of prime interest to Assistant Commissioner Hook and all manner of effing security agencies.' Jack also knew Trevarthen's son was ten years old, overweight like his dad, and unlikely to suffer any long-term harm by missing one training session. On the contrary, he'd be delighted to watch TV instead of running laps around a park.

'My wife won't be happy, sir. She already reckons I neglect Cornelius.'

'Tough shit.' *You already neglected the boy by calling him Cornelius,* Jack wanted to say but held his tongue. 'Talk.'

'Can I at least sit down again?'

'No. Please don't roll your eyes at me.'

Trevarthen drew a deep breath.

'And don't sigh.'

'Sorry, sir. Let's see. Noah, I mean Constable Semmens and I, met the neighbour Mr Mallick at the front door at 7:08am. I'd brought some liver treats to distract the dog we were told about. Staffies are great dogs but they can be aggressive. As it turned out, she's only a pup and her bark is definitely worse than her bite. The damn thing nearly licked us to death when we forced the front door open.' He described how Semmens got acquainted with the beast, tied to the railing of a deck out the back. He rustled up a feed of dog biscuits to keep it occupied. Turned out the mere presence of other humans in the house had a calming effect on the hound, who gulped down the kibble and promptly went to sleep. At that time, Trevarthen made his way to the basement and found the deceased in a drying puddle of blood next to the pool table. The constables, together with Smith, who arrived shortly thereafter, inspected every room of the house and found no other persons on the premises. At 7:30am an ambulance appeared in the driveway, paramedics made sure there was no sign of life left in the victim. Shortly after that, Dr Proctor and her team of forensics scientists arrived to make a sweep of the house.

'Did any of the neighbours other than Mallick come over for a sticky beak?' said Taylor.

'No. But a woman at number 5 and a couple at number 3 stood on their front lawns for a while, watching Proctor and her team arrive. I walked over to them, told them a person had died at number 2 and they could go about their business.'

'Did you say it was a homicide?'

'Of course not, sir. I know to wait till it's all official.'

'Good lad. Go on.'

'I asked them if they'd seen or heard anything, they said no.'

'Not surprising. There's a lot of space between those houses and Snyder's compared to Mallick's,' Jack observed.

'Yeah. Anyway,' Trevarthen pressed on, 'I told them there could be follow up questions about the deceased and they should be prepared for a knock on the door from CIB.

Of course, I didn't use the words "victim", but I'm sure they're smart enough to work out first responders don't arrive en masse when someone dies of natural causes, right?'

The detectives nodded.

'After I'd spoken with the neighbours, I went back inside the house to assist in any way I could. The scientists worked non-stop with only a short break, leaving just after 5:00pm. Us constables then secured the rooms containing primary evidence – the kitchen, bathroom and poolroom – as well as the entrance. It's been mind-numbingly boring for the most part and now, if you don't mind, I'd like to be on my way.'

Jack patted Trevarthen on his broad shoulder. 'See, Constable, that wasn't so hard, was it? Off you trot. See you in the morning for a debrief.'

'What about the neighbours?' said Taylor. 'Shouldn't we get the uniforms to knock on a few doors, rattle some cages?'

Trevarthen's eyes nearly popped out of his head. 'You can't be serious? I've been stuck here all day and I'm fucking starving!'

Jack opened the right-hand door of a stainless steel fridge, bent at the knees and peered inside.

'What are you doing?' said Taylor. 'You can't take the food.'

'Why not?' He unwrapped a foil-encased object, sniffed. 'Here, Constable. Fancy some leftovers?'

'Jack!' Taylor nearly shrieked.

'Wot? There's enough food in there to feed an army.'

'It could be evidence.'

'Don't be ridiculous. The bloke's been stabbed and hit over the head with a heavy object. You reckon this fried chicken might play a crucial role in the investigation?'

'Too early to say.'

'Don't be ridiculous, Claudia.' He held out the chicken to Trevarthen, whose eyes danced from one detective to the other. 'You want it or not?'

'Um, no thanks. I'll grab something on the way home. I'm free to go, right?'

'How can I resist those puppy dog eyes? Off you go then, sunshine.'

Trevarthen didn't have to be told twice. He donned his hat and scarpered.

'Back to the matter of the neighbours,' Jack continued. 'There's only four houses in the cul-de-sac, including this one. We interview Mr Mallick first, that leaves two. Easy enough for you and me to handle.'

'We won't be finished until after midnight,' Taylor groaned.

'Too bad. We need to solve this one pronto so I can jet off to Blighty at the end of the week.'

'It's going to cost the department a fortune in overtime.'

'Not my problem.' Jack twisted a thin plastic rod that opened the kitchen Venetian blinds. Streetlights shone circles of white onto the concrete footpath below. Fat moths battered into each other in their confusion. 'The lights are on in the other two houses.'

'Wilson and Smith can question them.'

'No. You and me, Claudia. This is too important.'

'Come on, Jack. They can handle it.'

'I said no!' Instant regret for the outburst, but Taylor's defiant stare told him she hadn't taken it personally. 'Look, sorry, but I don't want rookies buggering things up. They're tired and…'

'Jesus, Jack. We're *all* tired. It's been a bloody long day.'

'Just go with me on this. You can have a nice lie-in tomorrow morning.'

'Sure.' Sarcastic surrender. 'What about Mr Mallick, then? You'd better pop over and tell him we'll be over shortly. Wouldn't want him ducking out to the shops or anything would we? And why don't you have a quick word with the other neighbours while you're at it.'

'Smart thinking.' No *please*, no *would you mind*, but Jack barely noticed. Taylor's assertiveness sent a surprise tingle down his spine. 'Meet you in the basement in five.' He raced to the immediate neighbour's house. He introduced himself to the kindly-faced, nervous Raj Mallick, told him not to venture off anywhere until he and Taylor had questioned him. The man nodded vigorously, clearly eager to do his civic duty. Jack thanked him, repeated the process with elderly Pat O'Grady at No. 5 and a much younger Rex van der Klopp at No. 3 and headed back to the crime scene.

To get to Snyder's basement, Jack descended a long, narrow staircase which opened up onto a massive floor space. In the middle stood a full-sized pool table, and at the far end a bar with enough booze to require a liquor license. Around the periphery, racks of cues, triangles and chalk on string, shelving that hosted a myriad of statues, knick-knacks and memorabilia. An 80-inch TV sat high on one wall, surrounded by old-school cloth pennants from the 1980s and posters of sporting legends. An Australian flag draped over the top wooden frame of the bar. Next to a double-door refrigerator hung a flag Jack wasn't familiar with. Dark blue background with a central white symmetrical cross. There were five white, eight-pointed stars, one in the middle of the cross and one at each of its four ends.

'What's that?' Jack pointed at the banner. 'Very eye-catching design.'

'It's called the Eureka flag,' said Taylor. 'I'm a bit hazy on the history but it's popular among the trade union movement.'

'It's not a call to arms for rednecks is it?' For some reason the flag put Jack in mind of the American Confederate flag.

Taylor shook her head. 'If anything, it's more your leftie types who associate with it.'

'Really?' Jack decided to research the matter in more depth. 'I thought they were more into the hammer and sickle.'

Taylor shrugged. 'Are you sensing some kind of political motive for the crime?'

'Perhaps.' Jack searched his pants pocket till his fingers found the pack of gum. 'If the security agencies were interested in him, maybe there's a link to a right wing group. Or a left wing one, fuck knows with all the loonies about these days.'

'Interesting theory. Hook was vague with the details, but what you say could fit the bill. Political extremism's supposed to be on the rise in Australia, but I've seen no evidence of it in Yorkville.'

'It's just a thought bubble at this point, Claudia. Anyway, let's see what our esteemed colleagues have been up to here in the dungeon.'

A rapid-fire debrief with Constable Semmens confirmed Trevarthen's account. An initial inspection of the premises by both officers found no evidence other persons were living at the house. Constables Wilson and Kylie Smith were later arrivals, well after forensics, and their role had been limited to "fetching tea and biscuits and looking for anything suspicious". Jack sent Semmens, Wilson and Smith home. Told them to be at work bright and early next morning for some heavy lifting, in other words phone calls, door knocking and trawling data bases.

DS Lisbon's eyebrows dipped in the middle as he and Taylor approached the Inspector, leaning against the bar and tapping an iPhone with one finger. The tall man's head sat a millimetre under the Aussie flag, a whopper at around two and a half metres across. Jack coughed, Batista looked up with a slight shake of the head, like he'd been caught doing something he shouldn't. Jack wondered if he might be texting someone on a sensitive subject. Someone like Jabba Hook.

'Yes, Jack?'

'What's the deal, sir? I can't remember the last time you attended a crime scene. Especially at this late hour.'

The chief scratched his chisel-shaped chin. 'I'll be doing more of it in the future. I've been too bogged down in the administrative side of things. I need to get more hands on, so to speak.'

Jack sensed there was more to it. 'Is that the only reason, sir? Nothing to do with old Ray Hook, is it?'

'What? No, of course not. Besides, I was doing a bit of late-night shopping and this house happens to be on my way home.' That much was true. Batista's home was located in the next suburb. 'I kind of knew the victim, too.'

'You did?' said Taylor. 'How?'

'Only in a roundabout way. I played snooker in a social competition a few years ago. At the pubs around town. I've never been very good at the game, so I'd sneak in a few practice frames at Trick Shot so I didn't look too hopeless come match time. I'd seen Snyder there maybe once or twice. He was one of those in-your-face types. Smiling all the time, but you knew it was fake. Ingratiating himself with the clientele.'

'Yeah,' agreed Jack. 'I know the type well. London's crawling with 'em. They don't always deserve to be killed in their own homes, though.' He stepped around a rough outline on the floor where the body had lain. Not of chalk – the floor was carpet tiles – but one made of numbered yellow evidence markers in an approximate body shape. The largest blood stain was an inky black patch that wrapped around two of the thick legs of the snooker table and halfway under it. 'There are exceptions, though.'

'Deserved or not,' said Batista. 'We're going to find out who did this and bring them to justice.'

Jack leaned close to the Inspector, but spoke loud enough for Taylor to hear. 'You sure Hook didn't have a word in your shell-like, sir? Seems odd us getting the call up to Cairns, being told Snyder's of strategic importance, he winds up dead, and now you make an appearance as rare as the Yeti at the Sydney Opera House. You did look all sheepish when I caught you on the phone just now.'

Batista glared, turned the screen around to Jack and held it inches from his face. 'Look, I've had just about enough of your insolence, Jack. I was letting Marjorie know I'm going to be late for dinner. Satisfied?'

'Yeah.' Jack shuffled his feet on the spot. 'Sorry about that. Nothing personal. It's just that I don't trust that Assistant Commissioner, sir.' *Disingenuous, Lisbon. You haven't been straight up with your colleagues either.* 'I was flattered he sought us out to take care of a matter of national importance, but something stinks about the whole business.'

'Listen, as it's just the three of us, I'll be frank.' Batista glanced over Taylor's shoulder, as if making sure no one had returned unnoticed. 'I rang Hook to tell him about Snyder's murder, told him you officers were no longer to carry out his little job and I'd ordered you back to Yorkville.

He was all panicky, said the country's security would be even more at risk. I asked him how, but he started babbling on about CHOGM and Canberra and espionage and all kinds of nonsense. He still wants you to follow his orders, DS Lisbon.'

'But that's pointless,' said Jack. 'I'm pretty sure you can't slander a dead person.'

'That's exactly what I said to him. But he's even more agitated now the bloke's been killed. He said I was to order you back to Cairns to finish the job he'd given you.'

'What did you say?' said Taylor.

'No, of course. I told him if it really was a cloak-and-dagger operation, he'd have to get ASIO onto it. You and DS Lisbon are police detectives, for God's sake, not bloody spies.'

'Quite right, sir,' said Jack. 'Odd, though. I thought Hook'd be relieved. The bloke's dead, so you'd imagine any security implications would also...you know...die.' Jack decided to run his theory of political extremism up the proverbial flagpole. 'Reckon this paraphernalia suggests he was a nutjob?'

Taylor's phone rang, she excused herself and took the call on the other side of the room.

The chief jerked his head upwards and frowned. 'It's unlikely a couple of patriotic flags proves anything. Still, it's an avenue worth exploring.'

'Why do you think Hook's so antsy about Snyder?

'I wish I knew. I've had a quick look through the victim's record and it makes for short reading. Two driving violations. Also a restraining order filed by his ex-wife when they were living in Brisbane.'

'OK,' said Jack. 'Finally a possible motive. The ex-missus organising a hit against a wife beater.'

Batista pursed his lips. 'I doubt it. She retracted all her allegations the day after the domestic violence order was granted. Said she made it all up.'

'Maybe he forced her to retract, sir. It's been known to happen.'

'Yes, but that single incident was five years ago and they only separated the middle of last year. No interactions with the police since then.'

Jack folded his arms across his chest. 'I've known of men who've kept their wives cowering in fear for longer periods than that.'

'Yeah, I know that can happen. Only in this case I'm starting to think Snyder was up to something dodgy that involved Hook personally.'

'I wouldn't be surprised by that version either, boss,' said Jack. After a pause: 'What if he calls me again?'

'Refer him to me,' growled Batista, returning the iPhone to his pocket. 'I'll handle the fat fool.'

'Aren't you worried about your own arse if he's so... influential?'

'Not in the slightest.'

'Why?'

'Because I've got something over him. Something only I know about.'

'What?'

Batista touched the side of his nose. 'Let's just say his wife Juanita would raise hell if she found out what her devoted husband did on a police rugby trip to Sydney in the mid-1980s.'

'I can't imagine him as a footballer.'

'Believe it or not, Ray Hook was quite the athlete in his day. The higher up the food chain he went, though, the more obese he became. And more of a prick.'

'He's certainly that, sir. But surely his wife would forgive him something that happened over thirty years ago. It could be like your theory about Snyder and his missus. A misstep in the heady days of youth, but good behaviour thereafter.'

Batista shook his head. 'I don't think so.'

'What did he do?' Jack tried to sound blasé despite curiosity eating him alive.

'Can't say. How do I know you wouldn't blab it all over town?'

'Come on, Inspector. You know me by now.'

'Precisely.'

Jack smiled. Batista could keep his effing secret. The upshot – Jack wouldn't be dancing to Jabba's tune. The plane ticket was paid for, the letter for Sarah was signed and the boss had a mystery ace up his sleeve.

'I don't know what you're grinning for, Lisbon. When's your flight to London?'

'Four days away.'

'That gives you till the weekend to find the killer.'

'Wot? The airline won't be so generous about rescheduling me a second time. Plus I'll lose the bleedin' upgrade. Taylor can handle it with Wilson's help if I'm not here.'

'The weekend, DS Lisbon.' Batista waved away Jack's protestations. 'Your leave's in the balance. Make an arrest or it's rescinded until you do. Hook may be a fat fool, but he's got a reputation for ruining detectives' careers when things don't go his way. And I'd hate for him to ruin yours.'

'But you said you had…'

'Never mind what I said. I might have ammunition against Hook, but I don't want to use it unless I'm desperate. And I haven't quite reached that point yet.'

'I bloody have!'

'Your first job in the morning's a chat with the vic's ex-wife, Lydia. The uniforms who delivered the bad news said she broke down big time. More like a widowed newlywed than an estranged partner, apparently. Backs up my belief the violence back in the day was either a one off, or she made up the story.'

'Yeah. We heard she took the news badly. Maybe DC Taylor and I should pop around tonight, when we're done with the neighbours?'

'No. Let the woman get some sleep. You're likely to completely alienate her if you go at this hour.'

'Right.' He wants it solved fast, but puts the brakes on. 'Whatever you say, chief.'

'Don't forget, you've got until the weekend if you want that vacation, Lisbon.' Batista donned his hat and strode up the stairs.

'What was all that about?' said Taylor, rising from a plush sofa and gripping her mobile phone tight.

'Batista's threatened to revoke my holidays if we don't find the killer before I'm due to fly out.'

'He can't do that, Jack.'

'Don't matter. I'll take it as a challenge.' Jack wrapped tissue around a wad of gum, tucked it in his pants pocket and immediately got to work on another piece. 'Who was calling you just now?'

'Mum. About my sister.'

'She OK?' Claudia's older sister Annie had undergone surgery for skin cancer. 'Yeah. Turned out to be minor, thank God.'

Jack was genuinely pleased. He'd met Annie at a barbecue last month. A pleasant woman, shy and retiring, she was the antithesis of Claudia. A distant cousin had recently died from melanoma and Annie was terrified her diagnosis was going to be terminal.

'After I got off the phone to mum I did a quick online search, looking to see if Snyder was involved in anything political. I found a Reddit post about a right-wing organisation based in Cairns. They call themselves the Wild Colonial Boys, or WCB for short.'

'And you're telling me this because? And what the fuck's Rabbit?'

'Reddit. It's a website that's very useful for detectives.'

'Is it now? Why haven't I heard of it?'

Taylor shrugged. 'Because you're out of touch.'

'Leave off..'

'Back to this post. I couldn't find Snyder's name mentioned anywhere, but I found a photo. Look.' Taylor held the screen inches from Jack's nose. He took a half step backwards to remove the instant blur. The photograph was grainy and slightly out of focus. It depicted a group of seven grinning men in a tight bunch, four in the front, three in the back. They held green beer bottles aloft and brandished the sign of the horns with their free hands. All wore blue singlets emblazoned with the iconic Boxing Kangaroo, purple and black tattoos bloomed on muscular arms.

'What am I looking at?'

'I think it's our murder victim, middle of the back row.'

Jack clicked his teeth. 'No, it ain't him. Snyder's bald. This bloke's got hair. Plenty of it. Looks like bloody Brian May from Queen.'

'I think it's one of those novelty curly wigs. And the nose is the same.'

'Bullshit.'

'I'm sure of it. Look at the glint near his earlobes. The gold earrings.'

Taylor was bang on the money. Again. It was Snyder.

Chapter Seven

'WHAT CAN you tell us about Cameron Snyder?' Jack sipped on a strong coffee flavoured with cardamom. The fragrant exotic scents that swarmed Jack's senses the second Mallick opened the door weren't letting up. It transported him back to his neighbourhood in Peckham, where the aromas of Asian food cooking in the evenings were as familiar as a mother's touch.

'Apart from the gruesome discovery this morning, not much to tell.' Mallick rubbed his hands together like he was washing them.

'Was he a good neighbour?' Jack took another sip of his coffee, smacked his lips in appreciation.

The man shrugged. 'Not good, not bad. He tended to keep to himself. Over the three years we've lived here I think I exchanged words with him maximum half a dozen times. He was always polite, smiled and waved whenever we caught each other's eye. I can't believe he was...murdered.'

'Yes, shocking.' Jack nodded understandingly. Mallick wasn't describing behaviour typical of a racist man who's part of a right-wing outfit. Although Snyder could have been faking geniality towards his Indian neighbours.

'Nothing like that ever happened around here. This is a nice, safe, neighbourhood.' A small side-to-side head wobble. ' I'm going to be changing the locks on our doors, I can tell you!'

'I'm sure there'll be no need for that,' said Taylor. 'Nothing appears to have been stolen, so chances are high it was someone known to the victim. You and your family are in no danger.'

A portly woman in a colourful sari, springy grey hair tied back tightly over a round forehead, appeared beside Mallick. She rested a hand on her husband's neck and rubbed gently. Her eyes flickered as she flung a tea towel over her shoulder. 'Are you sure about that? I've been reading about Mr Snyder on the Internet. "Very crooked man" seems to be the majority view.'

'With respect, Mrs Mallick, you won't find the truth via online forums. It's mainly wild theories with no foundation.'

'No smoke without fire,' she said, turning to go back into the kitchen. 'And if there's no foundation, how come he got killed, huh?' She disappeared behind a wall before Jack could answer her question.

'Did he get many visitors? Delicious coffee, by the way.' If he played his cards right, he'd get a second cup. 'Groups of men, for example?'

Mallick beamed, the skin crinkling around his large eyes. 'Thank you, Detective Lisbon. Yes, He did. Sometimes he had friends over to play pool and the music and conversations got a bit loud, but nothing over the top. Perhaps he'd had run-ins with the authorities before.'

'Why would you think that?' said Taylor.

'Because he never went past 12 o'clock with the carousing. Like clockwork, the music would stop almost on the stroke of midnight and his mates would go home quietly.'

'A very thoughtful neighbour indeed,' Jack remarked.

'Yes, yes. No trouble at all.' Mallick's imitation hand-washing was relentless. 'Do you have any idea who did it?'

'We'll ask the questions if you don't mind.' Best to cut the curious types off quickly.

'Oh, yes, of course. A thousand apologies.'

'Were there any other visitors?'

'Yes. Men in suits. Probably to do with his business deal-ings. But of course,' he held out his hands, palms upwards, 'we don't sit here spying on our neighbours' houses, so anything's possible.'

'Was he away from home a lot?' asked Taylor.

'The house was dark some nights, but he was never away for more than one day at a time. I understand he often travelled to Cairns. At least that's what my wife tells me. She's always got her nose in the gossip pages. She told me there were rumours going around Yorkville that he was, like Miranda said…' Mallick made exaggerated air quotes … '*dodgy*, but he was respectful of us in the street. His dog was very well behaved, not a barker. That's why I knew some-thing was wrong this morning when she was howling. I've never heard her go off like that.'

'What do you know about his family?' Jack already knew the basics from a data base search Taylor requested on the drive back from Cairns. The ex-wife Lydia, separated but not officially divorced, a mother and brother, no children. Two registered businesses, one for the pool halls, the other a shelf company.

'Not very much.' Mallick turned his head to the side. 'Miranda! Come here for a minute please, love.'

Mrs Mallick reappeared, a broad smile on her face, like

she couldn't wait to put in her two cents worth. She flopped into a fabric rose-patterned armchair, placed her hands in her lap. Over the next five minutes, she detailed her extensive knowledge of Cameron Snyder and his shady business dealings. Internet rumours the detectives were already familiar with.

'What about his personal life?' said Jack.

'Oh, yes. He has a wife. Lydia, her name is. Lovely lady, a bit timid. I've spoken to her maybe ten times. They're separated, not divorced. She would drop by some weekends, stay for a few hours, then drive off again. Last time I saw her was last Saturday when I was working in the front garden. She'd just come out of the house with a big smile on her face. I cut a bunch of azaleas and took them over to her as she was getting into her car. She told me she'd dropped by to deliver a letter to Mr Snyder.'

'I wonder why she wouldn't simply re-address it?' Taylor ventured out loud.

'Just between us,' whispered Miranda. 'I got the impression she still carried a torch for him.'

'You're just speculating,' interrupted Mr Mallick. 'Keep to the facts.'

'Your wife's doing fine,' said Taylor. 'She's not under oath in court. Mrs Mallick, did Lydia live here before she and her husband separated?'

'No. She never lived in this street. Mr Snyder bought it after they separated. She's got the apartment across town in Thurston.'

'She must be very forgiving if she still loved him,' said Jack. 'Thurston's a shithole – pardon my French. At least compared to Mortimer.'

'And that's why I say Mr Snyder, rest his soul, was a dodgy character.' Mrs Mallick raised her chin. 'He came from that lower-class suburb straight to this lovely area. Apparently, his rise to riches was swift, but it's rumoured he's up to his eyeballs'… she bulged out her eyes… 'in debt.'

'Anything else you can tell us?'

'Afraid not.'

Jack realised with the conversation over, there would be no second coffee. 'OK, DC Taylor. It's getting on. Let's leave these good people in peace. We'll be in touch if we need to ask any more questions.'

Cutting across the Mallicks' well-groomed couch lawn to the next set of neighbours Taylor said, 'What did you make of that?'

'Most of it regurgitated gossip, but that stuff about the ex-missus coming for visits, gold.'

'I agree. I'll bet when Proctor analyses that condom she's gonna finds traces of Lydia's…um…'

Jack burst out laughing. 'You're probably right.'

'And the men in suits. Who could they be?'

'I plan on finding out before the weekend.'

Taylor gave a reassuring smile. 'They're probably a side issue, Jack. You and I know most murders are committed by people close to the victim.'

'I hope you're right, Claudia. It would certainly simplify things. The case already has too many variables, and I don't like it one bit.'

Chapter Eight

RENEE VAN DER KLOPP welcomed the detectives with frantic eagerness, waving them inside like she was directing traffic. 'Come in, come in, please. Oh, it's terrible, shocking. The ambulance, the people in those white suits. It's not good news, is it?'

Jack's lips pressed together as he gave a solemn shake of the head.

'My husband's in the lounge room waiting. Are you going to tell us what happened?'

'Of course,' said Taylor, wiping her feet on a coir mat. 'We'll tell you everything, don't worry.'

'Was he…murdered?'

'Yes,' said Jack. No point pussy-footing around with jittery people like her. 'And we need your help.'

The home owner stopped and turned around. Two stray tears wandered down her pink cheek, her lower lip trembled. 'Oh dear. Poor Cam.'

'Cam?' That was the first time anyone had abbreviated the man's name. 'You knew him quite well I take it?'

'No…no…not really.' She grabbed Jack by the elbow, steered him down a short hallway which opened into a spacious loungeroom, Taylor following on their heels. 'I'll get us a drink. Be back in a mo.'

The detectives held out their IDs, introduced themselves to Rex van der Klopp. 'Take a seat,' he replied in a barely audible grunt before fixating on the screen of his mobile phone.

'Excuse me, hello!' Jack flapped his hands about. 'We're here on important business. Can I have your attention please?'

'I'm texting me mum.' A dry sniff and a face wipe with the back of a hairy wrist. 'Just wait a minute, will ya?'

Jack silently cursed numb-nuts like Rex while he quietly assessed the surroundings. Open-plan layout, slow-turning fans, ultra-modern appliances. Floor tiles instead of carpet in the reception rooms. It all made sense to Jack. If he were to build a home in Yorkville, he wouldn't mind something like the functional ones dotting the end of Rogers Close.

Renee appeared with a tray. A jug of iced-water with lemon slices floating in it, four plastic tumblers. A letdown after the supreme coffee at the Mallicks'.

The van der Klopps presented as an ordinary working-class suburban couple in their mid-thirties to early forties. Hard to guess occupation, but judging by appearances alone, Jack could imagine Rex sorting screws all day on an assembly line, Renee waiting tables at a café. More likely they had good jobs, though, considering the price tags of homes in Mortimer. Taciturn Rex tended to overweight, a hairy muffin top peeking out from between a Yorkville Scorpions tank top and draw-string shorts. Raven haired and tanned, Renee was on the short side, perhaps five-four in her socks. She was plain featured in Jack's estimation, but he was picking up an underlying sexual vibe. Not directed at him, but hanging like a ripe apple, waiting to be plucked. Only not by her husband. Her eyelids fluttered rapidly, her generous chest rose and fell inside a ruffled floral blouse. Blips and beeps of computer games and snatches of teenagers' boisterous chatter filtered down the corridor. Jack spied a framed photo of two identical spotty-faced lads in blue-and-grey school uniforms on a side table.

The hosts sat on extreme ends of a three-setter corduroy sofa, torsos twisted away from each other. The detectives were left the matching two-seater couch opposite. Body language told Jack this couple had long ago exited the honeymoon stage. He sensed they couldn't stand each other.

Taylor took the lead, quickly explained that their neighbour had been killed yesterday evening between 10 and 12 o'clock.

'Oh my God!' said Renee. 'We were at home. The boys…Christ!'

'Don't stress, Mrs van der Klopp. We're certain the perpetrator was someone known to the victim.'

'How did he die?' said Rex, putting his phone on the armrest of the sofa. His voice and entire attitude were calm. Jack detected a touch of sadistic curiosity in the question.

'I'd rather not go into those details,' said Jack.

'Why not?' A furrowed frown from Rex. 'We're entitled to know. The bloke's our friggin' neighbour, for God's sake.'

Taylor coughed into her fist. 'That kind of information needs to be kept confidential for legal reasons.'

'Whatever. It'll all be in the papers soon enough. Or when that goofy Batista holds the inevitable press confer-ence.' Arms weaved into a tight fold across the man's chest.

Jack had been monitoring Renee as she observed the

exchange between her husband and the police with a disapproving eye and tiny head shakes. He'd string them along for a moment before lobbing in the hand grenade Mrs van der Klopp had herself supplied.

'How was your relationship with Mr Snyder?' Jack asked Rex.

'I said g'day to him, that's about it.' The arms across the chest tightened. 'He wasn't much bothered about engaging in conversation. Too up himself to ask me or the kids over for a game of pool. To be honest, I wouldn't be surprised if all the Internet rumours about his dishonesty were on the money.'

'And what about you, Mrs van der Klopp?' *Let's see if they're team players.*

'I'm the same as my husband. Just knew him to say hello to. He kept to himself, like we all do in the street. It's a sign of the world we live in, isn't it? Everyone too busy to take the time out to, you know, socialise and that. As for his business, I wouldn't know anything about it.' She gave a nervous titter.

'You called him Cam when we arrived,' said Jack in the flattest tone he could muster. The DS may have been addressing the wife, but his focus was on the husband. 'Rather familiar for someone you only know well enough to say hello to, innit?'

'I...ah... do that with people's names,' she replied. 'It's something I've always done.'

'No you haven't.' Rex released his self-administered bear hug and sucked in a deep breath. Jack guessed he was trying to control a mean temper.

'I have, too!' She spun in her seat, as if someone had poked her in the side with a hot iron.

'Bullshit.' The husband glowered, pointed an index

finger at his spouse. 'You've got nephews with great fucking long names. Sebastian and that other little shit, what's his name, Bartholomew. You never shorten them.'

'Only because my brother insists on the full names being used.' The claim sounded forced in Jack's ears. 'He's a snob like that.'

'Rubbish,' said Rex. 'I've heard him talking to his kids. He calls 'em Seb and Bart.'

'No he doesn't! Maybe I got things confused. Must be my sister-in-law Karen who insists on the full names.' The defensiveness in Renee's voice was palpable. 'You're just doing all you can to make me look bad.'

Jack cast a side-eye at Taylor. Her frown fighting against a wry smile suggested she was enjoying the train-wreck spectacle and feeling bad for their hosts at the same time.

'No, I'm not,' Rex insisted. 'Anyway, why do *you* use the full names when you're talking to me and your dumb-arse brother and his wife aren't even in the same bloody room? Puts the lie to your words.'

Tears welled in Renee's eyes. Her rib cage rose as she turned to her husband and glared. 'This is all irrelevant to the officers' questions. So just shut up, will you Rex!'

The sexual vibe Jack sensed emanating from Renee earlier had evaporated, replaced by desperation.

'Listen.' Rex readopted the crossed-arms pose, the pitch of his voice low and controlled now. 'I know you were fooling with him next door. Why not admit it finally? The bloke's dead. It's the decent thing for you to do.'

'Were you having an affair with the deceased?' Jack asked Renee, again with minimum expression in his voice. 'If you were, it might be enough of a motive for...' he switched his gaze to the husband '...*you* to murder the man.'

Rex van der Klopp morphed from lazy couch potato to

man of action. He leapt to his feet, eyes wide and jaw set firm. 'What the hell?' His arms windmilled about. 'You two come barging in here late at night, accusing me of killing my neighbour. Jesus Christ! I've heard about the lack of professionalism in the Yorkville Police, now I'm experiencing it for myself.'

'Oi!' Jack stood, extended his arms with the palms of his hands pointing to the floor. Time to regain dominance. 'Settle down, Mr van der Klopp. I ain't making no accusations. Just tossing theories about, like.'

'If you keep on like that, I'll be tossing you out the fucking door! What if the kids hear all this nonsense? I'll be suing you for harassment.'

'Hey, hey, hey,' said Taylor. 'Let's all calm down. Jack, apologise.'

'Wot?'

'I said apologise. Mr van der Klopp is right. You've stirred up some kind of hornet's nest here with no foundation.'

'Damn straight,' said Rex, brandishing his mobile phone like a gun as he resumed his seat on the end of the sofa. He glanced over his shoulder towards the hallway, dropped his voice to a whisper. 'If she was banging the bloke next door, which I'm sure she was, it wouldn't make me go over there and kill him.'

'But I wasn't, babe,' Renee pleaded with her eyes. *Believe me!* Jack noticed the unhappily married couple had jammed themselves even harder against their armrests at either end of the settee. The man shook his head before staring into space.

'OK,' said Jack. 'I'm sorry. But you have to understand, Mr and Mrs van der Klopp, we're talking about a brutal murder. You're unaware of this, but Cameron Snyder was a person of immense interest to Australia's security agencies. I'm under orders. We need to solve this crime, and we need to solve it fast.' He quickly popped two pellets of spearmint gum into his mouth before continuing. The blast of extra hot mint helped to clear his head. 'From where I sit, and please, I'm not making any accusations here, you, Rex, are the closest thing to a suspect we've got. Depending on the results of our scientific tests and other investigations, we may require your further cooperation. To quote the classic line, don't leave town.'

'As if I would! I've done nothing.' He flopped back into the couch, the weight of exhaustion dragging his eyelids down.

'And neither have I.' Renee's turn to bust out an angry arm fold across the chest.

Remembering the science lesson from Proctor, Jack couldn't resist. 'Let's see about that. We've got cutting edge forensics that can tell us everything, Mrs van der Klopp.'

'What are you talking about?' she said in a faint croak. She folded her hands together but the shaking fingers couldn't be concealed.

'We found a used condom over there. Modern methods can tell us who was shagging who, not just whose sperm is in the receptacle.'

Taylor buried her head in her hands. Jack smiled to himself. She couldn't handle the directness sometimes, but tough shit. Often it was the only way to get to the truth.

'You don't look so sure of yourself now, do you, *babe*?' said Rex. 'I can't wait to find out what the results are. If my suspicions are correct, you'll be packing your bags. Maybe you can move in with your brother and look after those little nephews of yours. The ones with the cute, short names.' He barked a sarcastic laugh.

'We're going to need DNA samples from both of you to run some tests.' Jack tapped the edge of his mobile against his thigh.

'Her, I understand.' Rex jerked a thumb at his wife. 'But why me?'

'Like I said, you're the closest thing we have to a suspect at this early stage.'

'What if we don't agree?' Renee's face was drained of colour.

'We can get a court order, not a problem,' said Taylor firmly. 'Why wouldn't you agree if you've got nothing to hide? If your DNA doesn't match, it'll go a long way towards eliminating you as suspects.'

'I don't want my name on record forever. It's an infringement of my civil liberties,' Renee pouted.

'Let me reassure you, if you aren't charged with anything we're obliged to destroy forensic samples after twelve months,' said Taylor

'So you say.' Renee took a long drink of water. 'How can I believe you?'

'It's the law, Mrs van der Klopp,' said Jack. 'And these things are closely monitored.'

'I'll only do it if he does,' said Renee, drilling a hole in Rex with her eyes.

'Bring it,' he challenged. 'I'm ready.'

No one spoke for a moment before Jack broke the silence. 'I'd like to see both of you at the station tomorrow to have swabs taken. Purely voluntary of course, but it's in your best interests.' He flicked his wrist to check the time. 9:45pm. 'It's getting late and we must press on. One last thing. Have either of you noticed any suspicious activity in the street recently?'

'No.' A confirmation in unison. Upon further questioning the van der Klopps backed up the Mallicks' account of Cameron Snyder, mentioned occasional parties that petered out before anyone felt the urge to call and complain, had seen no other guests and were aware of an estranged wife called Lydia although neither had met her. On face value, they took much less interest in the neighbourhood than Mrs Mallick.

At 9:55 the detectives bade good-night to the residents of No. 3 Rogers Close.

'I'd love to be a fly on the wall in there,' said Taylor, tucking her notebook into her jacket pocket.

'You reckon Renee was banging Snyder?' Jack asked as he opened the door of Snyder's Rav 4.

Taylor shrugged. 'If you base that assumption purely on her calling him Cam, I'd say that was a long shot.'

'What does your instinct tell you?'

'Renee van der Klopp was lying through her teeth. Anything in the car?'

'Yeah. A note from Proctor addressed to me saying not to touch anything.'

'And have you?'

'Only the effing note.' He clunked the door shut and blipped the lock. 'I should have realised she woulda been over the bloody car.'

'Maybe you should put that back where you found it, hey?' Taylor nodded towards Snyder's front door. 'I take it you have a key to get back into the house?'

A nod. 'Of course.' He held it up. 'Hang on, I've got an idea.' Jack called Wilson, made him an offer. Babysit the house until Procter and her entourage arrived in the morning for more toil at the murder scene. Jack would deal with Batista if there was flack about the exorbitant overtime the constable would be accruing for today.

'What was that all about? All you have to do is lock up the house. There's tape and stuff all over the place. I'm sure it's secure enough.'

'*A*, I don't trust Hook not to send someone down to poke about here and *B*, I wouldn't put it past the van der Klopps to tamper with the evidence.'

'Both of them?'

'Either or. They're both as dodgy as a three-dollar note.'

'Come on, Jack. Aren't you being paranoid?'

'No, I'm not. Murderers with blood still wet on their mitts tend to have elevated heart rates and impaired judgment.' Now wasn't the time to tell DC Taylor he'd been that paranoid person himself several years ago. The feeling still bubbled away beneath the surface. Knifing a bloke to death and then going to extreme lengths to cover his tracks was a path Jack had trodden by necessity. It kept him awake some nights.

'Still, Jack…'

He pretended not to hear as he pounded on the door of No. 5 Rogers Close.

It opened after the second knock. The smell of stale cigarette smoke whacked Jack in the face like a sparring partner getting in a sneaky one under his guard. The stench was at once repulsive and alluring to an ex-smoker. Taylor winced as the malodour entered her nostrils.

'About time you got 'ere.' The resident, Pat O'Grady, was a skinny woman in her seventies. Her abundant wrinkles reminded Jack of one of his favourite literary characters: Prune Face. 'I'm itching to hear what's happened across the street.'

A demonstration of police badges received a curt nod from Mrs O'Grady. Her eyes bulged in anticipation of meeting with the city's finest.

'May we come in?' said Jack.

'Of course, officers.' She gestured magnanimously over the threshold of her home, which looked very similar to the other two the cops had visited.

Taylor stood on tiptoes and whispered in Jack's ear. 'Perhaps we can conduct the interview out here on the patio? It's going to reek of ciggies in there.' O'Grady was wearing a chunky hearing aid, so the whispering was perhaps unnecessary.

'On second thoughts,' Jack smiled at the woman. 'Let's have a chat out here in the open air.' It was a warm, pleasant evening, low humidity and a half moon. Jack gestured towards a set of cane furniture set up on the front deck.

'Won't the neighbours hear us?'

'Don't worry. I made them brush their teeth and sent them all to bed.' Jack winked and the old lady blushed.

'I'll just fetch me smokes and an ashtray.'

Chapter Nine

JACK NOSED the patrol car out of the cul-de-sac onto a link road and then a major arterial leading to the Yorkville CBD. At close to 10:15pm on a Tuesday night, the streets were practically free of traffic. The radio announcer introduced someone with a Chinese name playing Hungarian Rhapsody No. 2 by Franz Liszt. Not sure if he knew this tune, Jack edged up the volume. It was oddly familiar, like he'd heard it long ago, background music in a cartoon perhaps.

He squinted and blinked to focus on the road. Dead tired after a day of drama, he still had a gym workout to complete before bed. The routine was not negotiable, written in stone. His sacred exercise plan. No excuses, no exceptions. He'd be smashing the heavy bag and jumping rope like a dynamo even if it was after midnight. To the accompaniment of some hardcore UK punk. Maybe *The Damned* tonight. "Smash it up". Yes, that would do nicely. His pulse picked up the pace at the thought.

In his peripherals Jack saw Taylor rubbing at the

corners of her eyes. Jack chomped on six pellets of gum at once, desperately trying to obliterate the taste of dry charcoal in his mouth. The speed at which Mrs O'Grady had puffed on cigarettes, billowing her CO_2 emissions in all directions, and the fact there was no breeze, meant it was only marginally more comfortable questioning the woman outside than in. A reformed smoker with occasional lapses, Jack often enjoyed passive fumes, but not this time. If he and Taylor tested positive for aggressive tumours on the lung tomorrow, he wouldn't be surprised.

'Holy mother of God,' said Taylor, dabbing at her wet cheeks with a tissue. 'I thought we were going to choke to death back there.'

'Me too. She's got some constitution if she can absorb that amount of poison and still live. Maybe she's related to Keith Richards. If we ever need to speak to her again, it'll be in the sterile environment of Interview Room 1 down at the station.'

'What did you make of her?' Taylor wadded the tissues and kept patting her face.

'Off her rocker.'

'She seemed pretty sure of herself.'

'Do you really think armed men in black suits spilling out of Hummers would have escaped the eagle eye of Miranda Mallick?'

'Maybe.'

'Bollocks. The Mallicks have a clearer view of the Snyder home, for one thing. And the very thought of such a scenario is preposterous.'

'You never know. Remember what Assistant Commissioner Hook said about CHOGM.'

'I don't care what Jabba said. And stop using his title, he

doesn't deserve that kinda respect. He was telling bigger porkies than Smokey O'Grady back there.'

'What do you mean?'

'Homeland effing Security,' Jack scoffed.

'What about it?'

'For someone so on the ball, Claudia, you've missed the bleedin' obvious. There ain't no such agency in Australia.'

'Jesus, you're right! It sounded a bit...foreign...at the time, but he's a top cop, y'know? I guess the natural instinct is to believe your superiors.'

'Quell that instinct immediately, DC Taylor.' Jack stopped the car to let a goanna slowly weave its way across the road. The hip-swivelling monitor lizard had fortuitously picked a well-lit pedestrian crossing to get to the other side. 'Except when it comes to me.'

'You always tell the truth, do you? Your record as my partner speaks otherwise,' Taylor smirked.

'If I've bent the truth with you from time to time, there's been a good reason for it.' *Like now.* Should he come clean with her? Perhaps it was time. He opened his mouth to speak, but Taylor beat him to the punch.

'I remember now. It's called Home Affairs!'

'Well done, sunshine. Speaking of affairs, are you still of the opinion Renee van der Klopp was having one with our murder victim?'

'At first I was sure of it. But you bringing up Neighbourhood Watch champion Miranda Mallick makes me unsure now. She never mentioned anything about that.'

'Look, even the most dedicated curtain twitcher can't see everything that happens. She might have been, I don't know, having an extended spell sitting on the toilet while young Renee waltzes into Snyder's place. Miranda makes a cup of tea an hour later, Renee leaves unseen. The only way

Miranda would be able to observe everything is if she's got a security camera set up. Which she hasn't.'

'Maybe Proctor's going to get all the glory on this one. Wrapping it all up with science.'

'Normally I'd be peeved at the prospect of her doing that, but this time I'd be glad if she found the killer before us.'

'Why?'

'Because I've got an effing plane to catch.'

Chapter Ten

'YOU GOING to be OK there, Constable?' said Jack into his mobile, towelling sweat from his armpit with his free hand. Limb stretching and warmup over, he'd decided to check in with last-minute night watchman Wilson before embarking on a proper hard training session.

'No worries, DS Lisbon. I had a power nap when I got home. I can hold the fort here until Proctor and her crew arrive in the morning. I've settled in on the couch in the lounge room. He's got an awesome sound system hooked up to his TV. You oughta…'

'No, no, no! You need to be in the car, opposite the house, about 30 metres away. Exercising discretion.'

'What? All night?'

'If need be. If you're sitting inside eating chips on the couch when the bad guys arrive, they'll have you hogtied before you know it. Plus you're going to contaminate the scene inside the house.'

'But Sarge, what if I need the toilet?'

'Bloody hell, Wilson, can't you think for yourself? There

should be a large empty bottle in the boot of the car. Pee in that if you feel the urge.'

'What about number twos?'

'Shit in your police hat.'

'You can't be serious, sir.'

Jack smiled politely at a supremely muscular female striding past on her way to a weight machine, gave a little finger salute. She snarled back at him. *Ouch.*

'Look. Go inside the house now if you need to evacuate your bowels. I've gotta get back to my workout. Before I hang up I've got one last question for you. Have you had your Glock serviced lately?'

'Last week. Wait…what? Do you think I'm going to need it?' Wilson chuckled uneasily, failing to mask the apprehension in his voice.

'With all that cloak and dagger malarkey from Jabba Hook, we gotta be open to the possibility of terrorism. And you must be prepared. I repeat, is your gun functional?'

'I guess. You're kidding about terrorists, right?'

'This is no joking matter, sunshine. If you see any suspicious activity while you're there, call the station immediately.'

'What if there's lots of 'em?'

Jack swapped the phone and towel to opposite hands, wiped his other armpit. 'Make sure they don't see you. Think of this as an undercover stakeout. We're all counting on you, Constable.'

'Geez… I'm thinking I should have said no to this job.'

'The odds are slim this is anything other than a common or garden murder, but you never know, innit?'

'Bloody hell. Are you sure I don't need someone with me?'

'Positive. See you in the morning.' Jack placed the phone

in his backpack and grinned. He may have gone overboard with painting the nightmarish scenarios, but at least Wilson would be wide awake until dawn, too terrified to nod off.

He slugged a draft of tepid water, labelled orange-flavoured but more reminiscent of rusty steel, put the bottle back in his sports bag and pulled out his favourite pair of black 16 oz Everlast boxing gloves. The Clash decided to make an untimely racket inside the pocket of his tracksuit pants. *Surely Wilson hasn't had an unexpected visitor already.*

Jabba. Again, curiosity overrode common sense and Jack answered the call.

'You better have a good reason to be interrupting my precious free time,' said Jack. A prickly heat ran down the back of his neck. 'It's five minutes to midnight and I haven't even got into my stride. What the fuck d'ya want?'

'Language, DS Lisbon.' Strained breathing rasped down the line. Hook wouldn't last five minutes on a walking machine at its lowest setting without keeling over from a heart attack.

'Oi! It was you who set the tone for our dealings, not me.'

'Do forgive me.' The man's words sloshed around in his mouth. He must've tucked away some booze before making the call. 'I just thought I'd give you a bit of advice.'

'Yeah, what's that? I already feel like a schmuck for deceiving my colleagues when I agreed to help you out.'

'But you never did what I asked!' Hook sounded desperate, almost teary. He must be close to plastered.

'Of course I never. The man went and got himself offed, didn't he?'

'Yeah, but…the retractions in the press. They never happened like we agreed.' Jack heard a crack and the sound of air escaping a pop-top can. 'That's what I needed from you, Lisbon. To clear Snyder's name. I ordered Batista to send you back, but he wilfully disobeyed me. He'll pay for that.'

'Don't be a mug, Hook. A murder investigation takes priority over everything else. You know that.'

'You can still do it, mate. Posthumously. It's essential for national security. CHOGM mustn't be compromised.'

'Piss off with your babbling nonsense. What's Snyder got to do with all that stuff?'

'Sorry, that kind of information is above your pay grade.'

'Nah-ah. There's something else going on here. What is it?'

'Shut up, Lisbon. I paid for your damn ticket re-scheduling, got you an extra week's holiday. You will do as I say!'

'I'd love to, guv, but it's gonna look very dodgy if I start doing your bidding while Snyder's the subject of a murder investigation. I have to stay objective, not run around trying to defend him against, what was it again?'

'Fraud. It's all manufactured lies!' Hook started making moaning, guttural noises that sounded like distraught sobs.

'And what if they are? You know full well you can't defame a dead person. And why are you crying?'

'I'm totally fine. Just hay fever.' The sound of a gulp as more alcohol was despatched down Hook's neck.

Then a thought occurred to Jack. 'Oi. You don't know about any connection between Snyder and radical political groups, do you?'

'More lies. Someone informed the security agencies he was associating with rebel bikers and had Eureka flags on display in his home. Is that a c-c-crime? No! And that's how he ended up on the radar of ASIO and the foreign agencies. It's all one big data base these days. A whisper of anything not a hundred percent politically correct and eyeballs are on you. I tried to convince the spooks he was no right-wing threat, because I...feared looking at Snyder so closely was...detracting them from their real job.'

'Who reported him?' Hook's explanations were garbage. 'And why do you seem so personally invested in this?

Ragged breathing, attempts to formulate words that came out as meaningless grunts. Finally Hook managed something intelligible. 'Because I, ooh....shit...'

Jack pressed his ear harder to the phone. 'What? I missed that.'

A muffled scream followed by a loud crash and pitiful groans. Jack disconnected the call, dialled the emergency number, informed the operator that Assistant Commissioner for Police Raymond Hook was in a spot of bother.

'Address please?' asked the operator.

'I don't bleedin' know, do I? Ring Cairns police station. Someone there'll be able to assist.'

'Sir, I'll need you to stay on the line for a moment.'

'Sorry, I've got some important training to do.'

'At this hour of the night?'

Jack hung up on the incredulous operator, tore his shirt off, donned the gloves and proceeded to knock the stuffing out of a 45 kg punching bag. The chain connecting the bag to the ceiling clanked with each ripping blow. The woman on the weight bench stopped and stared open mouthed at Jack. He caught a glimpse of her out of the corner of his eye, upped the ferocity. His peacock display must have impressed. She stepped off the machine and approached Jack, the previous snarl replaced by a cheeky grin and a glint in her eye. Muscly women weren't usually his type, but he was prepared to make exceptions.

Chapter Eleven

GET A MOVE ON, *Lisbon*. The case had to be solved in three days or Jack's trip to the UK was in the bin. Jack glanced at his wristwatch. 12:36 pm. Make that two and a half days. *Shit!* Last night's late-late romp with gym-nut Marietta Szabo had been fun, but now he regretted going back to her place instead of making a date for later. Like, post-UK-trip later. Now, his eyes shrunk to coin slots behind the Aviators as he stepped out of the Kia Stinger and headed down an alley leading to the back entrance of the pool parlour.

With urgency top of mind, he'd split the main interview tasks with Taylor. He'd speak to the manager at Trick Shot pool parlour, Cameron Snyder's primary place of business. Taylor got the grieving widow. She was better at handling recently bereaved women. After that, all they could do was throw darts at shadows and pray Proctor and her geeks would come up trumps with the scientific shit. Ray Hook had plenty of questions to answer, too, if he didn't die before his inevitable bypass heart operation. In reality, it was stomach stapling the bloke needed.

But Jabba's health was not Jack's concern. First job this morning, explore the business side of Snyder's life. That's where all the Internet heat was pointing, what all the accusations of impropriety centred on. Hook claimed it was all bullshit. But was it?

Jack gave three hard raps on the wide steel door of the establishment with the heel of his fist. He adjusted his sunglasses as the bright autumnal Yorkville sun beat down pleasantly on his head. He waited a minute, pounded again with twice the vigour. He pressed his ear to the door. *Yes, someone was there.*

Faint shuffling noises. The sound of lumbering footsteps grew louder until the door opened slowly. A man somewhere between 55 and 60 years old in a gaudy Hawaiian shirt and neat brown chinos stood in the doorway, feet planted shoulder width apart. He chewed the stub of a thick cigar, pushing it from one side of his mouth to the other with his tongue, resting a meaty hand on the edge of the door. His opal-blue eyes rose and fell as he gave Jack a reflexive up-and-down assessment. The DS did the same in return.

The man's body was an odd combination of a bloated beer drinker's gut attached to a slim body with toned limbs. Wiry grey hair stuck out in tufts from underneath a weather-beaten baseball cap that used to be red, now pink. His angular face bore ragged scars, his nose flared and flat. Not uncommon features on men who hang about in billiard halls. His eyes twinkled as his mouth broke into a broad smile that revealed teeth too white and symmetrical to be natural.

'Can I help you?' he asked in a pleasant baritone voice. 'We don't open for another six hours, sport.'

Jack showed his bona fides. 'Detective Sergeant Jack Lisbon. It's a rather delicate matter. May I come inside?'

The man's smiled flipped to a frown. He ushered Jack down a dim corridor that opened up onto the poolroom. It was almost a large-scale replica of what Snyder had in his basement. Even the flags and well-stocked bar were similar.

'I should've guessed by the cheap suit you were a cop. Plus the fact you didn't call to make an appointment like normal people do.'

'We like to be spontaneous.' *In other words, we don't give people the heads-up and a chance to disappear.* 'And you're no fashion expert by the way. This suit cost me a packet.'

'Sure it did. Like a drink?' The man reached for a bottle of overproof Bundaberg Rum from a shelf above the bar. 'We've got plenty of the good stuff to choose from.' He poured himself a shot.

'Too early for me.' Jack hadn't touched alcohol in months. It would take a fancier occasion than a chat with this bloke to fall off the wagon. 'Got any coffee? I prefer espresso, but percolated will be fine.'

The man shook his head. 'Not a popular beverage in here. If I look hard I might rustle up some instant.'

'That's OK, I'll go without. Do you know why I'm here?'

A shrug. 'No idea. Unpaid taxes?'

'No, nothing as trivial as that. Can you tell me who you are first?'

'Harry Sheffield. Trick Shot manager and general factotum for Mr Cameron Snyder.'

Jack knew that already. He and Taylor had spent two hours in the office this morning working out a plan of attack for this blitzkrieg investigation. Online photos of key players had been scanned and committed to memory.

'I'm afraid I've got bad news, sunshine. Majorly bad.'

'Jesus. It's not about the application to demolish the old fish factory, is it? I can't believe he never got that authority signed in time. But I promise, it's gonna get done. Just give us another week. Cameron's gonna be…'

'Cameron's gonna be nuthin' mate. He's dead.'

'Excuse me?' The shot glass shook in his hand.

'He's dead.'

'What? No!' The colour drained from Sheffield's face. He slumped onto a bar stool. 'I was just talking to him on the weekend. Jesus Christ. How did it happen? Car accident? He was always driving too fast.'

'Murder.'

The ashen face was now white as milk. 'When?'

'Last night between ten and midnight. Can you account for your whereabouts?'

'I was right here.' Sheffield's eyes narrowed in recollection. 'There were about six of us, preparing for the next series of roster matches.'

'Anyone able to confirm that?'

'Yeah. I can give you their names and addresses if you want.'

'You got closed circuit footage?'

'We've got a camera, yes.' Sheffield downed the rum, poured another and pointed the neck of the bottle at a second glass. 'You sure you don't want one?'

'I'm good thanks.' Jack perched himself on a stool next to Sheffield.

'Holy shit, I can't believe it. What's going to happen to the pool hall? Man, there's going to be chaos.'

The man was getting edgier and needed reassurance.

'There's always a lot of uncertainty when people die unexpectedly. But things sort themselves out eventually.'

'He employs people, you know? And not just me. People with mortgages, obligations. Shit, shit, shit.' He started chewing a fingernail.

Jack reached in his pocket, handed over a card for a counselling agency. 'If you're struggling, call this number. They can help you in many ways I can't.'

'Thanks,' Sheffield nodded. 'I understand.'

'My job is to find who did it. There's been lots of scuttlebutt about Snyder. Can you think of anyone who would want to see him dead?'

Sheffield pulled out a lighter. 'You mind?'

'No, go ahead.'

'A better question would be, who didn't?' Sweet Cuban tobacco smoke billowed around Sheffield's face. 'So many people had it in for Cameron, but he never did anything wrong. At least as far as his business went.'

'What about the accusation he bought Pilkington's fish plant without going through probate?'

'Nonsense stirred up by a dickhead called Randall Sowell. The property was obtained legally. No probate was required because the fella who died, Maurice Pilkington, wasn't the sole owner like everyone thought. There was a group of them, silent partners, and they decided to sell to Cameron for the price he offered.'

'Why would this Sowell character spread false rumours about Snyder?'

'Simple. Revenge. He wanted the property himself and couldn't afford it. He and Cameron go back years, knew each other at business college in Sydney when they were teenagers. When Cameron moved up here to make a go of it, Randall followed soon after. There's bad blood between them.'

Jack jotted down the rival's name. 'You got an address for this bloke?'

'I have. I'd be looking closely at him, Detective Lisbon. He's shifty as a bucket of eels, that one. Failed companies, ugly divorce.' He blew another cloud of smoke into the air before tapping a collar of ash into an empty beer bottle.

Jack pointed at a drinks fridge behind Sheffield. 'Actually, my mouth's gone dry. I wouldn't mind a Coke.'

Sheffield twisted the cap, handed Jack the soft drink.

'Speaking of divorce,' said Jack. 'Tell me about Lydia.'

'They're not—'

'Yeah, I know. It was a segue, like.'

'One 'o them things on two wheels?'

Jack shifted in his seat. 'No, not that. Yes, they were separated not divorced, I'm aware of that. What was their relationship like?'

Sheffield shrugged. 'He didn't speak about her much. They had a kid die on them back in Sydney before they moved up here.'

'How old?'

'Two, she was. They were never able to conceive again after that. They tried IVF, no luck.'

'That's the kind of thing to put a relationship under pressure,' Jack observed.

'Yep. I think Cameron had hopes they'd get back together one day. My opinion, it was a relationship doomed to failure. I reckon she still loved him, even though she was vindictive at times.'

'What do you mean?'

'Oh, she thought she was entitled to a bigger share of his money than he did.' Sheffield smiled but it was forced.

Jack expected the dam wall to break any minute. 'She even popped in here the other day, demanded to see the books.'

'What books?'

'The accounts. She screamed at me when I wouldn't hand them over. I told her it was impossible because they weren't kept here at Trick Shot. The accountant's got 'em all. Anyway, she stormed out with a bee in her bonnet. She's a feisty one, let me tell you.'

'What day was this?'

'Hmm. Exactly a week ago today. Cameron dropped by after Lydia's performance. He wasn't too pleased to hear what she'd been up to.'

'What reason did she give for wanting to see the accounts?'

'She said the divorce was going to leave her destitute. She said she wanted to show the figures to her lawyer, to prove Cameron had more money than he claimed he did.'

'And did he?'

'I believe he was always fair and he'd never leave his wife in the lurch, even after a divorce.'

'That's not what I asked. Did he have more money than he was letting on?'

Sheffield removed his hat, revealing a hairline receded halfway up his skull, gave his scalp a vigorous rub. 'I honestly couldn't tell you. I only manage this establishment. He's got – had – Chalkies in Cairns, too.'

'And a shelf company registered in the UAE,' Jack prompted.

The manager's blue eyes grew wide. 'Really?' he gave a half-hearted chuckle. 'Well, he always was a bit of a dark horse.'

'One more question, Mr Sheffield. Who was Snyder's accountant?'

Chapter Twelve

LYDIA SNYDER'S apartment in Bonnie Street, lowbrow Thurston was compact, clean and tidy. Not a luxury dwelling, but not a run-down dump either. Lydia lived in a tiny part of the suburb that nestled against a more salubrious section of town. People in this sector of Thurston liked to pretend they were really living in the adjacent suburb of Renouf, home to canal-front mansions, azure kidney-shaped swimming pools and prestige European automobiles. Taylor never understood the phenomenon of "post code snobbery", but it was as much a part of Yorkville as the saltwater crocodiles that sunned themselves on the banks of the estuary.

'Please, Detective Taylor, take a seat.' Lydia, her frail figure wrapped in a cream terry towelling dressing gown, gestured weakly to a fake-leather recliner. Her straight hair, closely matching the caramel tone of the lounge suite, hung about her face like a limp shower curtain. The hostess remained standing on shaky legs, eyes flickering. 'I'm not sure I can help you.' She sounded like a woman who'd lost everything.

'Why would you say that?' Taylor kept her voice level, trying to present a reassuring demeanour. She was looking into the saddest, reddest pair of eyes she'd ever seen. 'You were closer to him than most. I'm sure you can assist–'

Taylor's words hung in the air as Lydia let loose with a wail that came from the pit of her soul. Tears flowed in a bitter stream, racking sobs echoed around the apartment for three full minutes. Taylor was sure of that, because she timed it on her wristwatch. Finally, the woman summoned the will to stop crying. Lydia tucked a bunch of crinkled tissues into her dressing gown pocket and gave a quick nod. *I'm OK, I'm OK*, she mouthed silently. She straightened her shoulders and shuffled to the kitchen, visible from the living area. She poured herself a tumbler of water from the tap, took a large gulp, set the glass down. Taylor could only stare at the back of the woman's head, waiting for her to regain enough composure to continue the interview. *Maybe she couldn't.*

'Would you rather I come back another time, Ms Snyder?' Taylor offered, hoping like hell the woman would decline the offer.

'No, don't go. I'm actually glad of the company.' Lydia sniffed back a tear, chugging a ball of phlegm down her throat in the process. The gurgling sound made Taylor want to gag. Lydia slumped onto a wooden chair in the kitchen, not meeting Taylor's gaze but fixing her attention on a wall clock. She pulled a box of tissues across the dining table, plucked a couple and blew her nose, then turned to face Taylor. She tapped the top of the table with long fingernails. 'Please, sit at the table next to me.'

Taylor placed the strap of her handbag over the back of

a chair. As she sat, Lydia grasped the DC's right hand and gave it a squeeze. 'I apologise for my outburst.'

'Perfectly understandable.' No one Taylor knew personally had ever been murdered. She thought her reaction wouldn't be much different to Lydia Snyder's.

'What's the matter with me? I never even offered you a cuppa.'

'It's fine. I've already had my quota for the day.' Taylor gave a comforting smile. 'I'm going to ask you some simple questions. Your answers could help us find whoever killed Cameron. Firstly, do you know who might want to do such a thing?'

Lydia stood again, fetched the glass of water and brought it to the table. Taylor wondered if she could stay still from more than thirty seconds at a time. A foil of tiny white tablets appeared on the table. Lydia popped two and sluiced them down. 'Valium. I've been on them for years. I normally take one before bed, but...y'know.' She sipped again, wiped her mouth with the sleeve of her dressing gown. 'To be perfectly honest, I can imagine plenty of people would wish harm upon Cameron. But I can't think of anyone who'd want to...kill him. Oh my God, I never thought I'd be saying those words.' Her hands covered her face and she sobbed rhythmically behind them.

Taylor knew she should go in with the tough questions now, while the woman was at her most vulnerable. That's what Jack would do. But Taylor wasn't Jack. The hardest questions would come last. Ease into it, coax the information out of her. The DC took out her notebook, scanned the list she'd prepared at the station this morning. 'What about the rumours Cameron was, let's say, a less than honest businessman? Could one of his rivals have hated him enough to take the ultimate step?'

Lydia tapped her nails on the tabletop, twisted her lips. 'There's only one person I can think of. But even then... surely not murder.'

'Who?' Taylor's pen was poised.

'Randall Sowell,' Lydia hissed through gritted teeth. 'I'm sure it was him that started all the innuendo about Cameron. I fucking hate him. Look into Sowell. If he's not the killer, he might be behind it.'

'Did Cameron ever have this Mr Sowell over to his home?' Taylor arched a curious eyebrow. 'There's no evidence of forced entry into Cameron's property, so he most likely knew the person who killed him.'

'They were arch rivals. Why would they meet up? If they did, it would only have been by accident.' Lydia quickly explained the men's shared educational background at a New South Wales college, how Cameron was always one move ahead of Sowell and how it grated on the guy. 'Cameron tried to laugh it off, ignore the bullshit Randall stirred up. I told him to sue the prick, but Cam wouldn't. Too soft in my opinion.'

'You seem to know a lot about Mr Snyder's business. Did you give Cameron advice on how to conduct his affairs?' Lydia's last job was as a financial adviser, a fact listed on her public LinkedIn profile. She'd been in that profession until two years ago when the sparse resume stopped.

'I did, yeah. But he never listened to me. He could have got that Pilkington place cheaper if he'd held out longer like I told him, but he was worried someone – in other words Sowell – would steal it out from under him. So he rushed the deal. But I guess none of that matters anymore, does it?' Lydia honked into a tissue, then frowned at Taylor apologetically. 'I'm so sorry. I can't seem to stop this runny nose.' *Or talking.* She was on a roll and Taylor didn't want it to stop.

'No need to apologise. You're entitled to...' Taylor felt her mobile vibrate in her jacket pocket. 'Excuse me one moment.' Damn it. Jack was on his way. She put the phone away, pressed on. 'My colleague will be joining us shortly. He's not as pleasant as me, so perhaps we can motor along to spare you his gruff manner.' The words came out as a blend of statement and question.

'Of course. Ask whatever you like. And I'm sure I can handle your partner. If it's that Detective Lisbon I've seen on the TV, then I'm looking forward to it. He managed to catch the last couple of murderers in Yorkville. I pray he can do the same again.'

Taylor strangled the temptation to say she herself had more than a hand in solving those cases. Why did Jack get all the bloody limelight?

'How long ago did you and Cameron separate?'

'February last year. I took the break-up pretty badly, to be honest. The pills help. I quit my job, stopped seeing my friends and family, never went out anywhere. I was only just starting to get a grip on things when... this.' Lydia's face disappeared into a bouquet of tissues again as she wept softly for a few moments. 'Oh dear, sorry. Again.'

'It's fine. Go on, please. What caused the split?'

'His temper. Don't get me wrong, he was a good man.' She blew her nose into a tissue. 'We were childhood sweet-hearts, you know. We met in high school, we were inseparable.'

'Tell me more about this temper of his.'

'Don't get me wrong. He loved me, OK? But his bad moods when things went wrong scared the bejesus out of me. He used to shout at me, wave his arms about, throw things…'

'Do you know if he was a substance abuser?' Taylor wondered if a drug dealer owed money could have been the perpetrator.

'No way. He hated that kind of thing.'

'Alcohol?'

'Maximum two beers at a barbecue, then he'd stop. The mood swings were related to his business, I'm sure of it. All the stress messing with his head.'

'Did Cameron ever hit you?'

The head shake fast and emphatic. 'No, no. Never. I just got tired of his nagging. Yes! I see you find that odd, a man nagging. But it's possible. I could never do anything the way he liked it. But he was driven, you see. A workaholic. Always running around, putting out spot fires.' A big sip of water, another wipe of the lips with the gown cuff, now visibly damp. 'So his head was more focused on his businesses than me.'

Jack had mentioned a withdrawn restraining order in the Snyder closet, but nothing further. Taylor remembered it was from Brisbane, before the move north to seek their fortune. 'Tell me about the DVO you had out on Cameron.'

A wave of the hand. 'A complete overreaction on my part. I had the court cancel it after I calmed down.'

'So it wasn't a matter of domestic violence?'

'No, no. Nothing like that. He got frustrated one night and threw a glass. It hit me in the back of the head. At the time I was sure he aimed it at me, but later I realised he'd never have done it on purpose. I regret what I did.'

The story sounded fishy. Taylor scribbled in her notebook. *Check Snyder's interstate rap sheet.* She crossed the last "t", looked up at Lydia. 'I noticed a stack of packing boxes in a room off the hallway. Are you moving somewhere?'

'Ha! Where would I go? I've got no money. I quit my job six weeks ago, still waiting for the dole payments to kick in. There's a stupid waiting period when you leave employment voluntarily, even if said job sucks.'

That didn't tally with the LinkedIn record, but there's no legal obligation to keep your profile truthful and up to date. 'What job was that?'

'I had a part-time admin job with a local charity. Shit pay, but I needed something to keep me occupied.'

'Why'd you quit?'

'The boss was a bitch, kept bringing up Cameron in conversations, regurgitated all the online rubbish. She did it to bait me, I'm sure. Anyway, it all got too much and one day I told her to stick her lousy job up her fat arse.'

Taylor tugged her scrunchie. 'Would you call your relationship with Cameron post-breakup amicable?'

'Yeah, I'd say so. He was less inclined to shout at me, let's put it that way.' A wry smile penetrated the tear-stained face.

'From what I can gather his business was on the up.'

'He was doing OK, on the face of it. When he got the liquor licenses for the pool parlours, Trick Shot and Chalkies started to take off.'

'He didn't feel like sharing the successes of his business with you?'

'Listen, Detective, I might have worked for a charity, but I'm not one myself, you know what I mean?'

'But now you're set to receive a portion of his estate, right?'

'Ha! Like I said, on the surface he was successful. Why do you think we started off living here in Bonnie Street?'

'You tell me.'

'Because it's all he could afford when we moved up here. It's in a cheap suburb but at the "Paris end" as they say. Once the cashflow started to improve, his ambitions grew as well. He had plans of turning that old fish factory into some massive games centre.'

'That would've pissed off Randall Sowell.'

'Probably. But the project might never have got off the ground anyway.'

'Why not?'

'Because Cam was up to his eyeballs in debt. Borrowing money left and right to show the world he was the North Queensland Monopoly champion. Once the creditors get their share of his estate, there'll be nothing left for me. If you think I had a hand in doing him in so I could get rich, forget it!'

More shorthand notes. Conduct thorough investigation of Snyder's businesses and finances. Perhaps psychological evaluation of Lydia. Sharp mood swings could be indicative of….what?

'What can you tell me about the people he mixed with at the pool halls he owned? Could he have made enemies there?'

Lydia shrugged. 'Maybe. I never went to either of them. Places like that attract the wrong crowd.'

Taylor nodded. Another note. *Interview pool hall employees and clientele.* 'Just a few more questions and I'll be out of your hair.'

'Sure.' Lydia stared at the tabletop, massaged her temples slowly with the tips of her fingers.

'I'd like to ask you about the piles of boxes. If you aren't moving house, what's in them?'

'Photos of me and Cameron from happier times. Our wedding, honeymoon, holidays. I was going to give them to him. I didn't want them around here, reminding me of how good we used to have it.' Lydia stood unexpectedly. 'Just a minute, I'll make us a cup of tea.'

'Seriously.' Taylor shook her head. 'No need.'

Lydia gave a dismissive wave as she waddled to the kitchen, flicked on the kettle and dropped tea bags in chunky white mugs. 'How do you take it?'

'Milk, two sugars.' Taylor quickly texted Jack to stay away, she'd established a good rapport with the estranged widow Snyder and he'd only spoil it. A minute later came the curt reply. *OK. I trust you. Be there in an hour.*

'Now, where were we?' Taylor forced a feeble grin as Lydia placed a mug before her, the contents sloshing about.

'Discussing your relationship with Cameron.' No point delaying the inevitable. 'You're not going to like this question, but I'm obliged to ask. Were you having a sexual relationship with Mr Snyder even though you'd separated?'

Lydia drew her head back, her lips dipped at the corners. 'Excuse me?'

'One of Cameron's neighbours told us you'd occasionally visit the deceased for an hour or more at a time. I can only make assumptions until you put me right. Were you sleeping together?'

The woman cradled her head in her hands, the sleeves of her dressing gown slid down revealing thin, white wrists patterned with heavy blue veins. Like fragile, bone china porcelain. Taylor realised now how emaciated the woman was, a couple kilos shy of anorexic.

'Yes,' she whispered.

'Why?'

'Why? Because I still loved him despite everything, that's why!'

'Did you sleep with him at his residence on or around Monday night, March 4th, the day he was murdered?'

Bewilderment clouded Lydia Snyder's face as she picked at a loose thread of the chequered tablecloth. 'No. He was supposed to be in Cairns that night, checking out some faulty vending machines at Chalkies. I don't understand any of this.'

'There's something I have to tell you, Lydia. Something you're not going to like.'

'What?'

Taylor hesitated.

'What!' Lydia bellowed, thumping the table with her bony fist. 'What else could be worse than the love of my life being murdered, huh? Tell me that, smart-arse detective?'

For an instant, Taylor regretted taking this line of questioning. Lydia was already on the ropes. But no, there was a murder to solve. Her feelings were secondary, as Jack would have insisted.

'Forensics officers found a recently used condom in a waste basket in Cameron's bedroom.'

'What the hell?' Lydia palmed her forehead. 'Impossible!'

'So I take it you're saying that was not the result of an encounter between you and Cameron?'

'Oh my God! Oh my God! This can't be true.'

'Were you of the belief that you were a separated couple in a monogamous sexual relationship? Forgive me for saying, but that comes across as rather naïve.' Bloody hell, Taylor was sounding as callous as Jack right now.

'We were getting things back on track, how could he do this to me?'

'But you were about to take the boxes of photos back to him. I don't understand.'

A light switched on behind the red eyes. 'It's not your fucking job to understand, is it? It's your job to find out who killed Cameron. Our relationship was…complicated. We needed each other, but we also needed our own space. Him more than me, but I got it. We loved each other, and no one can tell me otherwise.' She pushed off against a table, shuffled to the kitchen sink and stared out the window. She continued to speak with her back to Taylor. 'You know, I wouldn't be surprised if someone planted a condom in Cameron's house to make him look bad in my eyes.'

An odd theory, Taylor thought. Why do that and then kill the man? Unless…they were two separate acts? But no. The likeliest scenario was that Cameron Snyder had sex with another person, most likely candidate at this point – Renee van der Klopp. She left and the killer paid their fatal visit later in the night. Time to disabuse the poor woman.

'It's a used condom, Lydia. There's semen in it. In a wastebasket in Cameron's bedroom. We're yet to confirm who was wearing it and who else was involved. Look, I'm sure you're telling the truth, but for our records, and to eliminate you as a suspect, would you consent to us taking a DNA sample from you?'

A drawer opened, cigarettes emerged and Lydia Snyder was soon surrounded by a cloud of menthol smoke. She popped open the window and blew the fumes outside. Half came back in, made their way up Taylor's twitching nose, but the DC said nothing.

'Yeah, of course. My fingerprints are on record from a misspent youth in Sydney, so you may as well have my DNA too. I've got nothing to hide.' To prove it, Lydia Snyder spent the next fifteen minutes opening up about Cameron Snyder's ambitions, other figures who were prominent in his personal and business lives, the child they lost to a rare disease, Snyder's unbridled patriotism that got confused with right-wing sympathies. *That explains the Reddit photo.* The information poured out like water from a burst dam. Taylor was glad she'd taken a course in Pitman shorthand, for those occasions when a witness might be less candid if they knew they were being voice recorded.

As she stashed the jotter away, Taylor noted Lydia's mood had shifted seismically since the interview commenced. The woman was now completely calm. She returned to the table and took a seat. Her eyes were much clearer. Perhaps the diazepam was taking effect. 'Thanks for your time, Ms Snyder. We'll be seeing you down at the station for those swabs, yeah?'

'I'll be there later this afternoon.'

A knock on the door. Jack. Like clockwork, exactly one hour after his text.

———

JACK RAISED his middle finger to a driver who cut him off at the Oliphant Street roundabout, pushed the button to lower the window and stuck his head out into the balmy 28 degree air. 'Fuck you!' He roared before calmly lowering the window. 'Sorry, Claudia, but did you see that arsehole? I'm sure he was looking at the mobile phone in his lap. Lucky for him I'm in a hurry to catch a killer and then a plane.' He tugged his seatbelt, looked left, indicated and exited the roundabout. 'So, what was the upshot of your wee chat with the bereaved.'

'First and foremost, she claims she didn't have sex with Snyder the night he died.'

'I'll bet London to a brick Proctor's chemistry set points us towards Renee.'

'You know this could be completely separate from the murder, don't you, Jack? I'm keen to check out this business rival, Randall…'

'Sowell.' Jack finished the sentence. 'I got the same tip from Harry Sheffield. Which sets my Spidey senses atingle.'

'Why?'

'Two persons of interest immediately finger the corporate enemy. Convenient.'

'Or it's simply the truth, Jack.' She relayed to Jack a summary of Lydia's tempestuous relationship with Cameron Snyder.

'The bit about the daughter who died. Did she say what the disease was?'

Taylor frowned. 'Huntington's. I've never heard of it.'

'Me either. Must be one of those rare ones.'

Jack pulled up at a chain-brand coffee shop, slipped the car into park. Taylor was left unsatisfied after Lydia's weak tea and readily agreed to the stop. The detectives placed their order, secured a seat by the window and watched the good citizens of Yorkville streaming past on their daily lives.

'I wonder how Wilson's getting along with the accountant,' Taylor mused as a waiter brought their drinks to the table. 'To be honest, I'm surprised you entrusted him with the task.'

'Time's of the essence.' Jack tapped the face of his watch. 'Besides, he's one of those types who can see patterns in numbers. I wouldn't be surprised if he was "on the spectrum", as they say.'

'I'm sure that would've been picked up in the recruitment process,' said Taylor dismissively. 'But you're right. He's up to the task. Even with sleep deprivation.'

'Be fair, Claudia. I let him lie in until midday.' Jack

slurped a cappuccino from a dark black-and-gold cup, gnawed on an almond biscotti.

'Let's hope he can find something useful. You think the secret lies in his business dealings?'

'My preferred option is it's a crime committed on the domestic front and Proctor can find the key among the physical evidence. It'll save us valuable time.' And when he said *us*, he meant *him*. 'I'm also keen to know what Hook was about to divulge before he keeled over on me last night.'

'I'm not sure you'll be speaking to him until you get back from the UK. If we solve the case before then, that is.'

'Oi! Your lack of confidence is unbecoming, DC Taylor. We *will* solve this case.' Taylor held up a laminated menu to shield herself from crumbs that flew from Jack's lips.

'Watch where you're spraying, will you!'

'Sorry. Anyway, I've got the latest update on Jabba's health. I rang Cairns this morning and was fortunate enough to speak to Constable Tinsdale.'

'The one Hook was bullying?'

'The very same. She passed on the news the Assistant Commissioner will require triple bypass surgery as a matter of urgency. And you know, there wasn't a trace of empathy in her voice.'

'Shit! When can we speak to him?'

'Apparently he's still sedated and not allowed to receive visitors. Word is he'll be released tomorrow. His wife Juanita will have to tend to the slob until he's lost enough weight to undergo the procedure.'

'Poor woman.'

'You got that right.'

They finished their coffees, paid the bill minus the traditional coppers' 10 percent discount, set sail for the office of Randall Sowell's company, FarQ2 Enterprises.

Chapter Thirteen

AS HE SAT in the accountant's pine-lined office, Constable Ben Wilson sensed his head nodding forward. He blinked, took a deep breath, rubbed his face hard with the palm of his hand. Sitting in the patrol car all night with only the radio for company, adrenaline pumping thanks to DS Lisbon's talk of terrorists, had depleted nearly all of his energy reserves. By 7:30am, when the forensics team arrived at the crime scene to conduct a second sweep of the house, all he wanted to do was sleep. He'd managed a couple hours of restless shuteye at home before DS Lisbon called on him to double-up with another shift. Eager to help crack the case, Wilson purchased a sixpack of highly caffeinated energy drinks and a bag of sugar-coated cinnamon donuts, headed to the station, grabbed a police car and set off to interview the accountant.

As he waited for Mr Yosef Soplyak to end a phone call, speaking in an accent thicker than mangrove mud, Wilson recalled the one incident that had added a modicum of interest to his lonely vigil. With eyelids drooping, at 02:47

Wilson was jerked into focus by the appearance of a dark, late-model sedan. It had crept into Rogers Close, high beams dazzling on approach, and jolted Wilson into full wakefulness. The vehicle slowed to a crawl as it glided by the murder victim's residence. Perhaps the driver clocked the police tape draped across the front door, maybe they had a change of heart about stopping for a closer inspection, or perhaps they were looking for another address and realised they'd turned up a dead end. Wilson had ducked low to avoid being seen as the car completed the circle at the end of the cul-de-sac and continued on its way, destination unknown. It happened so quickly and unexpectedly, he'd been unable to ascertain the licence plates or anything else that may have helped identify the car. The patrol car was equipped with automatic number-plate recognition, which uses infrared to capture images day or night. Only problem, Wilson forgot about using it until after the car was gone. The driver was nothing but a silhouette. There may have been a passenger, Wilson couldn't be sure. The urge was to pursue – it could've been the perp returning to the scene of the crime – but his job was to make sure no one got into the house and tamper with the scene. He dialled the station, requested another patrol car head to the area, but what would it be looking for? Too vague on details. Request denied.

All of this the constable had dutifully reported to Detective Sergeant Lisbon, who first berated Wilson for letting the car go but then forgave him for sticking to the plan. Then he rewarded the constable with the job in hand. Grill the dead guy's bean counter.

'Sorry, that was an important call to the Australian Tax Office.' Soplyak placed the telephone back in its cradle. He stood, reached across the table and shook hands with the police officer. Wilson pegged the accountant to be in his late fifties to mid-sixties. Clipped beard, sparkly green eyes, professional bearing. 'I'm at your service.'

'I'd like you to tell me everything you can about Cameron Snyder.'

'On what grounds? Do you have a warrant?'

Wilson shook his head. 'I'm not asking for documents – at this point. And you're under no obligation to divulge anything. But I would urge you to co-operate.'

'I am still in shock at the news, to be honest.' Soplyak tut-tutted, pressed his lips together and gave a slight shake of the head. 'I'm not even sure where things stand with his affairs now he's...dead.' A hand pushed back a twist of curly hair that flopped over a pale brow. 'That is a matter for his lawyer, I imagine.'

'I'll tell you where things stand.' The constable channelled his inner Jack Lisbon. Must have been the Red Bull working its magic. 'We've got a well-known pool hall owner who was, until his death, on the radar of Australia's top security agencies. With the CHOGM meeting coming up soon, this matter needs to be resolved quickly.'

Arms folded across a medium-sized chest. In fact, Wilson thought everything about Soplyak could be described as average. His own build and appearance, even the equipment and furnishings of his workspace, were as ordinary as white bread. The one stand-out was a bulbous nose that seemed to be constantly sniffing the air. 'I see. That puts a different light on things.'

'Getting warrants and such takes so much time. Time better spent investigating leads.'

'I agree,' Soplyak said with exaggerated alacrity. 'The security of the country is important. Would you like a drink of something? I have special Ukrainian *horilka*. It's like vodka, only better. You like to try?' He gestured towards a shelf lined with bottles containing clear liquids. Above it was a blue banner depicting a stylised gold design.

'No thanks, I'm good.' If not for the urgency of the case and the fact a drop of alcohol on top of no sleep would have knocked him out, Wilson might have tried a sip. He thought of himself as liberal minded, liked to expand his cultural horizons. 'D'you think you could summarise Mr Snyder's financial position?'

'His financial position was not good, not good. Terrible, actually.' Soplyak shook his head. 'There will be little to go around after the reading of his will. Lydia will get nothing.'

'In other words, we can rule out inheritance as a motive.' More question than statement.

'Not unless he had other accounts I am unaware of. Maybe offshore. But I doubt it. I'm pretty sure I have, how do you say, a handle on it.'

'Why are his affairs in such a state?'

'He kept borrowing money. More and more debt. He couldn't resist. It was like an addiction. Yes, his cash flow was finally picking up a little over the last two quarters, but it would have taken forever to pay off all the loans. He was struggling to even service the old ones. Profit margin was almost non-existent. Such a foolish man.'

'Didn't you advise him to take it easy on the borrowing?'

'Of course! I tell him time and again, but he don't listen. Too headstrong. He wanted to be king-pin of Yorkville. Cairns, too. He bought that stupid old fish factory to turn into a giant games centre. He paid way too much!'

'Were there any loans he was behind on? In other words, were there any angry creditors out there demanding their pound of flesh?'

'Not that I know of. He had no arrears, but liquidity was

tighter than a fish's asshole, excuse my language. Then again, he may have been doing things "off the books" that I was unaware of. Like I said before, I doubt it, but can you ever really know someone inside out, huh?' Soplyak showed his palms and shrugged.

'I guess not,' said Wilson. 'Does the name Randall Sowell mean anything to you?' Wilson received a text from Jack five minutes ago. *Ask the accountant what he knows about Randall Sowell.*

Soplyak coughed into a fist, as if preparing mentally to answer the question. 'Yes. I am aware of this man. Cameron would, how do you say, *beech* about him all the time. There was real hatred between them.'

'Why?'

'Hmm. Not sure exactly, but I think it's something that goes back years. Like Russia and Ukraine fighting over Crimea.'

'Any other people Mr Snyder bitched about?' Wilson remembered a trick Jack had taught him. Use other people's words back at them to make them think you attach value to what they're saying.

A head shake and a pair of honest eyes. 'I never pried into his personal affairs. I knew he was separated from Lydia and he was sometimes sad about that. But I never asked questions.'

'What about the gossip that followed him around?'

'He told me there were rumours on the Internet, even the papers, about him being a dodgy businessman, but I don't read the news. My love is the purity of numbers, tables and columns, not,' he waved his hand in the air, 'abstract things. Wait a moment, I'll be right back.'

Soplyak stood and adjusted cufflinked sleeves poking under a linen jacket. He walked through a door at the back of his office and returned hefting three black-and-white archive boxes, his chin resting on the top one. 'This is everything I have relating to the business affairs of Mr. Snyder.'

'Thank you. We'll be needing the electronic files too,' said Wilson. 'This will take too long to process.'

Soplyak placed the boxes on his desk, leaned back in his chair, cracked knuckles behind his head. 'No.' The answer was flat as a mill pond.

'I thought you were on board.' *What was the strange man up to?* 'I'll only be coming back with a warrant for them later.'

'Ha ha, you misunderstand me, officer. There aren't any.'

'Pardon?'

'I'm an old-fashioned operator. The only electronic documents I deal with are the tax returns I lodge for my clients. This computer on my desk, I hardly ever turn it on.'

'Seriously?'

'Yes. If you want full access to his bank accounts and insurance policies you need to contact the financial institutions. Maybe you can find what you're looking for on Cameron's own computers.' He pointed at the boxes sitting six inches from Wilson's face. 'Please return all those papers when you are finished. In there, you will find print outs of statements, invoices, receipts, everything like that going back five years, which is how long Cameron has been my client. As for stuff before that—'

'Yep. I got it. We'll talk to the institutions.'

'Precisely.'

'Before I go, do you have a copy of the will?'

'Why would I have that? No, you need to talk to his lawyer, Garfield Walters.'

'Got his number?'

Soplyak produced a business card from his wallet. 'Of course. He is also my lawyer.'

'One last question. That banner above the shelving. What is it?'

'Oh, that is Ukrainian symbol, the *tryzub*. I think in English it is called a trident.'

'Does it have any special significance?'

'You bet. It is the Ukrainian coat of arms.'

'You're proud of your homeland?'

'Of course! And also of Australia, the country I now call home.'

A vague idea occurred to Wilson. 'Are you involved in any patriotic organisations?'

Soplyak blinked like he was emerging from a dark tunnel into light, then his chest puffed out slightly. 'I am a fully paid-up member of the Queensland Ukrainian club. I have been for many years.'

'Do you know if Cameron Snyder was involved in any Australian version of that?'

'You are an odd person, officer. Why would he be a member of a club for ex-pats of the country he was born in and lives in? Makes no sense.'

'No, I meant, was he involved in any, ah, radical political organisations? Right wing in particular.'

Soplyak burst out laughing. 'Cameron was no Nazi sympathiser. You may have noticed, I myself am a foreigner, an immigrant.'

'Yes, but a white European one.'

'I have big surprise for you, Constable Wilson.'

'What?'

'I am also a Jew.'

Chapter Fourteen

'I CAN'T BELIEVE he'd have the temerity.' Taylor carefully peeled away cling wrap, nibbled on an egg and lettuce sandwich. Jack took two minutes to demolish his meat pie, known in the local lingo as a mystery bag, faint traces of tomato ketchup now lining his top lip.

'Me neither,' said Jack. Their visit to Randall Sowell's office was met with the surprising news that he and two advisors had headed to Trick Shot. When the DS asked why, the mumbling receptionist replied she had no idea.

'Got any theories?' said Claudia.

'Nope. Does Sowell own anything similar to Trick Shot?'

'Not than I can ascertain.' Taylor scrolled feverishly on an iPad. 'From what I can see on FARQ2's own website, the company acquires properties to lease out to small businesses. Fish and chip shops, hairdressers, that kind of thing. I can't get anymore details about the company's operations unless we get a production notice to serve on his banks.'

'We need to light a fire under this Sowell clown. I may have to call in a few favours from the magistrate.'

'Come on, Jack. We haven't even spoken to the man and you've got him behind bars already.'

The DS braked to give way at a T-junction, turned to face Taylor. 'But look who's mentioned him so far. Snyder's widow, the pool hall manager, and now his accountant. The Ukrainian told Wilson his dead client and Sowell hated each other's guts. Now this Sowell bloke's visiting Snyder's showcase establishment here in Yorkville before the victim's been buried. If that don't set alarm bells ringing in your head, I don't know what's required.'

'Or perhaps Sowell is an astute businessman who sees a golden opportunity to cash in on someone's misfortune.'

'Are there any other pool halls in Yorkville?'

'Not anymore. I remember there used to be one on the southside of town called Back Alley Pool. There were fights there on a regular basis. Constable Trevarthen copped a pool cue in the eye trying to break up a brawl one night, he couldn't see straight for a month. I'm pretty sure that joint closed years ago, before you arrived in town.'

'You know why?'

'Why you arrived in town? Of course. To take up the position of Detective Serg–'

'No!' Jack roared, then noticed Taylor's sly grin. 'I'm not in the mood for jokes, Claudia.' Her grin evaporated. 'Why did the effing place close down?'

'Give me a minute.' Scroll, scroll, scroll. 'Here's an old *Yorkville Times* article. An interview with the owner, a Mr Nik Koustas. Apparently he wasn't happy when Snyder opened his joint.'

'Not keen on competition, huh?'

'Doesn't look like it. You reckon he could have held a grudge badly enough to want to kill Snyder?'

'Men have killed for less, Claudia. I'm keen to talk to him.'

'I wouldn't bother. I just Googled his name. He died in a car accident middle of last year. He was in Brisbane for his mother's funeral, got drunk and drove into a power pole. And…oh no…he had two small children with him, one also killed, the other with permanent spinal damage.'

'Doesn't sound like an accident to me.' Jack shook his head. 'See what happens when folk let money rule their lives? Bad shit, that's what.'

A roadworker wearing a vest so bright you could probably see him from outer space directed the detectives around a pile of dusty rubble. He gave the detectives a perfunctory two-finger salute as they trundled past him. Further ahead a team of labourers toiled with shovels and rakes, buzzed around in skid steer bobcats and backhoe loaders, building a road that was meant to alleviate Yorkville's worsening traffic problems. The roadworks seemed to stretch for kilometres. 'Bloody hell, Claudia. We'll be here all effing day. I knew I shoulda gone the other way.' A yellow-and-black sign declared a 30km/hour limit. Jack flicked on the Stinger's flashing lights and sirens, nudged the speed up to 70km/hour. The detectives thrashed about like pebbles in a clothes dryer.

'Please! Go easy. You'll bugger the suspension.' Taylor's voice vibrated as the car careered down the rough surface, generating clouds of ochre dust in its wake.

Jack gritted his teeth, wrenched the steering wheel left and right, hitting more bumps and potholes than he avoided. 'Weigh it up, Claudia,' he huffed. 'Solving a murder versus a bill for a new set of sway bars.' Council employees watched open-mouthed as the fancy pursuit car tore along the round. Some laughed and pointed, others had their mobiles out to film the bizarre spectacle.

'At least drop the speed a little,' Taylor demanded. 'The way you're driving, you'll wreck the car and we won't get there at all.'

Jack sighed, eased off a fraction. Five jolting minutes later they exited the roadworks area onto a smooth asphalt surface. 'See? We made it. You can relax now.'

'Bloody miracle,' Taylor whispered under her breath.

'Did you find out any more about Sowell on the Internet?'

'You must be joking? The iPad screen was jiggling about so much I couldn't read it. Why didn't you take the 4x4 from the compound?'

Jack shrugged. 'I didn't know we'd be traversing a war zone, did I? Anyway, Oliphant Avenue's a minute away. Ready to apply the blowtorch to Mr Randall Sowell?'

'I'll leave that up to you. If your flame throwing skills are anything like your driving, the man's in for some punishment.'

'Thanks, DC Taylor.' Jack thumbed open a plastic bottle of Extra peppermint gum, tipped half a dozen pellets into his mouth. 'Right, we're here. Follow me.'

Chapter Fifteen

HEATED WORDS REVERBERATED from behind the front door. Muffled, indistinct. At least two unique voices, perhaps up to four. An argument about to descend into violence or a spirited difference of opinion. Whatever it was, Jack didn't like the sound of it. He remembered the battle-scarred face of Harry Sheffield. Those markings weren't earned by diplomacy and tact. The door was ajar. Jack pushed and went inside, Taylor on his heels.

The corridor to the main hall ran for 15 metres, the cops covered the distance in seconds. Inside the main pool hall four men stood beside a billiard table the size of a small hippopotamus. Three of them were squaring off, dancing on tiptoes. One, a man in a suit, stood back a fraction, as if preparing to let the others get stuck in while he watched from the sidelines. Jack immediately recognised Harry Sheffield, who spotted the detectives and gave a curt nod that said *I've got this covered*. The sweat beading on his brow and the shaky hands told another story. Tough man or not, he was severely outnumbered by younger opponents. "Advisors" the receptionist said. Like hell they were.

'Police.' Jack held his badge aloft, Taylor did the same. 'Whatever you're all doing, step back and take a breather.' A brusque introduction by Jack, the combatants stood at ease.

The well-dressed man hanging off to the side held up a hand. 'All under control, officers. I just dropped by to pass on my condolences for the tragic loss of Cameron Snyder. He was a pillar of Yorkville's business community and a shining light for all.'

'Will you get a load of the bullshit pouring out of this guy's mouth, Claudia?' said Jack, now a metre from the man who spoke. 'It looked like your musclemen were about to tear poor old Harry here a new one.'

'Not at all. Just a slight misunderstanding, right Harry?'

'Fuck you, Sowell,' Sheffield jabbed a finger at the unwelcome visitor. 'You're such a lying prick.' He turned to Jack and said, 'He's here casing the place 'cos he thinks he can buy it now Cam's dead. Fucking suspicious if you ask me!'

'I didn't ask you,' Jack replied calmly.

'You must be Randall Sowell,' Taylor said to the fashion plate. 'We've heard so much about you.'

'All good, I hope.' The man thrust slender hands into his trouser pockets. The graphite-grey suit looked like it cost over a thousand dollars. He appeared gym-fit, average height and owned a baby face for a man in his early thirties. His goons, both sporting jet-black bushranger haircuts, were at least ten years younger. Clad in blue denim jeans and white t-shirts, the lads' attire reminded Jack of London thugs from the 1980s, except these guys wore Paco Rabanne cologne behind their ears instead of razor blades in their lobes.

'As it happens, no,' said Jack. 'Well, let me rephrase that. We've heard the same thing from different sources. You hated Cameron Snyder.'

'We had our disagreements, for sure. But hate is such a...strong term.'

'We're not going to waste anyone's time,' said Taylor, stepping up next to Jack. 'Where were you on Monday night?'

'At home.'

'All night?'

'Yeah. What are you alluding to? Surely you can't think I had something to do with whatever happened to Cameron. He and I may have had our disagreements over the years, but nothing so bad that I'd...Jesus. To be perfectly honest, his death has me rattled.'

'Like hell,' said Sheffield, shaking his head, still encased in the fuchsia-coloured cap. 'You were pissed off he got hold of Pilkington's fish factory. Now Cam's dead, you probably think you can get your hands on it.'

'Is that right?' said Jack. 'Will you be seeking to buy it?'

'How can he?' said Sheffield. 'It'll be part of Cameron's estate now.'

Taylor shook her head. 'We've received reliable information Mr Snyder was drowning in debt. Whoever loaned him the money to buy the plant will own it now. I'd imagine they'll put it to auction, where Mr Sowell will have a chance to purchase.'

'Yes,' said Jack. 'Very convenient.'

'What do you mean?' Sowell had produced a nailfile from somewhere and was buffing his cuticles. 'No idea what you're all talking about.'

'Look,' said Taylor. 'Your friends here are making me uncomfortable. How about they take a hike.'

Sowell nodded and the men disappeared.

'Want me to go too?' said Sheffield. 'I'd rather be far away from this creep.'

'I'd rather you hung around, if that's OK,' said Jack. 'I don't want Mr Sowell making accusations about the way we treated him.'

'Look.' Sowell made a fuss of looking at his watch. 'I've got other matters to attend to, so…'

'They'll have to wait. We can carry on the conversation at the station if you'd prefer, only that'll detain you from your business even longer.'

'Very well.' Sowell sighed like a stroppy teenager. 'Can we at least sit down?'

Jack asked Sheffield to clear a space in the back office, bring them some drinks. The manager was reluctant, but a fifty note on the top of the bar secured his agreement. Taylor queried the generosity. Jack had one word: expedience. Sheffield returned carrying a tray with a large bottle of Coke, a mini bucket of ice, but only three glasses. Sowell scoffed at him, called him a petty, pathetic old fool. Sheffield glared a laser beam of contempt at Sowell, who averted eye contact with him and avoided it for the duration of the interview.

'OK, tell me all about your relationship with Cameron Snyder.'

'Not until the charming Mr Sheffield brings me a drink.'

A head gesture by Jack, a scrape of a chair, Sheffield departed, returned with another glass, clunked it down in front of Sowell. 'There. Happy now?'

'Wow, you really seem to piss everyone off, Mr Sowell.' said Taylor. 'Or can I can you Randall?'

'*You* can call me Randy,' Sowell leered at Taylor and gave a rapid wink.

Jack's fist came crashing down on the table, rattling the glasses and ice cubes. 'And now you've pissed *me* off!' He reached out, twisted the collar of Sowell's crisp, white shirt and dragged him halfway across the table, sending glasses and cola spilling onto the floor. A loud crack sounded as knuckles made "incidental" contact with the interviewee's jaw.

'Ease up!' Taylor cried. 'No need to get offended on my behalf.'

'Sorry,' said Jack, shoving Sowell by the shoulders back into his seat. 'Now, just answer my questions without any lip, OK?'

Sowell nodded obediently, rubbing the side of his face.

'Can anyone confirm your whereabouts on the night of the murder?'

'Yes. My mother.'

'Excuse me?' said Taylor. 'Does she live with you? If so, you'll have to prove she was awake between 22:00 and midnight.'

'No I don't.'

'Don't be cheeky,' said Jack. He was itching to land a punch square in the middle of Sowell's pasty mug.

'My mother lives in Perth. We had a Skype chat that ended, lemme check my calendar.' Sowell pulled out his phone, pressed a few buttons. 'That's right. It was 10:30pm here, so it must've been 8:30pm there. Not too late for an old woman to be up, you'll agree.'

'You keep records of phone conversations with your mother?' Jack asked incredulously. It was almost as if he'd set out to give himself an alibi.

'As it happens, she's in a care facility, doesn't have a lot of time left.' His voice trailed off, barely audible.

'Sorry, I missed that,' said Taylor.

'She's fucking dying, all right! That's why the calls are in my diary. They're scheduled by the home she's staying at, not me.'

Jack almost felt bad about roughing up the man. But not quite. He side-eyed Sheffield, who wore a slightly remorseful expression. A terminal mother, enough to evoke sympathy for even the biggest of arseholes. He could still be capable of murder though. 'That doesn't account for the time until midnight. I calculate a maximum half-hour drive from your house...yes, we looked up your address...to Snyder's residence. That gives you a window of one hour or so to enter the house and murder your worst enemy.'

'That's a little melodramatic, don't you think?' Sowell laid his iPhone faceup on the table. 'Please, you can see here I was in a teleconference with a partner of mine who's currently in South Africa. I know it's only a diary entry, but I'm happy to hand over my laptop on which the call was made.' He pocketed the mobile and smiled.

Jack couldn't decide if the man was telling the truth. His alibi could very well check out, but his behaviour here with bodyguards in tow suggested he was the type of snake who'd order a hit rather than carry it out. 'I'm going to take you up on that offer.'

'No problem. We can go back to my office now and fetch the computer.'

'Excellent. Plus we'd like DNA swab and fingerprints. You prepared to head down to the station later this afternoon?'

'Of course.' Sowell made a quick call, cancelled a

meeting with someone called Deepak. 'Let's go then, officers.'

———

'I THOUGHT you only wanted physical samples and a look at my devices? I've handed everything over, cooperated in full. Now you've dragged me in here. This is an outrage!' Sowell's china-blue eyes darted about the walls inside Interview Room No. 1. 'I demand to call my lawyer.'

'And so you shall. But not yet.'

'Why the fuck not?'

Jack tapped the side of his nose. 'CHOGM.'

Genuine surprise elevated Sowell's eyebrows. 'What the fuck's that?'

'I'll tell you, as long as you promise to stop swearing. My partner is watching and listening behind that pane of glass there. So behave yourself, *Randy*.' Inspector Batista was there too.

'Sure.' Arms folded defiantly across his chest. Jack had to admit, Sowell was the best dressed person he'd ever had in the interview room, not counting his on-again-off-again girlfriend lawyer Denise Hutchinson, who always scrubbed up a treat. But a nice suit wasn't going to be enough to save Sowell's sorry arse.

'I'll explain to you what CHOGM is and why it's important.' Jack embarked on a theatrical monologue about visiting dignitaries, threats of assassination, mayhem on the streets, bombings, linked it all with Cameron Snyder's supposed implication in matters of national security. 'So you see, Randy.' Jack smiled and Sowell winced each time the DS used the epithet. 'You, my friend, are also under the eye of our agencies.'

'Give me my phone back. I want my lawyer.'

'Not yet, mate. I've got special powers when security's at stake.'

'Bullshit. Under what Act?'

'The Special Security and Terrorism Act, 2006, gives me the power to restrict your right to a lawyer for a period determined by me at my discretion.' Total bollocks, but it sounded legit.

'You know I'm going to report you for assaulting me back at Trick Shot, don't you?'

'An empty and stupid threat, sunshine. Your word against mine, DC Taylor's and Harry Sheffield's. No, son, it's you who should be worried.'

Sowell massaged his temples, stared at the table, muttered under his breath.

'Let's assume for a moment you had nothing to do with the murder of Cameron Snyder, shall we?' Jack continued.

'Why assume? I *did* have nothing to do with it, for fuck's sake.'

Jack had quietly walked behind Sowell, still fixated on the tabletop. The DS yanked the back of the steel chair, Sowell stumbled to the hard floor, banging his head on the table legs on the way down. Taylor would be fuming behind the glass, but Jack couldn't care less. Time was ticking, he only had two and a bit days to figure this out. Missing out on being reunited with Skye at the end of the week was *not* an option. He half expected Batista to come barging through the door, but the Inspector had promised some extra leeway. As long as Jack didn't strike the man or draw blood, the boss would leave him undisturbed.

'Hey, what did you do that for?' Sowell whimpered.

'You promised not to swear, sunshine. Then you went back on your word. Doesn't engender respect or trust, know what I mean? Now, sit still, look at me when I'm talking to you, and keep the language clean. Got me?'

'Yes.' Sowell was defeated. Without his goons to hide behind, he was weak.

'Let's play pretend for a moment. I'm a crown prosecutor, looking to nail your backside to the wall. You've got...' Jack counted off on his fingers, '...a long-standing feud with the deceased, one that goes back to college days, at least three independent people pointing at you as the most likely suspect. Finally, we discover you running your envious eyes over Trick Shot not two days after the owner is killed in his own home, from what we can surmise by someone he knew well enough to let inside. How would you respond to those accusations?'

'They're nonsense. Once you've got the results back from my swabs and devices, you'll see everything I've said is the truth.' He wriggled uncomfortably in his chair. 'I agree, it may appear a bit...ghoulish...checking out the pool hall so soon after Cameron's death.'

'That's an understatement. It's disgusting.'

'Perhaps. But not illegal.' Bravado was creeping back into Sowell's demeanour. 'Check my record. I'm clean as a whistle.'

That much was true. Jack was starting to get that gut-wrenching feeling he was barking up the wrong tree. Sowell was a slimeball, but that didn't make him a killer.

Jack spun a chair around, sat on it backwards, smiled politely. 'OK, Randy. Let's imagine I believe you. You've known Cameron for years. Who do you think might have had it in for him?'

'I can rattle two names off the top of my head. Keith Lynch and Tommy Thomson.'

Those names meant nothing to Jack. 'Who are they?'

'Lynch is small time dope dealer.'

'I know all the suppliers in Yorkville. Never heard of him.'

'That's because he deals out of Mareeba.' A town nearly 100km inland from Yorkville, Mareeba came under the jurisdiction of Cairns Police. 'He hangs out at the Cane Cutters' Arms Hotel with a bunch of other low-lifes.'

'Why do you know so much about him?'

'He used to work for me, but I found out he was a coke-head redirecting company funds into his own account. I fired him because I don't like users and thieves on the payroll.'

'Fair enough.'

'Rumour on the streets is Snyder owed Lynch. Cameron had tapped out all his official lenders, so he borrowed off another guy.'

'Lemme guess. Tommy Thomson.'

'Correct. A slimebucket of the first order, lives in Cairns.' Sowell grinned with self-satisfaction, leaned back in his seat. 'So you've got two crims owed money by the same guy. Maybe they teamed up to off Snyder.'

'Anything else you'd like to tell me?' Jack almost regretted asking. He needed the list of suspects to get smaller, not bigger.

'Yeah. Look on the other side of the family tree.'

'Explain.' The regret intensified.

'Lydia's mob. She's got a brother in Cairns, Trent Gillmeister. A physical education teacher if memory serves me correctly. He was very protective of little sis when they were teenagers.'

'Protective and murderous aren't exactly the same.'

'You must know there were some domestic violence issues back in Brisbane.'

'The DVO was withdrawn. It's ancient history.'

Sowell shrugged. 'Yeah, I know. I'm just giving you another lead you might like to chase up.'

'Any evidence Lydia played around on Cameron? Maybe there was a boyfriend who wanted Lydia all to himself.' It was a long shot. From what Taylor said, the woman was devoted to Snyder, in her own unique way.

'Wouldn't have a clue. She was pretty unstable mentally. Probably still is. From what I knew of them as a couple, she loved him and vice versa. But look at how they split, the relationship couldn't handle the turbulence.'

'What about you? How's your marriage? Happy wife, happy life?'

'You need to do your homework better, Detective Lisbon. I'm a single gay man without a care in the world. I tried marriage, to a woman, turned out it wasn't for me.' Sowell wore a grin like a split pumpkin. 'My focus these days is on growing my business, not breaking hearts.'

Jack *had* done his homework. More precisely, Taylor had. And what Sowell said stacked up. He'd shunned settling down in a relationship, preferring to indulge his whims. Fancy cars, boats, jet skis, the man had more toys than Santa's workshop.

'What do you know about the Wild Colonial Boys?'

'Not much. I can already anticipate your next question. Yes, Snyder's pool halls are decked out in all that patriotic Aussie shit, but I don't believe Cameron had any involvement with radical politics. The guy who managed Trick Shot before Sheffield was a WCB member, and when Cameron found out he got rid of the bloke. The dude left in a huff, pissed off back to Melbourne.'

'Maybe he bore a grudge, came back to kill Snyder?'

Sowell shook his head. 'I doubt it. Check it out if you

like, but I reckon you'd be wasting your time. Believe it or not, I want this matter cleared up as quickly as you do. People murdering businessmen in my home town makes me nervous. Why do you think I have those two body guards around me? I only hired them yesterday.'

'OK, Mr Sowell. You're free to go.'

As Sowell sauntered out of the interview room, escorted by Constable Smith, Jack rang Wilson. 'Thanks for that emailed report from your visit to the accountant. Very useful.'

'You're welcome, sir.' Wilson sounded chuffed. Rightly so, Jack was spare with his praise.

'You talked to the lawyer yet?'

'No, sir. There's been a hold up. He's only just arrived back at his office.'

'Shit. Don't waste too much time with him. Make sure you get a look at the will's beneficiaries.'

'What if he refuses?'

'Ring me and I'll have a word.'

'Yes, sir.'

Jack ended the call, smiled awkwardly at Taylor and the Inspector as they entered the interview room. 'That went OK, don't you think?'

Batista's lips formed a tight line. 'Not so sure about the pulling-out-the-chair prank, though.'

'Come on, sir. No damage done. He won't say boo about it.'

'Let's hope so.'

Taylor flipped open a notepad. 'I made some very quick enquiries about all the people Sowell named. Want my opinion on how to tackle that?'

'Sure.' A frisson ran down his spine as Taylor took the reins. What the hell was that about?

'Don't bother driving to Mareeba to talk to Keith Lynch. He fronted Cairns Court late January and copped six months jail for dealing coke. Turns out he was using more of the product than he was selling. A quick read of the case notes tells me he's a minnow among minnows. No friends and stone broke. Hired a pro bono lawyer from Legal Aid.'

'Thomson?'

'Another kettle of fish. Very dangerous, a long list of priors, quick to resort to violence. He's served a combined six years for GBH and extortion. Yet he's somehow managed to keep his nose clean since 2015.'

'Where can we find the charming Tommy Thomson?'

'He was based in Cairns, as Sowell said. But he's recently reported to his parole officer that he's moved to Yorkville.'

'Saves us a long drive.' Jack managed half a smile.

'Maybe even a short one.' Taylor tucked her notepad into her handbag. 'He's working as a grease monkey at the Subaru repair shop in Fulton Street. One block away from here.'

Chapter Sixteen

THE SLEEK OFFICE of solicitor Garfield Walters was as modern as accountant Soplyak's had been old hat. Wilson could feel electrons buzzing around him from the myriad of computers, printers and God knew what other gadgets that were running. Or perhaps it was elevated caffeine levels induced by several litres of Red Bull. The Constable had read in *New Scientist* magazine that sleep deprivation can cause a temporary high. Perhaps that was what he was experiencing right now. He prayed he'd still have enough focus to get the information DS Lisbon had asked for.

'Thanks for taking the time to see me, Mr Walters.' Wilson sensed his face spasming as he stifled a yawn.

'Don't mention it,' said the lawyer, waving the matter away. 'This is a horrible, horrible thing to happen. I'll cooperate in any way I can to help the police find the killers.'

'Glad to hear it.' No time to waste on pleasantries. 'I'd like to see a copy of the will, if you don't mind.'

'Except that.' The lawyer rested his elbows on the table and steepled his fingers. 'Confidentiality considerations.'

Wilson held up a finger. Exactly what he didn't want. 'Just one second while I call my—'

'Only joking.' A fleeting pink smile emerged from behind a luxuriant russet moustache. His mien immediately returned to serious. 'The poor man's dead, murdered most violently from what I heard on the news. I quite liked Cameron and I want to see the culprit caught. Confidentiality be buggered.'

Walters left his desk, returned with a thin plastic folder. He opened it and proceeded to mark bands across selected parts of text with a bright yellow highlighter pen. He slapped the cap back on the pen with a flourish and turned the will around for Wilson to read. 'Here, I've highlighted the beneficiaries and the percentage of Cameron's estate they can expect to receive.'

The person to gain the most was Lydia, with 80%, followed by a charity dedicated to researching Huntington's disease getting 10%, and the remaining 10% going to Lydia's brother, Trent Gillmeister. 'Rather surprising to see the widow's brother listed here,' said Wilson, forefinger resting on the page. 'And this annotation. *A small token by way of an apology.*' Wilson's droopy eyes looked up at the solicitor. 'An apology for what?'

'No idea. I've never met the brother. Just Lydia five years ago. A lovely woman. At least she was back then. Such a shame the marriage broke up.'

'You think the breakup could have anything to do with the murder?'

Walters narrowed his eyes, scratched an earlobe. 'I'd be the last person qualified to offer a theory on that. My dealings with Mr Snyder were not particularly frequent. Middle of last year was the last time, when I made that slight change to the will by adding Trent.'

'A pity none of the beneficiaries will receive anything.' Wilson handed the will back to Walters.

'Excuse me?' The lawyer looked genuinely surprised. 'I'm not aware of anyone filing an injunction against the estate. Do you know something I don't?'

'No, it's nothing like that. I mean there's nothing left in the war chest.'

'What do you mean?'

'The accountant showed me the books. Well, he handed me three whacking great boxes full of papers. The upshot is, the man died almost broke, with liabilities far exceeding his assets. Big creditors will get first pick of the crumbs.'

'How interesting. I had no idea he was in such bad financial shape.'

'Looks like Lydia's not going to be moving into that nice house in Rogers Close.'

Walters adjusted his glasses. 'No, but I reckon she's going to be OK. At least for the foreseeable future.'

'What do you mean?' From what Wilson knew, the woman was unemployed with no prospects other than a miserable life on welfare.

'There's a special trust fund set up for Cameron and Lydia. It's got a healthy balance of $250,000. I won't bore you with the details, but it was established by a check I received from someone three years ago. It's also structured in such a clever way that creditors will not be able to touch the funds in the trust. Safer than Fort Knox. Another condition of the trust is that neither beneficiary shall be made aware of the founder's identity until that person passes away.'

'Wait a minute, back it up. You said "from someone". The money didn't come from Snyder?'

A head shake.

'Who then?'

'I've most likely overstepped the mark already in terms of the old confidentiality thing. But as my old grandad used to say, you may as well be hung for a sheep as a lamb.'

'Who, dammit?' Wilson heard his voice almost as an out-of-body experience. 'Don't muck me about, man!'

Walters jumped slightly in his seat. 'Oh, sorry. I actually can't remember the name. Once second.' Walters tapped on his keyboard, adjusted his glasses. 'Yes, here it is. It's a Suncorp bank check signed by a Mr Raymond Ogden Hook.'

'Can you repeat that, please? I'm not sure I heard you right.'

The solicitor repeated the name, slowly and clearly. It was a name that carried much weight, almost as much as the man who bore it. For a split second Wilson thought his forehead was going to crash onto the top of Walters' rosewood desk.

Chapter Seventeen

'SIR, I want to speak to that loan shark, Tommy Thomson.'
Jack could feel his pulse quickening. 'Time's of the proverbial essence and he's only around the corner. I think he may
be the link we're looking for.'

'Calm down, DS Lisbon. It can wait half an hour.
Wilson just texted me. He's done with Snyder's lawyer. I'd
like a quick debrief with all officers before everyone scatters
off in different directions. Let's consolidate what we've got.'

'But, chief...'

'There's a bombshell.'

'What?'

'One second.' Batista held up a forefinger as the
uniformed constables filed into the room. Smith,
Trevarthen, Semmens. No sign of Ben Wilson.

'What's the bombshell, sir?' said Taylor, invading the
Inspector's personal space so much he had to take half a
step backwards.

'Just a second, the pair of you. I'll fill you all in as soon as…actually, here he comes. He can tell you himself.' Batista clapped his hands, stuck fingers in his mouth and blasted out a shrill whistle. 'OK, everyone take a seat. Wilson's got some interesting news for us.'

The constable that walked in the door wasn't the same man Jack remembered from yesterday. It was a zombie in a crumpled cop uniform. The officer needed sleep, but he may have to postpone that luxury. There were still leads to follow up, people to talk to. Jack grabbed him by the elbow, escorted him to a spot in front of the whiteboard, about where the X would be marked on the floor for a singing audition.

'Thanks, DS Lisbon,' Wilson muttered without a trace of thankfulness.

'No worries, sunshine. We're all eager to hear about the bombshell.'

'What? Jesus, have the terrorists struck? Is it CHOGM?'

'No, you twat. Your big news. What did you learn at the solicitor's office?'

'Oh, I…'

Batista coughed loudly into a fist to quell the developing hubbub coming from the back row of plastic chairs. 'Everyone shut up. Constable Wilson, if you please.'

Choking back yawns and wobbling like a blancmange, Wilson delivered news that sucked the air out of the room.

'Wait, wait, wait.' Jack was out of his seat, the loan shark from next door suddenly a character of secondary importance to the case. 'Jabba gave this solicitor a check for a quarter of a million dollars to set up a trust account for Snyder?'

'Yeah. And Lydia too. They're joint…whatever you call them, benefactors.'

'Beneficiaries,' corrected Batista. 'Like in a will. And Walters presumably would be the trustee. Thanks for that, Ben. Take a seat, you look knackered.'

'Any theories on this development, chief?' said Jack, remembering the Inspector's "dirt" on Assistant Commissioner Hook.

Batista caressed his chiselled chin.

'Well?' said Jack as the pause dragged on. 'I know you know something juicy about the fat lizard. Let's be hearing it.'

The chief took a deep breath, motioned for Wilson to take a seat as the chief took centre stage. 'Frankly, I've got no idea where Hook got $250,000. But I do have a theory about something else. Back in 1989, Hook and I played in a mini series of rugby league matches in Sydney against the New South Wales cops. They beat the crap out of us. Anyway, Hook took a gift from his wife down to her sister Carrie, who lived in inner Sydney in those days. A cardigan or something, can't remember exactly. Ray Hook and I shared a hotel room. I went out with the lads for a pint while he was meant to be delivering the present, and when I came back to the hotel I opened the door to see Hook's bare arse pumping up and down like a fiddler's elbow, the sister-in-law underneath him squealing with delight.'

Jack side-eyed Taylor, blushing at Batista's colourful description of the event. 'What's that got to do with Snyder?'

'It could have everything to do with him. Now his name and his widow's name pop up as beneficiaries of a trust set up with Hook's money, it's time to do the maths. Claudia, could you please check the years of birth of Snyder and his wife?'

'Sure. What month were you in Sydney?'

'Winter, for the footy season. Without double checking I'd say it was late July 1989.'

'You reckon he fathered Snyder or Lydia after that one encounter?' said Jack, barely believing the scenario.

'It's not beyond the realms of possibility,' said Batista. 'It only takes one time.'

'It all makes perfect sense,' said Taylor, her eyes darting over the iPad. 'The way Hook was so keen for us to clear the man's reputation. Before and even after his death. That CHOGM stuff was probably a smokescreen. Yep, you were right sir.' She glanced up at Batista then back to the screen again. 'Cameron Snyder was born in April 1990, nine months after July 1989. But his mother's not called Carrie. She's a Suzanna Snyder.'

'Carrie must have adopted him out.' The Inspector sounded like he'd made a Nobel prize winning discovery.

'Here, I've pulled up random photos of him and Hook. There's definitely a resemblance.'

Jack took the tablet from Taylor's outstretched hand. 'Well I'll be. The eyes, the nose. Bloody hell, if you strip the lard away from Hook's flabby face, add some hair to Snyder's bald noggin, the similarity's remarkable.'

'The question is, what do we do with this information?' said Constable Trevarthen. 'It's all well and good knowing the link, but does that get us any closer to finding a culprit?'

Silence. Of the dejected kind. Pressing Hook for answers right now was out of the question. Batista quickly explained the Assistant Commissioner was in a critical condition, slipping in and out of consciousness. The doctor in charge was hopeful Hook could be stabilised enough to undergo heart surgery within the next few days.

'I guess that brings us back to physical evidence,' said

Taylor, who seemed to be forcing optimism into her voice. 'What's the latest from Proctor? Did she get anything from the second sweep of the crime scene?'

Batista picked up a stapled document from the top of a filing cabinet and flicked it open at the first page. 'Indeed she did. Behold the object used to strike Snyder over the head before he was stabbed.' He turned on an overhead projector connected to a laptop, an image of a shiny bronze trophy filled the screen. 'This stylised eight-ball trophy weighs 950 grams and is hard as a rock. Proctor found minute traces of Snyder's blood and skin on it, even though it'd been wiped. Not thoroughly enough, it seems.'

'Prints?' said Jack.

A shake of the head from Batista.

'Any sign of the weapon used to stab the guy?' said Constable Noah Semmens.

'A couple of possibles. Proctor matched the minor wound patterns below the left clavicle and the deep lethal cut with three knives found on the premises.' Batista pressed a key on the laptop and the knives appeared. They were spaced apart evenly and had been photographed on a plastic sheet laid out on Snyder's kitchen table. 'All are non-serrated, stainless steel knives of German manufacture. Two found in kitchen drawers, one in a barbecue kit on the back deck. No traces of anything on them.'

'Come on, sir.' Jack screwed up his lips. 'The killer's taken the weapon with him and chucked it somewhere. None of those blades are the murder weapon, are they? This was a psychotic attack. The murderer's not gonna tidy it all up, is he?'

'Or she,' said Taylor.

Jack sighed. 'All right. Or *she*. I guess a woman's more likely to embark on a quick tidy-up than a man after murdering someone, so the perp's probably female. I'll bet she even vacuumed the place and did a spot of dusting before fleeing the scene. Congratulations on the breakthrough, Claudia.' He regretted his sarcastic words the instant he uttered them, felt his face flush.

'Stop it, Jack. You're losing the plot,' said Batista. 'No need for cynicism when your partner raises a perfectly valid point. No one needs to listen to your outmoded notion of gender roles, do they?'

Jack folded his arms and frowned. 'Don't get all uppity with me, sir. You're the one holding me hostage with this crazy deadline. I can't help it if my brain's wandering off on wee excursions, can I?'

'I'll pretend you didn't say that.' Batista straightened his shoulders, shot Jack a laser stare. 'You want to catch that plane to London, don't you? Then stop wasting time.'

The chief was right. 'Sorry, won't do it again.'

'Glad to hear it. Now, as disappointing as that all sounds, there is some encouraging news. Strands of long black hair were found in a set of bedsheets in the laundry hamper. They don't match Lydia Snyder.'

'Could be Renee van der Klopp,' said Taylor. 'She's a brunette.'

'Could be the other neighbour, Miranda Mallick,' said Jack. 'She's got a generous head of thick, black hair on her.'

'Do you seriously believe that she would've been sleeping with Snyder?' Taylor was incredulous.

'Anything's possible.' Jack pushed his hands into his thighs, still sore from his "leg day" gym session from last weekend. Right now he was itching to get into the ring to spar with someone. Anyone. This case was doing his head in and he was spouting nonsense.

'Proctor promises to have the DNA results back

tomorrow from the used condom, and also these new hairs.'
Jack counted off in his head. Tomorrow's Thursday. Two
more days to find the killer. He decided if the case was
unsolved he'd take the plane anyway. Fuck Batista, his
daughter was more important than this job. If he got sacked
Jack could always pick up security work, set up a private
investigation company, drive Ubers. He still had money
stashed away, the cash he stole before fleeing England. He
could live off that for at least six months.

Getting his mind back on the job, Jack said: 'Snyder's
phone and laptop. Anything found on them?' The Inspector
had arranged for them to be couriered to the QPS's digital
forensics team in Brisbane with a request for expedited
examination.

'There was little in the way of security or encryption on
the victim's devices, so it was easy to access everything,' said
Batista. 'Most of the content is innocuous. Financial transactions, all above board, some video games, photos of his
pool halls, happy snaps of customers. He rarely posted
anything on social media, especially since the nasty online
rumours started. However, of particular interest is a text
conversation between Snyder and loan shark Tommy
Thomson. The language used by Thomson is "careful", like
you'd expect from a seasoned crook.' Batista clicked a
mouse and part of an SMS conversation between Snyder
and Thomson was reproduced on the screen.

Don't 4get the 450 OK mate
I'll get it to you ASAP
That wood b appreshiated
Don't stress. Next week

'And that's where it ends, eight days before Snyder's

death,' said Batista. 'We don't know if the money was repaid or not.'

'Not a sum to kill a person over, is it?' Trevarthen pointed a ballpoint pen at the screen.

'Wanna bet, sunshine?' Jack snapped. 'I've known payday-lenders who love it when their small debtors don't cough up. Gives 'em an excuse to flex their muscles, break some bones. And yes, even kill.'

'Jack's right, Aden.' Batista switched off the laptop and the roll-down screen went blank. 'People have different motivations.'

'He might've been following the Internet attacks on Snyder,' added Taylor. 'Leaning on a man in the public eye might have given him a thrill, too.'

'Talk to him after this meeting.' Batista gestured at Jack and Taylor. He cast his eyes over the uniforms. 'You guys, talk to some of the business owners around Trick Shot, see if they've heard anything, watch their body language. That's about all we've got to go on at the moment.'

'Don't forget the brother,' said Wilson, his voice indistinct, like he'd just awoken from a long slumber.

'What?' said Batista.

'I...ah...forgot to mention something from the interview with Garfield Walters. There was a notation in Snyder's will. Wait a second.' Wilson checked a small spiral notepad. 'Yeah, it stated the 10% – of nothing, by the way – left to Trent Gillmeister was by way of apology.'

Jack thumped a fist into his palm. 'Jesus, that could be it. Sowell said the brother was protective of his sister. What if Lydia's downplaying Snyder's treatment of her? What if that's why they lived apart, he was more violent than she led us to believe. The "apology" is him saying sorry from the grave for roughing up the guy's sister.'

'I agree,' said Taylor, putting the iPad into sleep mode. 'Lydia spoke of a "complicated" relationship. Should we check hospital records, see if she was admitted for any unusual injuries?'

'Yes,' said Batista with more enthusiasm than he'd started the briefing with. 'I'll arrange a warrant with the magistrate. Constable Smith. Get your butt over to Yorkville General.'

'Yes, sir!' She was halfway out the door before she turned around. 'What if the hospital tries to give me the run-around?'

'Say the matter is linked to a threat to national security. Give the Director my number if she tries to block you,'

'You bet.' Smith nodded and strode out the door.

'Change of priorities.' Batista stood hands on hips. 'Semmens and Trevarthen, talk to this Thomson character. It'd just be our luck for the murderer to be working less than 200m from the station, thumbing his nose at us the whole time. Lisbon and Taylor, hustle up to Cairns and grill Trent Gillmeister. You know where to find him?'

'Sowell said he's a PE teacher in Cairns. I'll research the schools on the drive there,' said Taylor. She and Jack were out the door before the rest of the officers could blink.

'What about me?' Wilson stood slowly, putting on his police hat with fumbling hands.

Batista gripped Wilson by the elbow and steered him out of the squad room. 'I need you to speak to Snyder's neighbours, see if they saw that car you witnessed on the stake out.'

'But, sir. I…'

'Just kidding, Wilson. I rang them myself and they saw nothing. Go home and get some sleep. I need a fully fit and alert squad if we're going to crack this case. I don't know what Lisbon was thinking making you work a double shift.'

'Thank you, sir.' The relief was almost palpable. 'Can I make a request?'

'What?'

'Can you drive me? I don't think I can make it all the way home without crashing into a telegraph pole.'

Chapter Eighteen

CONSTABLES TREVARTHEN and Semmens ducked under a roller door and entered the fluoro-lit interior of Marco Campari's Subaru Repair Shop. The heady scents of oils, grease and lubricants together with the noisy clanking of metal on metal greeted them as they surveyed the area. The shop floor was about the size of two tennis courts placed end on end. A man was busily looking and poking under the hood of a canary-yellow WRX, two others inspected chassis of SUVs raised on hydraulic hoists. Although the name of the enterprise suggested it specialised in a particular Japanese make, neither of the elevated 4X4 vehicles was a Subaru. Elsewhere but unseen, a mechanical chain pulley was running and someone was operating a drill that set your teeth on edge. To the righthand side of the repair shop proper was a narrow glassed-off area. A stout middle-aged woman inside spoke animatedly on the phone and tapped coloured squares on a computer screen.

'Let's start with the reception,' said Trevarthen, heading for the open door to the office with Semmens half a step behind. Before they got there, a round, moon-faced man with a cherubic smile and a grubby rag tossed over his shoulder appeared from behind a rack of tyres. He casually approached the constables, smiling politely as if the police were the most welcome guests he could imagine dropping in. 'Can I help you, officers? Need your cars serviced?'

'Are you the owner of this place?' Trevarthen took the lead while Semmens crossed his arms, spread his legs in an at-ease stance.

'Yep. Marco Campari. Like the drink.' He held out a large hand, the entire surface black with grime.

'You expect me to shake that?' said Trevarthen, slightly recoiling.

'Oh, sorry.' Campari spat on his hands, wiped them down the front of his blue overalls, thrust out the right mitt again. 'How 'bout now?'

Trevarthen looked the man directly in the eye, ignoring the proffered hand, which, if anything, had attained a higher level of filthiness. 'Where's Thomson?'

'Who?'

'Don't play dumb, mate.' Constable Semmens consulted the screen of his iPhone. 'The bloke is registered as working for you. Full name, Thomas Earl Thomson, aged 42, covered in jail tatts, built like a brick shithouse. Ring a bell?'

'Oh, that'd be Tommy.' Campari chuckled uneasily. 'He's supposed to be checking the circuits on that Forester over there. He prob'ly ducked out the back for a smoke.'

'Really?' said Trevarthen. 'Looks like you're flat out with work.'

'Yeah, well. Tommy tends to set his own rules. He's got a bit of a temper on him.'

The constables exchanged a look. 'Really?' said Semmens. 'Then why'd you take him on?'

'Because he's a shit-hot auto electrician. He can fix any problem with alternators and batteries. The bloke's the best, so I don't care if he needs an extra smoke break.'

'You didn't get any financial incentives for hiring a man on parole, did you?' said Semmens, looking back at the cell phone.

'What?'

'The government's started this new program of offering wage subsidies for taking on ex-offenders. Sure you're not taking advantage of that?'

'OK, maybe that does help a bit with the cashflow. But he's still an excellent worker. You know, officers, you should bring your police vehicles to me. I'm a huge fan of those Kia Stinger pursuit vehicles. I can offer a 10-percent—'

'Look, Mr Bacardi...' said Trevarthen.

'That's Campari.'

'Yeah, sorry. We're getting way off track and we don't have all day.' Trevarthen pinched the bridge of his nose. 'Reckon you could fetch Mr Thomson so we can have a chat with him?'

Campari despatched a lanky youth in overalls two sizes too big to get Thomson. A minute later a human beast, standing at least 6'3" and sporting a shaved head, cauliflower ears and abundant blue and green neck ink, emerged through the plastic strip door at the end of the garage. Oddly, his overalls were so clean it looked like he'd just taken them out of the packaging. The errand boy trotted behind obediently, at a safe distance. The cops exchanged an anxious look. Yes, they were armed with Glocks, but Thomson looked like he could chew up both weapons until they were the consistency of porridge. The closer he got, the more frightening he became.

'You do the talking,' Semmens whispered, his fingers

twitching. Logically, the man wouldn't take on two armed policemen, both of them big men by any standards. Yet Thomson's mere presence set pulses and hearts racing, and not in a good way.

'OK,' Trevarthen whispered back.

'Wadda you dickheads want?' The beast snarled. 'You better not be wasting my time.'

'We're just here to clarify a couple of things. How about we sit down somewhere?'

'How about we don't.' Technically it was a question, but the intonation said statement. 'I gotta get back to that Volvo over there.' Thomson pointed at a Holden Commodore. Trevarthen's eyebrow jumped as he realised the man was here for the easy pay check and a tick on his record, not his expertise when it came to automobiles.

'Righto. I'll keep it brief.' Trevarthen explained the content of the texts found by digital forensics.

'Youse have no right accessin' my phone!' Thomson's lip curl was on a par with Billy Idol's. 'Not wiv'out my permission.'

Semmens pointed out there were two sides to the conversation, and they only needed to access Snyder's records to also see what Thomson himself had contributed.

'Still shoulda consulted me about it.'

Trevarthen struggled to hide his exasperation. 'How can we do that beforehand if we don't know who Snyder's been in communication with until we look into his—'

'You're not hearin' me, boys. I don't care!'

Thomson jabbed his finger to within a millimetre of Trevarthen's name badge. His breath stank of cheap stale tobacco and something rotten, like there was old meat stuck and decomposing between his uneven yellow teeth. The temptation was strong to cuff the unpleasant man, but even with Semmens on hand it would be a tough job to subdue Thomson. Besides, Thomson had technically done nothing wrong other than be an obtuse prick. 'Please put your hand down.' Trevarthen could hear the quavering of his own voice. 'We're all civilised here, right?'

'Course we are.' Thomson plucked a match from his pocket and started chewing it. 'It's still an invasion of my privacy, no matter what path you took to get there. Now, get to the fucken point. What do you want from me?'

'Where were you on Monday night gone?'

'With me mum.'

'Can she verify that?'

'Yeah. And so can the other fifty people who were there.'

'What? At you mum's place?'

'I never said that. I was helping her out at the Bingo hall. She has trouble keepin' up with the caller and marking the numbers on her card,' Thomson sniffed.

'When did the Bingo finish?'

'Hmm. I'd say about 9:30pm. I took mum home and stayed the night at hers.'

'Cameron Snyder was killed between 10:00pm and midnight. With all due respect, you could have tucked your mum into bed with a warm cocoa, dashed over to Snyder's and murdered him, then returned to your mum's house before–'

'Leave my mother out of it!' The brute bellowed. Both officers recoiled half a step. 'You blokes are off yer fucking rockers, ya know that? Cameron Snyder, God grant him eternal rest,' Thomson made the sign of the cross, eyes closed, 'owed me $450. Do you really think I'd go to the trouble of killing a bloke for that pissy little amount?'

'Others have killed men for less.'

'I've never killed no one. Not even when people owed me thousands. You think I'm stupid?'

'We have to ask these questions.' Trevarthen couldn't look Thomson in the eyes, which seemed to be darting independently of one another.

'Yeah, doing your job 'n that. I've heard it a million times from pissant coppers like you pair of losers.'

Trevarthen felt his core body temperature inching upwards. Instinct told him Thomson had zero to do with the murder, but the constable wouldn't let him off that easy, even if his voice was quavering. 'We'll be double-checking your alibis with all the relevant people, including your mother. If there's even the slightest discrepancy, we'll be back with a warrant and arrest you for obstructing the course of justice.'

Thomson's fingers trembled before forming a pair of hard-boned fists the size of house bricks. 'How about you fuckwits take a hike before I lose my shit and start massaging you with that tyre lever over there.'

'We'll be in touch if we have any more questions,' said Trevarthen handing Thomson a business card. As he did so, he imagined how much differently DS Lisbon would have handled this arsehole. Thomson would've been on the ground moaning before he could blink. 'I'm thinking of having a word with your parole officer about your impolite behaviour.' The officers turned and headed for the roller door. 'You'll be back behind bars before the day's out.'

Thomson tore up the card, laughing as he watched the little white pieces flutter to the floor. 'Please, do tell him,' he called to the officers' retreating backs. 'That pussy's even more scared of me than you two wankers.'

Chapter Nineteen

'WE'RE a little underprepared on Gillmeister. We need good background material.' Jack ran a hand through his close-cropped hair as he and Taylor waited at the MacDonald's drive-through counter. He surreptitiously checked the new 'do in the mirror. After a series of dud barbers in Yorkville hellbent on giving everyone a hipster cut, Jack had finally found one who could style his hair short enough without making him look like a neo-Nazi. 'I've got a feeling about this guy.'

'Like you had about Randall Sowell?'

'Yeah.' Jack took the coffees and fries from a too-happy teen in a headset, arranged them in the console already overcrowded with detritus of on-the-go snacks. 'Just like him.' *Why did she have to be such a smart-arse all the time?*

'I'm just bringing the details up now on the school's website,' said Taylor. 'Here we are. Teaching staff list. Trent Gillmeister, physical education teacher. An email address and a small passport style photograph. That's all.' Taylor turned the tablet to show Jack the man's profile photo:

genial face atop a collar and tie, gap-toothed smile and a thatch of curly blonde hair.

'Looks a nice enough bloke,' said Jack as he buckled his seat belt. 'Although I knew a baby-faced killer like him back in the UK. Check out the eyes. Too close together.'

'Are you serious?'

Jack shrugged. 'What else can you find on him?'

She scrolled, typed something into a search engine, pressed a combination of on-screen buttons. 'Plenty. He used to be a personal trainer in Sydney with his own consultancy. Lots, and I mean lots, of photos. Make a single woman weak at the knees.'

'What?' Jack failed to hide the faint jealous note in his voice. 'Gimme a look.' He reached for the iPad but Taylor gripped it tight, wouldn't surrender it.

'Ooh, would you look at this. Rippling muscles coated in sweat, lifting big heavy weights. What's this move, a biceps curl?'

'Show me, dammit.'

She handed him the tablet with exaggerated care and a beaming smile. 'Be my guest. Didn't know you were so enamoured of the male form, DS Lisbon.'

'Don't be daft, Claudia. But you're right. He could make a certain type of woman swoon.' Jack had to admit to himself, the handsome Trent Gillmeister looked like a model out of a glossy fitness magazine. And on closer inspection, his eyes weren't too close together at all. Chiselled features, buff body. Granted, filters could have been used on the professional-looking shots, but you still needed the raw material to work with. One thing was for sure, the man's face was too pretty to be a fighter. Unless he was so good no one could lay a finger on him, like Ali. Doubtful.

'You got the phone number for the school there? I think we should make an appointment before barging in.'

'That's not your usual style, Jack, giving people advance warning of our impending arrival.'

'Agreed. But Cairns is a fair drive, innit? I don't wanna turn up at the principal's office to find the bloke's not there.' As Jack stirred a sachet of brown sugar into the takeaway coffee, Taylor dialled the number of the school on the dash comms display. A woman answered on the fourth ring. Jack introduced himself and Taylor, said they were an hour away, requested Gillmeister's mobile number.

'Sorry, I'm not authorised to give staff members' phone numbers,' said the haughty female.

'This is an urgent matter.'

'You could be someone pretending to be the police, how am I to know?'

'I assure you, we're—'

'Just one moment while I consult the timetable.' A rustling sound, some coughing. 'He's in the middle of conducting a self-defence class for the senior girls at the moment. Would you like to leave a message?'

'No. Get him to call me back when the class finishes.' Jack left his number and disconnected. He glanced at the time on the dashboard. 2:10pm. It was a 45-minute drive to Cairns from their current location, barring road accidents and other mishaps. He turned to Taylor. 'What time does school finish in this part of the world?'

'3:00pm.'

'Jesus, we'd better get a move on then. I don't want him missing the memo and disappearing before we get there. Tell me more about Gillmeister on the way.' Jack gulped down the remainder of his coffee and tossed the cup over his shoulder. He rammed the gear into drive, depressed the accelerator hard. The rear tyres squealed on smooth concrete as the Ford Territory exited the car park and lurched onto the highway, miraculously missing an open-mouthed elderly tourist behind the wheel of a rented camper van.

Settled into a cruising speed at a smidgin over the speed limit, Jack received a call from Trevarthen over the two-way. 'Thomson's an absolute prick, sir. He's denying involvement. Said no way he'd kill a person for such a paltry sum.'

'Was he credible?'

'Hard to tell. He was fucking scary, I'll say that much. Threatened to attack us with a tyre lever! I called his mother, she backed up his alibi.'

'As you'd expect.'

'Yeah. Semmens and I reckon he's worth pursuing further. He's a loose cannon, could easily have killed Snyder for reasons other than a loan debt. Insulting his mother, for one.'

'Thanks, Aden. If we get stuck with other enquiries, we'll have another chat with Prince Charming.'

'Sure. Only do you reckon you could talk to him next time?'

'Come off it, man. You're an armed policeman, working with another armed policeman.'

'Yeah, but you'd be better at messing the bloke up with your fists, hey?'

'Jesus, Aden. That's not what I'm all about. Diplomacy's more my thing.' Jack heard Taylor chuckle, he turned and frowned at her. He instructed the constables to continue door knocking businesses around Trick Shot, and when they'd finished that, research the hell out of potential cuckolded husband Rex van der Klopp, maybe even pay him a visit at his workplace. Jack still had nagging suspicions about the couple with the odd Dutch surname.

Fifteen minutes later and Taylor had run out of coffee. She'd also run out of information to tell Jack about Trent Gillmeister. He'd documented his life highlights on social media, but been spare, verging on silent, in his posts over the last two years. 'That wraps up his bio, Jack. A single man focused on body image. And…shit, you nearly hit that guard rail. Will you slow down, for goodness sake?'

'Calm down, Claudia. I missed it by miles.'

'Right,' she muttered, shaking her head.

'Let's back this up.' Jack ignored his partner's exasperation. 'I promise I was listening hard, but I missed a bit when that semi-trailer tore past. How long did you say he's been in the state teaching?'

'One year.'

'And how long's he been up here in North Queensland?'

'Three. Two years at teachers' college on a fast-track program and then into the job in Cairns. Cameron and Lydia Snyder moved to Yorkville five years ago.'

'It's a wee bit odd, innit? Sowell said Gillmeister was super protective of his sister. If that was the case, he would've come sooner than that, hey? I reckon either Sowell was exaggerating about Gillmeister's care factor or…'

'Or maybe there was an incident that drew him here? Taylor finished the thought for Jack.

'That's what I'm thinking. And you said he unsuccessfully applied for a job teaching in Yorkville first, didn't you?'

'Uh huh.'

'Something's triggered the relocation. Any news yet from Kylie Smith on Lydia's medical records?'

'Be realistic, Jack.' Taylor eyeballed the digital dash

clock. 'She would've only just finished up at the hospital. She's not a magician.'

'Wishful thinking, I know. I'm just anxious to get this tucked away so I can fly home to my kid.' Jack turned in his seat, fixed Taylor with puppy dog eyes. 'Know what I mean?'

'Of course, I understand. Sometimes you have to let things take their own course, Jack. Smith will contact us the minute she's got anything.'

'Yeah, yeah, I know.' The DS needed air, pressed the button to wind down his window. A cool breeze carrying the warm, sweet scents of the tropics filled the interior of the car. He fumbled in his pocket, unwrapped a stick of gum and jammed it in his mouth. They had reached the leafy suburb of Redlynch on the western fringes of Cairns. Not long now.

'Take that left turn,' said Taylor. 'According to the GPS, St Hilda's Catholic School for Girls is half a kay up that road.'

———

THE TWO DETECTIVES sat in a sparsely furnished anteroom. Jack wriggled, trying to find some comfort. The only decorations in the narrow space were wall-hung portraits of the stern-faced principle, Ms Ruth Havlik, and Queen Elizabeth II. Both were taken when the subjects had fewer wrinkles. The hard and unforgiving wooden benches transported Jack back to his school days in inner London. To pass the time, Jack absentmindedly flicked through a dusty St Hilda's yearbook from the 1980s. He soon tired of looking at pictures of teenage girls sporting ridiculous perms and returned the book to the shelf it lived on. He noticed Taylor's face contorting as she tapped away on her iPhone.

'Who're you messaging?'

'None of your business.'

'Come on, tell me.'

'If you must know, it's a guy I met on Tinder. He's asked me on a second date tonight and I'm saying yes.'

'Who is he?'

'What do you care?'

'I don't.' *Boy, did he care.* 'Only you were miserable as hell after that last dating fiasco.'

Taylor lowered her eyebrows. 'That's my problem, not yours. Besides, he was a cop, this man isn't. And he's not married, I double checked this time.'

Jack had already gone too far to turn back. 'I don't want you distracted while we're working on this urgent case.'

'What, I'm not allowed to have a personal life because it's inconvenient for you?' She swung her head back to her lap, completed the message and pocketed the mobile.

'That didn't come out the way I meant it,' Jack mumbled. 'I worry about you, that's all.'

'Bullshit. You need this case tidied up ASAP and if I have to put my life on hold, too bad for me. You're a selfish prick sometimes, Jack.'

She was right, so he said nothing further about it. Instead, he dialled Constable Kylie Smith. The call went to voicemail and he left a message to get back with Lydia Snyder's medical information if and when she got any. He hung up, turned to Taylor and said, 'Sorry, sunshine. You're right. I was thinking of myself, but half of what I said was God's honest truth. I do worry about you.'

'I know,' said Taylor softly, a pink blush spreading across her cheeks. 'Let's not argue, hey?'

A loud trilling bell signalled the end of the school day.

The fussy receptionist who'd answered the detectives' initial phone call and greeted them on arrival opened the creaky door, ushered in Trent Gillmeister and disappeared. It was clear the use of filters in the man's online pictures had been minimal, if they'd been used at all. In real life he was bursting with health and vitality, and no less handsome. One major difference. The neat, mid-length beard framing dazzling white teeth had been grown after he'd sat for the staff photo.

'I'm pretty sure I know why you're here.' Gillmeister approached Taylor first and shook her hand, then Jack's. Dressed in a white polo shirt and shorts, the man reminded Jack of a health resort tennis professional. 'It's a terrible business about Cameron.'

'This room reminds me of my sadistic headmaster,' said Jack. 'Is there somewhere else we can talk that ain't so oppressive?'

'Sure. Staff room?'

'Suits us.' Taylor stood, smoothed her trousers and opened the door. 'Let's go.'

As they crossed an expansive quadrangle enclosed by sandstone buildings, dozens of girls in maroon and navy uniforms, alone, in pairs or chattering in groups, scurried in multiple directions. Some home, others to after-school activities. Jack thought of his own daughter. Skye had been attending school for four years now. Not a posh private one like St Hilda's, but a government comprehensive. He'd fled the UK before she'd even started Year 1. He'd missed so much of her life it made his heart ache. Christ, she'd be entering Year 5 in September. Easter would coincide with his trip home – assuming it even happened –and he'd be able to catch up on so much of what he'd missed. Sarah said if he kept his nose clean in London she'd consider bringing Skye to Australia for a holiday. At Jack's expense, of course, and that was perfectly OK with him. But that was all hypothetical stuff. First he had to find a killer.

Gillmeister brought the detectives instant coffee, a can of soft drink for himself. Jack took a sip and winced. 'Geez, you'd think an elite school like this would have better coffee for its teachers, wouldn't you Claudia?'

Taylor tasted her drink and smiled. 'Don't know what you're talking about. Mine's fine.'

'No, I agree with Detective Lisbon here,' said Gillmeister. 'It's a running joke. But the focus is on spending money for the benefit of the students, not the teaching staff.'

'Wouldn't happy and contented teachers be a better proposition than ones pissed off about the facilities?' said Jack.

'That's my argument, but it falls on deaf ears. I'm just a humble PE teacher who's only been tenured for a year. Who's going to listen to my complaints?'

Jack tapped a forefinger on the tabletop. 'Time's marching on, Mr Gillmeister, or may I call you Trent?'

'Trent's fine.'

'The thing is, Trent, we're a wee bit concerned about the lack of progress in our investigation into the murder of your sister's ex-husband.'

Gillmeister gestured with open palms. 'I'm at your service. My sister is a mess, so you know I'll do anything I can to help.'

'Good, good.' Jack absently scratched his chin. 'Now, what was the first thing I wanted to…hang on, you didn't have a beard in your staff profile, did you?'

'Very observant, Detective Lisbon. I was clean shaven when I started working here.'

'Props to you, Trent. A very dashing beard it is. I'm not sure a delicate Pommy like me could tolerate one in this climate.'

Gillmeister gave half a laugh. 'That's the exact reason I did it. The heat was starting to give me a nasty rash when I shaved. I tried all kinds of creams and lotions. The only thing to stop it was this crop of facial hair.' He fired a wink so fast Jack nearly missed it. 'You think it suits me, Detective Taylor?'

'Sure,' she said as if she couldn't care less. 'I don't go for bearded men myself, but each to their own.'

Good one, Claudia was what Jack wanted to say but bit his tongue.

'I do like honest ones, though.' Taylor added as she opened her notepad. 'Men, that is.'

'Actually,' said Jack, reaching into his pocket. 'Speaking of honesty, do you mind if I record you on my phone? Mainly for your protection, you understand.'

'Not at all.' Gillmeister produced his own mobile, pressed a few buttons and placed it on the table. 'As long as I can do the same. Then we'll cover all our arses.'

'OK,' Jack continued, realising he wasn't dealing with a fool. 'I'm going to get the unpleasant questions out of the way first. Can you explain your whereabouts on the night of Monday, 4th March?'

'Easy. I was with Lydia.'

'What?' said Taylor. 'In Yorkville?'

'Yep. She was having a particularly bad night. She'd taken a couple of tranquilisers but they weren't doing the job. She told me Cameron was in Cairns checking on some machinery at his other pool hall, so she couldn't go over to his place for,' he made air quotes, *"comfort"* like she some-times did.'

'Do you often travel all the way to Yorkville when Lydia's feeling out of sorts?'

'When I can, yeah.'

'Even with school the next day?'

'Why not? It's only an hour each way. When I lived in Sydney, that was considered a reasonable daily commute. I'll be frank with you, officers. I warned her time and time again not to go back to him. You know he had a domestic violence order taken out on him, right?'

Jack nodded. 'Of course. But Lydia withdrew it and she denies Snyder was violent with her. He's got no history of police attention since that DVO was cancelled.'

'Did you check his record as a younger man back in New South Wales?'

'We're onto that. But while we're waiting, tell us what we can expect to find.'

'Numerous police visits when Lydia called triple zero, scared Cameron would kill her. He was never charged with anything to do with that, always knew how to manipulate her into backing down.'

'I'm not sure all of those call outs are going to be kept on file, Trent,' said Jack, shaking his head, as if disappointed in Gillmeister's answer.

'There's definitely a break and enter charge for a burglary. He and Lydia did it when they were in their late teens. He had her hypnotised, she'd do anything he said. And that's basically never changed.'

'Until now,' said Jack.

'That backs up Lydia's statement about her fingerprints being on record,' said Taylor. 'I'll be making a request to the NSW police for access tomorrow, see if there's more in the storybook. I'm a little puzzled, though, Trent.'

'Oh really, why?'

'You painting a picture of Snyder as a violent man, coupled with the fact his nemesis Randall Sowell told us you were a highly protective brother, is doing you no favours.'

'Indeed,' chimed in Jack. 'The more you rub the dirt into poor deceased Cameron Snyder, the more motive you're giving yourself.'

'As I said, I was with Lydia the night Cameron was killed. All night. Plus,' he smiled broadly through his neat beard, 'DC Taylor here said she liked honest men, so I'm telling the truth.'

'Are you saying all this just so I'll like you?' said Taylor, scribbling in her notebook. 'I'm not in the habit of being picked up by persons of interest in murder enquiries.'

'I…no…oh Jesus, it's nothing like that.'

Good one, Claudia, Jack thought again. Putting him on the spot nicely.

'Then what?' she added.

'I'm co-operating, OK? I can only tell you what I know. Apart from Randall Sowell, I'm not aware of any other people who might've wanted to kill Cameron, for whatever reason.'

'Didn't Lydia talk to you about Snyder's work?'

Trent laughed. 'No way. Why give me ammunition to support my argument she should stop seeing him? She protected Cameron, his reputation. Even after it got to the point where she couldn't handle his temper tantrums and had to leave him, she still carried a torch. Love is blind, officers.' He paused for a second. 'If I asked about him, she'd always steer the subject in another direction.'

'What was your own relationship with Mr Snyder like?' said Jack. Time to suck the wind out of Gillmeister's sails. 'You must've hated his guts the way he roughed up your little sister.'

'He wasn't on my Christmas card list, let's put it that way. I've known him for years, Lydia and Cameron got together when they were in high school. I'd see him at the odd social function. I always had my suspicions he was beating her, but no proof. Even if I had, my energies were spent trying to convince Lydia to leave Cameron, not taking revenge on him. I'm not a violent man, detectives.'

'You look physically strong enough to have handled Snyder easily,' said Jack. 'You and he never got into any altercations over the years?'

Gillmeister shook his head, locked eyeballs with the DS. 'I've resisted the temptation.'

'You've got amazing restraint,' said Jack. 'If someone was hurting a person close to me, my daughter for instance, well…I'd be putting a stop to it whichever way I could.'

'That's you, not me. And you know what? There were times the charming bastard almost had me fooled, made me question if I was wrong about him. He'd have me convinced everything was in Lydia's head. That she mistook his "excitable nature", as he himself put it, for mental instability. If I was at a barbecue or a party or something at their house, he was the friendliest, nicest person you could hope to meet. But deep down, I knew he was putting on a show. And if I knew, officers, then others must have known. A two-faced snake like him would have made a ton of enemies in all walks of life. I'd go back to that Randall Sowell, if I were you. Or maybe Cueball Snyder wasn't redneck enough for his ultra-patriotic mates. They don't like traitors in their ranks.'

'Anyone else?' said Taylor, placing the pen neatly on the notepad.

Gillmeister shrugged. 'He ran two pool halls. Those

places attract the dregs of society. I wouldn't be surprised if a customer took exception to something he did or said.'

'Could you two excuse me for one minute?' said Jack. 'Can you tell me where the little boys' room is?' He screwed up his face like he was about to wet his pants.

'This is a girls-only school,' said Trent. 'But I get your meaning. Out the door we came through and you'll see the restrooms for staff clearly marked halfway down the hall.'

'Cheers.' Jack scooped up the phone, stopped the recording and strode down the corridor, smiling politely at a couple of female teachers clutching folders and text books. He passed the bathroom and exited onto the quadrangle. A quick call to Lydia Snyder was in order.

'Yeah, what is it?' A weary voice answered.

'Were you alone on Monday night?'

'Ah, who's this?'

'DS Lisbon. I repeat. Were you alone at your house on the evening of Monday 4th March?'

'No. Trent was with me.'

'You sure?'

'Of course I am. He drove down from Cairns to keep me company. I was on edge, almost having a panic attack. Maybe I was having a premonition about what was going to happen that night.'

'Why the hell didn't you mention it before?'

'I didn't think it was relevant?'

'DC Taylor briefed me on her chat with you yesterday. You talked about a lot of things. But not your brother.'

'Why would I?'

Calmly, Jack, or she'll hang up on you. 'Because, potentially, he has a motive for murdering Cameron.'

'Bullshit.' The sparking up of a lighter, inhalation of smoke, a cough. 'Trent never hurt anyone in his life.'

'Was he with you the whole time?'

'Yeah.'

'How did you spend the evening?'

'He got here around 7:30pm I guess. He brought some red wine, take-away chicken and chips. We watched TV and chatted until we went to bed about...ah...geez, I dunno. Midnight, maybe?'

'Are you sure it wasn't earlier?'

'Listen, Detective Lisbon, I wasn't exactly watching the clock. Why would I?'

She was telling the truth as she knew it, Jack sensed. And her alibi was enough to get Trent off the hook unless Proctor could find something linking him to the crime. Or a witness came forward. Gillmeister may well have despised Snyder, but was that hatred enough to spur him to murder?

'Did you see Trent the next morning?'

'Nah. I didn't wake up until after he was gone. In fact it was....' Sniffs, blubbering, ragged breaths. 'It was the cops knocking on my door...with the news...that woke me up.'

He waited for her breathing to normalise. 'Lydia, what do you know about Cameron's mother and father?'

'What's that got to do with anything?'

'Just background. With murder enquiries information that seems insignificant can prove to be critical.'

'His mother Suzanna developed early onset dementia. She's in a care facility in Sydney somewhere.'

'And his dad?'

'No idea. His mum brought him up on her own. She told Cameron his father was an American sailor she met at a bar, but I always thought that was a lie. So did Cam, but he never bothered about it too much.'

Now wasn't the time to tell her about surprise daddy Ray Hook. She'd find out soon enough when he croaked and she got her hands on the trust money. 'Once again, sorry for your loss.'

———

'IS TRENT GILLMEISTER TELLING THE TRUTH?' said Jack, indicating to overtake a Prado towing a caravan up a winding section of the highway.

'He wanted me to like him, remember.' Taylor expanded a scrunchie between her fingers, looped her black hair through it. 'So that means no.'

'Pardon?'

'Do you tell the truth when you want women to like you?'

'Yes…ah…no. Damn it, Claudia, you're in the wrong job. You should be a prosecting QC, giving criminal defendants merry hell.'

'I'm thinking of starting a law degree next year, as it happens.'

Another slow vehicle made Jack ease off the gas again. 'Please don't leave me for greener pastures until Wilson gets a transfer. I couldn't handle him being my partner.'

'It's a part-time course that'll take me ages to complete. I can't see myself abandoning you for a while yet.'

'Glad to hear it. But back to Gillmeister. What if he snuck out after Lydia fell asleep? He could've waited until she was out like a light, then raced over to Snyder's house and done the deed. That's the only plausible scenario I can see if he's the killer.'

'Really?' Taylor's eyebrows formed a V. 'I can see another.'

'What?'

'Brother and sister acted together to kill Snyder.'

'I don't like that theory. She loved Snyder too much. Either that, or she's missed her calling as a Hollywood actress.'

'Still, can we completely rule it out?'

'No, damn you, Claudia. On second thoughts, maybe Wilson *is* a better proposition.' They crested the top of the hill. A clear view of the opposite lane gave Jack the chance to overtake five cars in a row, taking the Territory 30kms beyond the speed limit. 'What we need is some proper evidence. Talking to people ain't getting us diddly squat except information we can't use.'

'Could you convince the chief to get a warrant for Gillmeister? He's got a brand new phone, there could be incriminating evidence on it. Plus the GPS record. If he's gone to Snyder's and offed him, the data will support that theory. His house could be worth searching, too.'

Jack shook his head. 'I've stretched Batista's friendship with the magistrate to breaking point. Apparently she told the Inspector she's going to be needing a lot more of that "reasonable grounds" bullshit in future. There's been a legal audit and our station's been too slapdash in requesting warrants.'

'He could talk to the police chief in Cairns, get them to chase up the warrant. They can seize the property and conduct the search and we tag along. With Snyder's businesses in two locations, the matter of jurisdiction is blurry.'

'We've got no reasonable grounds for Gillmeister. Only speculation.'

'Come on! This is a high-profile murder case. And don't forget the national security implications.'

He had to come clean eventually. It may as well be now. 'Listen, Claudia. There are no security implications.'

'What? Hook said CHOGM was under threat because of this.'

'He made all that shit up. It was Hook who asked me to take the drive up to Cairns, engage you and Wilson to help out and try to salvage Snyder's reputation.'

'I beg your pardon?' Taylor yelled so loud Jack instinctively tucked his ear close to his neck.

'Listen, Claudia. I didn't mean to deceive you, but Hook promised to upgrade my flight and arrange me an extra week of holidays.'

'Did you ask him why Snyder was important to him? And was your flight even cancelled?'

Jack gritted his teeth so hard he thought he'd snap a tooth. 'No and no.'

'Christ, Jack, why didn't you just say? Ben and I would've agreed to help you out in any case.'

'How was I to know that? You would've called me a selfish prick.'

'But you *are* a selfish prick, Jack. We all know that.' She managed a meagre smile. 'Just be honest with us, OK.'

'I'm sorry. Anyway, at least we can be sure about Hook's motives now, knowing he was the victim's father.'

'If it weren't for the fact the trust was secret, you could almost elevate Lydia as a suspect, at least in orchestrating the murder.'

'How do you mean?' Jack popped the lid of a packet of orange-flavoured Tic Tacs, swallowed a pair.

'With the only other beneficiary dead, she'd get the lot.'

'Do you think the lawyer let her in on it, maybe for a cut?'

'Couldn't rule it out. I think I'll swing by his office.'

'Want me to ring him?' Taylor's hand reached for the dash comms screen.

'Not this time.' Trees whizzed past as the Territory thundered down the highway. 'I'm done with politeness.'

Chapter Twenty

BACK AT HER DESK, Taylor took a gulp of water from a plastic bottle. The speed-limit-breaking drive from Cairns had left her mouth dry, her stomach rolling and her head spinning. She'd screamed at Jack to slow down, which he did. At first. Then somehow, gradually, the pace picked up again as he weaved in and out of traffic, honking at everyone. Four times she told him to chill before she could take no more. Twenty kilometres out of Yorkville she yelled at the DS to pull the hell over and she took the wheel. To Jack's fidgety frustration, she stayed five under the limit until she dropped him at Garfield Walters' office. God help that lawyer.

Heart-rate now normal, she opened the printed report from Brisbane digital forensics. As usual, the specialist unit had done a thoroughly professional job. The file contained an overview of the analysis plus a couple of bonus annexes jammed full of rows and columns. There was an electronic version in her inbox, but for close-up inspection you couldn't beat paper, a ruler and a ballpoint pen. She licked a forefinger and began leafing through the file. She wasn't optimistic. Ninety-nine percent of the time the officers who prepared these reports laid everything on the line, there was no guess work required by detectives. Occasionally, very occasionally, something slipped through the cracks. Fingers crossed it had happened this time. Blinking hard to focus on the hiero-glyphics before her, she wished Constable Wilson was on deck. This tedious aspect of police work was more up his alley, the man was borderline savant when it came to the minutiae of data. Unfortunately, young Ben was at home, exhausted, probably tucked up in bed and pushing up a stream of Z's.

Taylor flicked to the back of the thick document to get to the meat of this data stew, grabbed a ruler and scanned line after line of text messages and emails, stopping at specific trigger words. These were highlighted by an algo-rithm some big tech companies would pay the Queensland Police Service big money for. Judging by the laser-targeted advertising rammed down her throat, maybe they already had, with ads for scrunchies and chocolate truffles flooding Taylor's Facebook feed.

As she checked off the seemingly endless list of texts and numbers, Taylor prayed she'd pick up a telling crumb of information. Either something the chief had missed in his summary or a gold nugget the team down south had forgotten to mention in the findings. An hour and thirty minutes later and nearly cross-eyed, Taylor reached the last entry. A text from Cameron Snyder to Lydia telling her not to come around tonight, he was heading to Cairns to check on a malfunctioning vending machine. Exactly as Lydia claimed.

Batista's gangly figure hovered into view, the shadow of

his elongated chin encroaching onto the cover page of the report. 'Afternoon, Claudia.'

'Sir.'

'See anything that eluded everyone else?'

'Fat chance.' She frowned. 'I found no lovers, angry loan sharks or offshore bank accounts. Why would I? The experts have been through this with a fine-tooth comb and come up empty.'

'Wilson did it last year.' The Inspector gave a half-hearted wink.

'Yes, but that hardly counts.' Taylor remembered the constable's Eureka moment. Yorkville CIB had relied on phone records they were sure would lead to a conviction. Wilson realised the mistake when a warrant was issued to arrest well-known country singer Lesley (woman) Chandler instead of violent career thief Leslie (man) Chandler.

'I don't know about that. He saved us from potential embarrassment.'

'That wasn't in the same ball park as Snyder's murder in the seriousness stakes.'

'Of course not.'

'Anyway, like you said already, there's nothing on Snyder's devices incriminating anyone he's been communicating with.'

'Damn it.'

'One thing to bear in mind. The data doesn't go back forever.'

'How do you mean?'

'People change their phone numbers, email accounts. They pay some bills with cash, others with PayPal or similar services. That can make it tough for us to track down transactions without a court order.'

'But we don't need a court order for a dead man. We've got all the authorisation we need.'

'True, however Snyder could've had email accounts years ago that have been closed and all records erased.'

'Is that realistic?'

'Absolutely. I had this secondary Yahoo account, didn't use it for two years. One day I decided to log on to check something and, lo and behold, the whole history of the account had been wiped due to inactivity. Every single email was gone.'

'Jesus, it's amazing they can do that. Aren't your emails personal property?'

'I guess not. But Snyder was only in his early 30s, so I'd hazard a guess he's been using this same Gmail address since he left high school.' Taylor opened the file and pointed. 'See, this one goes back to the mid-2000s. He's got another one that's linked to his business name's website.'

'More or less an open book.' Batista rubbed a pen behind his ear.

'Yep. Same with his SIM card. He's used the one phone number for a decade.'

'That's not to say he didn't have an enemy with a long-standing grudge who never communicated with him. Say, someone he bullied when he was a kid.'

'But what evidence do we have for that? Lydia's been his partner since they were at school. She'd have told us.'

Batista pulled up a chair, sat next to Taylor. 'Does Jack have any hunches?'

'Only everyone!' She laughed. 'Sowell the jealous business rival, Gillmeister the protective brother, maniacal thug Tommy Thomson. Then there's Rex van der Klopp…'

'Wait a minute. I thought you told me earlier the neighbour wasn't the jealous type.'

'Not on face value. But even if the love's faded between him and his missus, the bloke next door shagging your wife's gotta be a huge blow to a man's ego.'

'True.'

'Then there's the latest possibility, the lawyer.'

'Why him?'

'I aired the theory he may have spilled the beans to Lydia about the secret trust, and the pair of them acted together with Walters getting a slice of the action.'

'What's your feeling?'

'I'm open to it. Jack's at the fellow's office as we speak, giving him the third degree no doubt.'

'Excellent.'

Taylor took a deep breath, placed the digital forensics report on top of a pile of other papers. 'With time running out on this investigation, Jack's willing to interrogate the school lollipop lady.'

'Which one?'

'The proverbial one, sir.' Taylor rolled her eyes.

'I knew that.' Batista coughed into his fist. 'I'll let you in on a little secret, Claudia. Jack can go on his holiday whether we solve the case by the weekend or not. I was never going to stand in his way.'

'You must be kidding, sir! He'll blow a fuse when he finds out you've lied to him.'

'I know. Perhaps I should ring him, ease his anxiety. What do you reckon?'

'Like hell. He works better under pressure.'

Batista's phone rang. It was his wife, Marjorie, priority number one, trumping all other matters, murder enquiries included. Taylor overheard the name of their son, Jordan, a man-baby who'd worry Mr and Mrs Batista into early graves. The Inspector strode to his office to continue the call, a worried edge to his voice. Taylor took the opportunity to check her emails. An update from Semmens and Trevarthen. Intensive door knocking around Trick Shot brought no joy. People either knew nothing or weren't willing to talk. Not a huge surprise. A phone call by Semmens to Thomson's mother confirmed the loan shark's alibi. A message from Cairns CIB's Chief Inspector contained disheartening information. In response to a request from Batista, a squad of Cairns uniforms pounded the pavement around Chalkies pool hall. They came up with some names, but the leads were vague. But, the station's boss promised his team would dig, dig and dig some more. Tomorrow and the next day and the day after that until all leads were exhausted. Taylor smiled to herself. She and the Yorkville team would do the same, with or without Jack Lisbon.

The repercussions of this case would be enormous. If and when the killer was found, there'd be internal investigations into where Hook had come up with a quarter of a million dollars in spare cash. The press would have a field day.

Taylor checked the time. Ten minutes after the end of official business hours. Still, she buzzed Proctor. The woman was a workaholic and most certainly would still be hard at it. 'How are the tests going, Margaret?'

'Not even a good afternoon, DC Taylor?'

'Good afternoon.'

'That's better.'

'How are things looking in the lab? Found the smoking gun?'

'Not yet, but you'll be pleased to know I've pulled out all stops on the DNA analyses. This new testing gear we acquired from America last month certainly speeds things up. With Rapid DNA testing we can get basic information within two hours. Isn't that amazing?'

'Marvellous.' Get to the point, Margaret.

'This technology was unheard of just a few years ago. But for more detailed, accurate information, we need at least 24 hours. Do you know if all your suspects intend to supply samples? We don't have anything from the widow, yet.'

'She wasn't feeling up to it today. She's promised to call by tomorrow.'

'Fine. We did get cheek swabs from Rex and Renee van der Klopp. The officer who took the samples told me the wife wasn't at all phased by the process. On the contrary, she was rather excited by it, which leads me to deduce...'

'Leave the deducing to us, please, Margaret. But I know what you're thinking. That the neighbour's genetic material is not going to be among the samples collected from the crime scene.'

'You read my mind.'

'What about her husband?'

'He came by separately, about an hour ago. Apparently his demeanour was less pleasant. Complained about his precious time being wasted.'

Taylor rubbed her forehead, a tiny ache building into a bigger one. Perhaps she ought to cancel tonight's date. 'Yeah, he's a grumpy git, all right.'

'Nevertheless, he did comply with your request, and rather quickly.'

'Thanks for that, Margaret.' *Also a pointer towards innocence.* 'Talk to you tomorrow.'

Taylor tidied her desk, pulled her scrunchie tight. She decided she would go on that date tonight. James the bank teller was a nice, safe option for dipping her toes back in the water. They'd been out once before, the evening ended with a peck on the cheek at Taylor's front door. Maybe tonight passions would ignite. She composed a quick text to Jack. *Let me know how you go with Garfield Walters. I'm done for the day. Talk soon. I've got to get ready for my hot date tonight.* She re-read the text, was about to hit send, then, she had no idea why, deleted the last sentence.

———

JACK HADN'T ENJOYED the cool interior of the Pelican Pub in months. In prime position on Yorkville's waterfront, the place attracted a wide range of clientele, from rusted-on locals to excitable tourists. Tonight the sports bar, where Jack preferred to roost, was only at around one fifth capacity. Perfect.

Now a non-drinker but, if he was going to be honest with himself, still an alcoholic, Jack only visited when he wanted to glean gossip out of Dave the barman. He was a nosy, chatty type who had his finger on the pulse. His information had proved crucial in a number of previous cases. For Jack, though, visiting the Pelican Pub was a classic Catch-22 situation. A great place to get leads, but the temptation to slide back into bad habits here was strong. So far, Jack had resisted the urge for, he counted in his head, thirteen months and twenty-four days. Let's *not* drink to that!

He draped his jacket over the back of a barstool, fished out his phone. An SMS from Taylor. He started to reply when a familiar voice asked, 'What'll it be, Detective Lisbon?'

He looked up and frowned. 'Didn't I tell you last time to call me Jack?'

'Buggered if I can remember, it's been so long since I've seen your battered nose around here.'

The DS tilted his head to the side. 'Oi. Enough of your cheek. Get us a ginger ale and a shot of Bundaberg rum. And a packet of your finest peanuts.'

Dave's expression was a question mark underneath a tight man-bun, then he smiled and nodded. Jack would do the usual *can I resist* routine: buy a rum with his soft drink and leave the booze on the bar when he departed. Dave poured the two drinks, unnecessarily adding ice to the rum, shook roasted nuts into a bowl, then strode to the other end of the bar to attend to another punter. The man waved a fifty note around like he was about to die of thirst. Jack took the opportunity to complete the text to Taylor, fill her in on his meeting with lawyer Walters. *Hi. Lawyer's a stuffed shirt but no grounds to suspect anything. C u tmrw.*

A quick reply. Hope u were nice to him

Jack: Of course. As always

He waited for the conversation to continue, but Taylor clearly had more important things to do. Then he remembered. She was going on a date. He had no right to feel jealous, he had his own dinner rendezvous lined up with Marietta, the Amazon woman from the gym. Still, something gnawed at his heart, the thought of another man and Taylor....*No, stop it.*

Jack recalled the bollocking he'd just given Garfield Walters. Accused him of all kinds of treachery: breaching confidentiality by telling Lydia about the trust, conspiring to murder Snyder in order to share the spoils. Walters, to his credit, never buckled under Jack's onslaught of hyperbole and empty threats, smiled throughout the entire interrogation. Walters claimed he'd been grilled in court by cops more belligerent than Jack. Walters held firm, denied,

denied, denied. Solid as a rock. Getting physical with Walters was out of the question, the wall separating them from the receptionist was paper thin. Not only that, if there was one breed of person who knew their rights better than others, it was damned lawyers. After half an hour of bellowing, Jack thanked the man for his time and stormed out of Walters' office. Despite leaving with nothing concrete, the energy expended on the tirade somehow left Jack on a high. To stay there, he pushed all thoughts of Taylor out of his head, beckoned to Dave.

'Another drink? Oh, you've barely touched the first one.'

'Cameron "Cueball" Snyder.'

'Pardon?'

'You must have heard about the murder. It's been all over the newspapers and TV.'

'The pool hall guy?'

'Yeah, him.'

Dave shrugged his slim shoulders.

'There's been some rumours.'

Jack's ear pricked up. 'What?'

'Stupid ones. Fake news, as they say. He assaulted the daughter of a biker gang's boss, he's part of a Mexican drug cartel, runs with Nazis, things like that.'

'Nothing about a rival businessman bumping him off in order to get his hands on the Pilkington Fish Factory?'

Dave raised a forefinger to his chin. 'Actually, yeah, I did hear something like that. Well, not exactly. It was months ago, before the guy was killed.'

'Got a name?'

'Nope, it's eluding me. Geez, I'm not being very helpful am I?'

'That's fine, mate. Snyder was busy running his own

businesses, unlikely he'd waste time frequenting the pubs around Yorkville.'

'I saw photos of him on the news. To be honest, I don't think I ever saw him in here. He's fairly distinguishable, with that shiny bald head and hooped earrings.'

The last one was a hail Mary. 'Anything about him being a wife beater?'

A shake of the head. 'Nah, nothing like that. To be honest, the punters that come here are more interested in the fate of the Yorkville football team. They're six and oh this season, so that's about the only thing people are talking about right now.'

Jack didn't give a damn about the town's football team. It was time to leave. He gulped down his ginger ale, shrugged on his jacket and placed twenty dollars on the bar with an exaggerated flourish. 'The rum's all yours, mate. And keep the change.' Not a generous monetary reward, the tip would have been less than five dollars. But pouring the alcohol down the sink would be more of a sin than someone else consuming it.

'Sorry I couldn't be of any more help.' Dave had a quick look left and right, slammed down the shot.

'Don't mention it, sunshine. I'm sure I'll be back.' Jack took two steps before turning around. 'Oh, one more thing, and it's very important.'

'Sure, Jack. Anything to help Yorkville's finest.'

'You know any good restaurants where I can take a big strapping woman with an appetite like a bleedin' bear?'

Chapter Twenty-One

DAVE'S SUGGESTION turned out to be an inspired choice. Genaro's Grill House and Oyster Bar sat at the far end of The Esplanade, quiet compared to the middle section where rowdy bars and clubs crowded into each other. It had been open for only four months, but in a small city like Yorkville that was enough time for word to spread. The restaurant couldn't have suited a woman of Marietta Szabo's immense appetites any better. It boasted a menu loaded with high-calorie options, a groaning salad bar and a wine list longer than the white pages. The only downside was the astronomical prices.

'I've been thinking about coming here for a while.' Marietta held her glass up to the light, gave a tiny nod of approval and took a sip of French pinot noir. 'It's had some excellent reviews already.'

Jack smiled. 'Yeah, me too.'

'You've had excellent reviews? Where can I read them?'

'No. I mean I've been keen to check out the restaurant.'

He'd not heard of Genaro's until Dave gave him the rundown on the joint.

'Only teasing,' she laughed. After a considered swirl of wine inside her mouth and a satisfied swallow she added, 'You know, Jack, I can't believe you asked me on a proper date so soon. We only met yesterday!'

'I'm not known for wasting time.' Although he had ulterior motives, he wasn't prepared to reveal his hand. Let the evening progress naturally, ease the request into the conversation. *Don't let her think you're using her.*

Marietta readdressed her dessert, an elegant slice of lemon cheesecake dwarfed by a plate the size of a manhole cover. Jack couldn't imagine where she put it all. She'd already wolfed down a 600 gram ribeye steak with half a dozen oysters au naturel while Jack still had half a chicken schnitzel left on his plate. Most impressive, though, was the way she tilted back her head and let the salty bivalves slide down her long neck. If those babies worked their aphrodisiacal properties, Jack was in for a wild night. She'd also gulped down a carafe of deep purple cab sav before switching to the lighter pinot. The alcohol appeared to be having little effect on her, speech clear and movements coordinated.

'How is everything?' said an eager waiter, hovering over Jack's shoulder like a mosquito.

'Fine,' Jack forced himself to reply politely. He would have obtained immense satisfaction by giving the runt a slap about the ears.

'And you madam?' Marietta looked at the fawning server sideways, pointed a finger of one hand at the cake-laden fork she was holding in the other. She emitted a low growl and the man minced to another table, the tail of his apron flapping behind him.

'Well done, sunshine,' Jack smiled. 'You sent that fussy little toe-rag packing.'

'I don't suffer fools and I don't like being interrupted while I'm eating.' Marietta laid the spoon on the side of her dish. 'Or when I'm doing…other things.' She grinned, ran her tongue around her bright red lips, dabbed the corners of her mouth with a linen napkin.

The display made Jack blush. 'I…ah…ah…' he stammered.

She reached across, rested her hand over the top of his. Her hand was slightly bigger, minus the gnarled knuckles. 'What, don't tell me the wild boy I took home the other night has gone all demure on me, has he?'

'No, no, of course not. I'm just not used to women being so…forward…in public.'

'Are you intimidated by strong, liberated females?'

'Not at all. I'm rather old school in some ways, I guess.'

The glib answer seemed to satisfy Marietta, who enthusiastically dug back into her dessert. Jack skipped the last course, having already let his belt out a notch on a trip to the bathroom. If romance was on the cards tonight, he didn't fancy approaching the task with a distended stomach.

'The press are hinting this murder case has got the Yorkville police baffled,' said Marietta, rounding up stray pastry crumbs with a finger. 'Do you reckon you'll find the killer soon?'

'To be honest, no. Which is a right pain in the arse. If that plane takes off for London without me I'll be lucky if I get speak to my daughter again before she's fifteen years old.'

Marietta nodded. 'I've got a daughter myself. She left the nest a couple of years ago. Danila's a daddy's girl who'd prefer to spend her free time with my ex-husband. She doesn't want much to do with me.'

'That's a shame.'

She shrugged. 'It is what it is. Danila's much more feminine than me. Make-up and clothes are her thing. Always taking duck-face selfies and posting them online. She can't relate to me and my obsession with natural physical health and exercise.' She paused. 'Or my pansexual lifestyle.'

Jack gulped. 'Excuse me?' He wasn't even sure what that word meant, but it didn't bode well.

'Does that shock you?' she laughed. 'Not a good fit with your old-school values?'

He didn't know what to say, so he closed his eyes and took a long sip of his cappuccino. He tried to marshal his thoughts so he could add something apropos to the conversation. No good, nothing clever came to him. Instead, he grinned like an idiot and said, 'Not for me to judge.'

Mariette smiled back, perhaps satisfied with his diplomatic answer. But no, there was more. 'I'm only joking, Jack.'

'What?'

'Despite my androgynous appearance, I only go for men. Big strong ones like you, complete with their outmoded morals. Hairy chests are a bonus.'

'Phew,' he ran the back of his hand across his forehead. 'For a moment there I was...'

She squeezed his hand. 'Getting back to the case. I think I might have a juicy lead for you.'

If Marietta had told Jack she was Arnold Schwarzenegger in disguise he wouldn't have been more shocked. 'I beg your pardon?'

'You haven't forgotten I used to work in a law firm, right?'

Marietta had indeed given Jack a patchwork description of her background. She'd worked as a paralegal in a Cairns law firm, Robinson, Brinkworth and Clayborne, before she left the job two years ago to become a florist. Jack had planned to ask her to make enquiries around the North Queensland legal fraternity, perhaps she could turn up something useful. But this was even better. She was offering up information without being asked. 'I remember, sure. You told me last night before we had se... ah...made love.'

She tossed her head back and snorted before gathering her composure. 'You are a dead-set prude, Detective Lisbon.'

'I am not!' Jack thought of himself as being an open-minded man, however the Amazon across the table was having a disconcerting effect on his machismo. 'Anyway, what's this lead and why didn't you tell me last night?'

Marietta screeched with laughter. Jack said, 'It's not funny.'

'It's hilarious. Whether you want to admit it or not, we were both horny as rabbits and only had one thing on our minds.' She slowly leaned across the table, put on a serious face. 'I can't believe I didn't see the connection before.'

'What connection?'

Marietta folded her napkin and leaned back in her seat. 'The law company was approached, maybe four years ago, by this young businessman. He'd just moved to Yorkville from Brisbane with his wife. One night he was out with a bunch of new friends he'd made and got involved in a bar-room brawl. He put another man in hospital with serious head injuries.' She drained the rest of her wine, beckoned the waiter and he refilled her glass. Jack kept silent, determined not to interrupt.

'Now, where was I? Oh yes, this guy was desperately

seeking someone to defend him against a charge of aggravated assault. He was shit-scared, claimed there were witnesses lined up to testify that he whacked the other bloke, who was just an eighteen-year-old kid, with a barstool, then stomped on his head. Look, I can't be sure, it was a while ago and we had a lot of clients, but I think the man could have been Cueball Snyder. I saw the mug shots in the paper this morning and, well, the likeness rang a bell.'

'But Snyder has no record in Queensland.'

'That's the thing. He should have. A week before the matter was scheduled to go to court, we got a call from Cairns police, a man saying the charges had been dropped.'

'Who made the call, do you remember?'

'Ray Hook.'

'You can be sure of that but not the name of the client?'

'Of course. Hook spoke to me at length. His name is well known, always got his fat face on the TV. At that time he was the most famous person I'd ever spoken with. Of course I'm going to remember that.'

Jack rubbed his face. 'I knew it. He's either paid off those witnesses or threatened them. Probably even the effing victim. Jesus Christ, what a snake.' Jack drained his coffee, called the waiter over and paid the bill. He could almost hear his bank account crying out in pain, but Marietta deserved the treat. For a number of reasons.

Chapter Twenty-Two

TYPICAL, *Lisbon. A dream date only you could fuck up.* Tonight's workout was supposed to be in bed with Marietta, not alone in the cramped gymnasium of his apartment block at quarter past midnight. His last dinner date, with then girl-friend hot-shot solicitor Denise Hutchinson, had ended in unmitigated disaster, so it should have come as no surprise when this one did too.

Roughing up villains and scaring the bejesus out of witnesses, that was a piece of piss, as the Aussies say. Women, though, that was a tough audience. Jack had no problem telling bawdy jokes and being crude with men, but the minute a woman starts licking her lips like a vamp, he goes to water. Why the hell did he suggest her higher-than-average libido was a result of promiscuity? Only an idiot would have said what Jack said. A complete fucking moron. He knew it the instant it was out of his mouth, but it was too late, the damage had been done. *I suppose you've slept with tons of men, hey?* And just like that, the date was over. Marietta storming out of the restaurant, all eyes on her, was an image that'd be haunting Jack for a long time.

Would he ever learn how to read the room?

Perhaps not.

But he'd work on it. Maybe read some self-help books.

The evening wasn't a complete disaster, thankfully. The information about Hook getting Snyder off a serious assault charge was worth its weight in gold. It was insurance for the future, should Hook pull through and start making demands on Jack.

Tomorrow, he'd go to Marietta's old employer, Robinson, Brinkworth and Clayborne, get the names and addresses of the witnesses who retracted their statements, maybe pay them a surprise visit.

First priority, however, was to get the frustration out of his system. Time to beat the horse hair out of the heavy bag. Stretching exercises and a set of barbell squats over, Jack slid his hands into his Everlast boxing gloves. He pulled the Velcro flap of the left glove over with his teeth, pushed it snugly into place with his chin. Same with the right. He stood, waggled his head from side to side, rolled his shoulders and addressed the bag. Jack's stance and snarling expression would have scared off a robber's dog. He started slowly, tap, tap, dab, dab. Left jabs, then switched the stance to southpaw, right jabs, nice and relaxed. *Ease into the task until the sack attains some momentum.* He imagined the swinging object was Assistant Commissioner Raymond Ogden Hook, proceeded to thwack the damn thing with lightning combinations, mean jabs and savage rips and, fittingly, brutal hooks. The DS punched and punched and punched until he hadn't the strength to hold his arms horizontal or the breath left to continue.

Sweat poured from Jack's skin, splashed onto the floor in droplets the size of ball bearings. His body temperature climbed, neared the maximum possible before blood boiled and steam emerged from orifices.

He collapsed in a heap on the floor, thought of nothing for a couple of minutes, then clambered to his feet.

Upstairs, showered and rehydrated, Jack was easing his weary body into bed when The Clash decided to split the silence of the night. "London Calling", demanding an answer.

No way! He was supposed to be on death's door. Jack picked up his mobile. 'Is that you, Lazarus?'

'What,' came the croaked reply. 'No, it's…me…Ray…'

'I know it's you, you pillock. Don't you know your bible stories?'

'No.'

'Pity, 'cos I reckon you'll be meeting the good Lord sooner than you'd counted on. If not because of your dodgy ticker, it'll be because of the shit storm I'm gonna unleash on your sorry arse.'

'What the hell are you talking about?'

'Where do I start? Lies about a secret child…'

'Stop right there. I don't know what you've heard, but it's bullshit.' The most unconvincing denial Jack had ever heard from a high-ranking police officer. And he'd heard a few.

'Whatever,' Jack scoffed. 'Nothing a paternity test and a re-examination of an old assault case won't clarify.'

Silence, apart from the faint blips and bleeps of medical equipment.

'Are you there?'

'Yes. Where else would I go? I'm in a hospital bed, for

fuck's sake. None of what you said matters to me right now, Lisbon. What matters to me is that whoever murdered Cameron is caught and punished. Get back onto Randall Sowell. He's your man, I know it.'

'He might be, yeah. But there's no concrete evidence.'

'Lean on him harder. I've heard how you operate. Beat a confession out of him. They say you're free and easy with your fists.'

'Rumours, Ray. Anyway, I'm hamstrung at the moment. We're still awaiting final forensics results. If the science points to Sowell, I'll have him in cuffs before you can say triple bypass. Now, what can you tell me about a sum of $250,000 that was used to set up a trust fund? You've got some explaining to do, sunshine.'

Breathing laboured, as if each inhalation could be the last. 'It's the subject of a confidentiality agreement. National security. I can't comment on it, I…'

'Bullshit!' Jack roared. 'Tell the truth for once in your life.'

Click.

Fuck you, Jabba, you coward.

Jack placed his mobile on the bedside table next to the book he'd been reading, one agonisingly slow chapter at a time. He thumped a fist into his pillow. Sleep was elusive, his mind filled with visions of Snyder lying in a pool of blood, the blurred face of his killer hovering above the body. *Who is it?* No good, he couldn't shake the imagery. He switched on the light, picked up the paperback, a biography of champion boxer Rocky Marciano, removed the bookmark and started reading. Two minutes later, the book dropped from his hands and landed on his face. He closed the book, rolled over and within minutes was fast asleep.

His dreams were not of Snyder. They were of sweetness and light, of innocence and love. Skye spoke to him, begged him to hurry home, she could hardly wait to see her daddy again.

Chapter Twenty-Three

JACK SAT IN THE COOL, austere waiting room of Robinson, Brinkworth and Clayborne. The hard plastic chairs were only marginally more comfortable than the wooden pews at the girls' school. The senior partner on duty, Elmore Brinkworth, was dealing with a serious matter and, the receptionist promised, would be out shortly to speak with the detective.

The digital clock on the wall glowed a green 10.13am. Jack had rushed directly to the law firm after oversleeping, no time to call in at the office for a catch-up with the team. Fit as he was, late night workouts weren't agreeing with his middle-aged body. His raucous Sex Pistols alarm tune, "Anarchy in the UK" on full volume, had failed to wake him up. That job was done by sunlight pouring through his bedroom window. Had it been overcast, Jack would still be asleep. Now, he'd have to debrief with Taylor over the phone instead of face-to-face at the station.

He pulled up his phone contacts, pressed the button marked Claudia and she answered immediately. 'Have you seen Snyder's NSW criminal history?' said Jack, not one for telephone small talk. To ease nagging discomfort in his upper thigh, Jack crossed one leg over the other, outside left ankle resting on right knee. The extra set of barbell squats had been a bad idea.

'Affirmative,' said Taylor. 'Our southern colleagues sent the email last night as per Batista's request. Snyder's rap sheet shows a total of three court appearances resulting in three good behaviour bonds. Batting a thousand, as the Americans say. Somehow, he's avoided custodial sentences altogether, even though he was over eighteen years of age when the offences occurred. Two charges were for assault, one of them GBH only six months after the first charge. The third, get this, was for breaking and entering in the company of a Miss Lydia Bourke, who acted as a lookout.'

'Not a very good one, since they got caught 'n all.'

'Right. She was let off with a caution. Can you believe it?'

'Yes I can. I'm assuming that's our Lydia Snyder.'

'Geez, Jack. I bet you won all the games of Cluedo with your little pals when you were a kid.'

'No need for sarcasm, DC Taylor. Not the rarest name in the world. I mean, it's not beyond the realms of possibility that he knew two girls called Lydia, is it?'

'No, Jack. But it *is* the widow Snyder, as it happens. We matched the fingerprints data base with the ink blotches she provided us this morning. She also left a buccal cheek swab that Proctor's pushed to the front of the queue. I asked Lydia if she had anything further to add to help us out. No joy. I could barely get a word out of her, just more tears.'

Jack gnawed on a fingernail. 'A death in the family and a tranquiliser breakfast will do that to a person.' He paused a couple of seconds then said, 'This reeks of interference. If

Snyder breached a good behaviour bond and landed in court again soon after, he should have copped a jail sentence, even a suspended one.'

'Yep. Amazing.'

'But not unsurprising.'

'Why?'

Jack explained where he was and why he was there.

'All that information courtesy of a date with your new gym buddy?' said Taylor with a pronounced rising inflection.

'Yeah.' *Let's not dwell on that catastrophe.* 'Hook was able to exercise his influence not only here, but in another jurisdiction when his kid was younger. I'm not too much bothered by the historical charges in NSW, but I am going to amass all the evidence I can to prove Hook perverted the course of justice in Queensland.'

'Then what? You figuring on getting him charged? The guy he got off is now dead. A jury might sympathise with a person his defence portrayed as a father who cared for his long-lost son, even to the extent of breaking the law. Seriously, what would be the benefit of prosecuting Hook?'

Taylor had a good point, but Jack had a better one. 'Maybe none. But he's grossly abused his power on numerous occasions.'

'You've never done that, right?'

'Not at that level, sunshine.' He'd done worse, much worse, but it was another country, another lifetime, and Taylor must never find out. 'Look, you may have a point. But I'm gonna gather evidence, just in case.'

Taylor sighed. 'None of this is getting us any closer to who killed Snyder.'

'How can you be sure? Maybe one of those lads who saw Snyder in action took revenge later for belting a mate half to death? It's my duty to pursue and exhaust this lead as part of a thorough investigation.'

'Sounds like you're trying to convince yourself.'

'Maybe. Hang on, the lawyer's free now. I'll call you back.'

———

HALF AN HOUR LATER, Jack was armed with the names, phone numbers and last known addresses of four witnesses to the bar-room assault. Plus the victim. The latter would never be interviewed. According to Brinkworth, Jarred Fox, an apprentice plumber and promising cricketer, never fully recovered from his injuries. After the attack, he suffered blackouts, chronic headaches and permanent ringing in the ears. He committed suicide last July by taking a long swim into the Pacific Ocean with all his clothes on and a belly full of alcohol. Any sympathy Jack may have had for Cameron Snyder evaporated like mist. He was an arsehole with a short fuse who got his comeuppance. No matter his distaste for the victim, the crime still needed solving, especially if Jack was to get on the 777 to Heathrow this weekend.

The construction area was crawling with men in hard-hats toting tools and materials. Somewhere amongst the hive of activity was witness number one, Gabe Snowden, a plumber like Jarred Fox. They'd attended the same trade school. Jack had rung the mobile number provided by Brinkworth on the drive over. Snowden confirmed he was at work, installing hot water systems in the new apartment block going up, ironically, a stone's throw away from the now infamous Pilkington fish factory.

A quick word from the DS to the site manager in his demountable office and an underling in an orange vest was despatched to fetch Gabe Snowden. Jack retreated to the relative quiet of the dirt car park and leaned against the patrol car's driver door. He closed his eyes and let the gentle rays of the sun warm his face, a moment just to let go. Crunching footsteps approaching made him open his eyes. A young man with blonde dreadlocks was making his way over to Jack, shoulders slumped and a vacant expression on his face.

'I'm the cop you spoke to on the phone,' said Jack, holding out his credentials. 'I haven't got all day so I'll cut to the chase. What can you tell me about Cameron Snyder?'

'Nuthin.' A large Adam's apple rose and fell in Snowden's throat.

'You don't watch the news?'

'Nope.' Getting Snowden to open up was going to be a challenge.

'What about Jarred Fox?'

The man's face fell, his mouth drooped at the corners like he was about to burst into tears. 'He was…my…mate.'

Jack noticed a stylised animal tattooed just below the man's left ear. A dog? No, it was a fox. And then, the penny dropped. Vengeance for a fallen comrade. Meek and mild on the surface, Gabe Snowden had a ton of motive to slay Snyder. Advertised on the boy's damn neck. Maybe all four lads were complicit in Snyder's murder. It wouldn't have surprised Jack, young men with a strong bond, together organising the execution of the man who destroyed the life of a close friend. 'Tell me what happened to Jarred?'

'He died.'

'Listen,' Jack said through gritted teeth. He fought the instinct to scream at Snowden. This was not the time or place. Kid gloves now, sledgehammer later. 'Here's the deal. I know you know who Snyder is. He's the bloke who caused so much damage to your mate that he ended his own life. And even an out-of-touch tradesman like you must have heard on the grapevine Snyder's been murdered. You're probably thinking to yourself, *Finally, justice for Jarred. I've got my closure and I don't have to say any more.*'

Snowden scratched an arm. 'Say any more about what? I dunno what you want from me.'

'I want you to tell me why you withdrew your statement about what happened at the Red Lion pub.'

'I never.'

'Yes you did!' Jack thundered. He kicked the dirt, creating a mini dust cloud. *Rein it in Jack.* 'I just visited the law firm who was supposed to represent Jarred until...well, you know what happened.' It was tempting to put Hook's name into the kid's mouth, but he had to let it come out naturally. 'I know you and your pals were all lined up to testify but retracted.'

'Re what?'

'Retracted. You took back your statements and agreed not to testify.'

'Only after Jarred said he never wanted to take it any further.'

'Was he scared of Snyder?'

'Nah. I can't tell you.'

'Why not? Did someone threaten you?'

Snowden turned his head, gazed at a forest of scaffolding embracing the apartments. 'Like you said, Jarred's dead and nothing will bring him back. I've gotta get back to work. The boss'll be fuming.'

'No he won't. Look, what if I told you the mongrel who leaned on you, Jarred and the other fellas, has one foot in the grave?'

'What does that mean? Is he working at the cemetery now?'

Were young people these days that thick they only understood things literally? 'It means he's probably going to die soon. He's had a massive heart attack and the doctors don't fancy his chances of survival beyond a few weeks.'

'I'm not surprised. Jarred said he was a fat fuck.' A half smile crept across Snowden's freckled face.

'Tell me his name please, Gabe.'

Snowden studied his boots and whispered. 'Hook. Ray Hook.'

'OK.' Jack took a deep breath. 'Would you agree to make a formal statement to that effect?'

'Fuck no.'

'What if I guarantee nothing will happen to you?'

'You can't.'

'Oh, believe me, I can.' Jack's phone, set to silent in his jacket pocket, vibrated insistently against his ribs. Then it stopped, two sharp buzzes. Someone's left a voice mail. Ignore for now. 'Even if by some miracle Hook survives, I've got enough dirt to put him away until he croaks in a prison cell. That's if the crims don't finish him off first.' Jack added he would make the same guarantee of protection to the other lads who saw Snyder's vicious attack. With all four on board, Jabba would be at Jack's mercy from now on.

'Liam's working here with me. Wanna talk to him now?'

'Is the effing Pope catholic?'

The two trudged through a chicane of wheelbarrows and pallets of bricks, got Jack a hard hat and located Liam Renner, a tiler, on the first floor. In a tribal conversation of gestures and grunts, Gabe convinced Liam to also provide a statement about Hook's threats. Jack kept an eye out for "tells" as they spoke, signs of guilt. He saw none.

'OK,' said Jack, rubbing his hands together. 'Are the other two boys also working here?'

'Nah,' said Liam. 'Robbo's pissed off to Melbourne to become a pastry chef and Jeb's gone back to New Zealand to live. Dunno what he's doing now. Those guys couldn't stand being in the same state as Hook or Snyder, let alone the same region.'

Jack had a thought. Perhaps he could add bribery to the Assistant Commissioner's list of misdeeds. 'Did Ray Hook pay you fellas any money to keep quiet?'

Two heads shook in unison. 'He didn't have to,' said Liam. 'He shouted down the phone like a madman. It was obvious he wasn't bluffing. Even if he was, we were too scared to take the chance.'

'OK, one more thing. I'll need you to pop down the station to make this official. You prepared to do that?'

Liam gave his friend a wink of reassurance. This pair would be solid as a rock. Hook, on the other hand, would be properly fucked.

Jack shook the boys' hands, thanked them for their cooperation, agreed on a time tomorrow when they could pop into the cop shop for a chat. In Interview Room 1, he'd holler at them, bang the table with his fists, throw accusations around like hand grenades. They were well-mannered, respectful young men, not hardened career criminals. If the lads were guilty of killing Snyder, there's a good chance an Academy Award winning performance by Jack would see them crumble and confess.

He strode back to the car, listening to the voice mail message as he went. Batista. *Get your arse back to the station. I've called a snap press conference.*

Chapter Twenty-Four

HOLLY MAGUIRE, Channel 11's hotshot news anchor and chief crime reporter, stood and spoke into a big black microphone emblazoned with her news outlet's logo. 'Inspector Batista. Is there any truth to the rumours the murder of Cameron Snyder is linked to the upcoming CHOGM meeting?'

'None.' The single syllable flew out of Batista's mouth.

'No links whatsoever? Why should anyone take your denial on trust?'

'Let me state from the outset, this get together wasn't my idea. I would never call one so early in an investigation unless we were totally stumped, which we aren't.' He took a sip of water, made the crowd wait a moment before continuing. 'The Police Commissioner herself tasked me to brief the media today. She's worried by the frenzy of Internet chatter about terrorism coming to our shores. I can assure you, nothing is further from the truth.' The chief was resplendent as always for press conferences, uniform starched and ironed to perfection, necktie in a fancy double

Windsor knot Jack could never master. The embodiment of law and order. 'The Commissioner asked Yorkville Police to allay those baseless fears. Because that's all this is, hysteria stirred up by people with nothing better to do than post garbage on social media.'

Jack sat to the Inspector's right, scanning the assembled sharks as they sniffed the air for traces of blood. They might be predators, but old Joe Batista was an expert in defending the integrity of the force from hostile outsiders.

'There've been stories in foreign newspapers.' Maguire again. 'The press in India and Canada have picked up on the murder of Cameron Snyder, and the fact it happened virtually on the eve of CHOGM. There's fear abroad government representatives are potentially in danger. Are you saying they're worried about imaginary threats?'

Batista nodded, coughed loudly into his fist. He then cleared his throat like he was going to hack up a snot-ball the size of a scoop of ice-cream. Jack watched the twisted faces of the crowd of journos and smiled. *Off to a flyer, sir.* 'Thanks for the follow-up question, Ms Maguire. I know the public, both here and abroad, are concerned. But let me assure you, all security arrangements for the Heads of Government meeting in Cairns are being taken care of by the Federal Police and ASIO and there are no, I repeat, no threats.'

A newspaper hack from Brisbane, shirt half hanging out of his pants and hair protruding in all directions, raised a hand and Batista acknowledged him. 'With all due respect, Inspector, the venue for the meeting in Cairns is only an hour's drive away, close enough for Yorkville's citizens to be anxious. Are authorities prepared for terrorist attacks here?'

Well done, dickhead. Whipping up panic when the chief's

appealing for calm. Jack wanted to scream at him to shut the fuck up, drummed his fingers instead.

'Listen, my friend,' said Batista in the patronising tone he reserved for the media. 'What you are suggesting is so unlikely as to be laughable.'

Jack nodded and grinned. *Good one, sir.*

'Can you give a guarantee that—'

'As I already said, these matters are being handled by the appropriate agencies. The safety of the citizens of Yorkville is my number one priority. If that were being compromised, do you think I wouldn't say something about it?'

The man's mouth moved like a goldfish but no sounds came out.

'We are treating this terrible homicide as we would any other and are investigating in our usual professional manner, calling on other departments within the Queensland Police Service to assist us as and when required.'

'So there's no connection to domestic loonies, far-right movements? I heard rumours Snyder had ties with various patriotic groups. The Wild Colonial Boys, for example.' Macho reporter Johnno Peroni, ex-rugby professional now a gopher style reporter for Channel 3, scowled like a negative answer could elicit violence.

'There were such no links,' said Jack. 'You know, sometimes I wonder whether you people even listen to the responses you're given.'

Peroni's face flushed red. He was about to say something else when Jack pointed a finger at a seasoned journalist from the Yorkville Times. 'Yes, Fiona, you were next.'

Fiona Wagstaff, caught off guard, flicked through a notebook. 'Oh, yes. Detective Sergeant Lisbon, could you please tell us if you have any leads?'

Bless you Fiona. A nice, normal question people want answered. Not doomsday nonsense about non-existent terror groups. 'Yes, we do. A number of them, in fact.' Jack consulted a printed sheet, prepared an hour ago by Taylor. 'As we already revealed via a press release on Tuesday evening, Mr Cameron Snyder died from a single, deep stab wound to the neck after suffering non-fatal blunt force trauma to the crown of the head. So far no weapons have been recovered but the search continues. Persons of interest have been interviewed at length, some of them providing us with information that is helping progress our enquiries further.' Jack looked up and blinked a couple of times. *Christ, Taylor, how do you come up with this?* 'More key individuals are expected to be questioned over the next 48 hours. Our forensics experts are still analysing a large quantity of samples, some taken from the crime scene, others supplied voluntarily by persons we are seeking to eliminate as suspects. We are hopeful our scientific experts will find conclusive evidence leading to an arrest.' Jack dropped the piece of paper back on the table, tucked back in his pocket the pen he'd been running down the side of the page as he read aloud. 'That's about all we have for you today, folks.'

'Persons of interest are one thing, but do you have any *actual* suspects?' Maguire wasn't ready to wind things up.

Jack rested his elbows on the table, steepled his fingers. 'Sure we have suspects.'

'Can you elaborate?'

'Not at this stage. To do so would compromise our enquiries.'

'Is that so? How do you respond to comments I obtained from one of Snyder's neighbours? She claims several days ago she saw men wearing dark suits arrive at

Snyder's house in armoured vehicles. She says they entered the building, exited ten minutes later and drove off.'

'With or without AK-47s?' said Jack, cocking an eyebrow. Maguire offered a deep frown as the rest of the gallery laughed. Peroni the loudest of all.

'She didn't say.'

Jack shook his head. 'I think I know which neighbour you're talking about, and with all due respect, her statement hasn't a shred of credibility.'

'Have you checked it out, though?' Maguire would not be deterred. *Her skin must be thicker than a rhino's arse.*

'Look, if she was that concerned she would have called the police, wouldn't she?'

'Perhaps she was too scared to. Why aren't you following this up? It sounds like the potential link to terrorism you're so keen to dismiss,' said Peroni, supporting Maguire's pointless onslaught.

'No other neighbours have mentioned mysterious visits by groups of men,' chimed in Batista. 'I'm sure the person Ms Maguire spoke to was mistaken. There's been a lot of file footage on TV lately from previous CHOGM meetings, secret service men running about and whatnot. I reckon the dotty old dear's started to confuse what she's seen on television with her own version of reality.'

The back row of reporters chuckled at Batista's description of the neighbour. Jack prayed Pat O'Grady wasn't watching the press conference. She'd be entitled to file a suit against Batista for defamation of character.

'It could be a top secret operation the neighbour witnessed,' said Fiona Wagstaff. 'Can you be certain the spooks wouldn't keep some things from the QPS?'

Batista rolled his eyes, signalling it was time to end this press conference before it turned into a complete circus. 'As

Detective Sergeant Lisbon told you already, Yorkville CIB is pursuing a number of leads and we have yet to interview all persons of interest. In conclusion, I'm going to repeat the key message. There are no grounds to believe our city and its citizens are in danger from terrorist attacks. End of story. Thanks all for attending.' He turned to Jack and whispered. 'C'mon, let's get out of here.'

Chapter Twenty-Five

'THANKS FOR THE SCRIPT, CLAUDIA.' Jack flopped into the revolving office chair at his corner work station, spun a half rotation. 'Helped me keep those jackals at bay.'

'No worries,' said Taylor from her neighbouring desk. 'Anything for the cause. I'd hate for Holly Maguire to get one over on us. For what it's worth, I thought you and the chief handled those numpties with aplomb.' She shuffled papers before securing them with a paper clip. She leaned across and passed the bundle to Jack. 'I've located Robert Gillon, the pastry chef who witnessed Snyder assaulting Jarred Fox. He's working at a bistro in Melbourne's Southbank. All his details and some background are in there.'

'Impressive.' Jack grinned. 'What about the Kiwi?'

'No joy.'

'Seriously? The bloke's name is Jebediah Heatherington-Smythe. Shouldn't be too hard for a sleuth like you.'

'I found a relative in Auckland, a cousin. She reckons Jeb's a loner, has nothing to do with the rest of the family. I found a Facebook account with his name and sent a message for him to contact me. No response as yet.'

'You call the New Zealand cops for assistance?'

'Yes, Jack. All twelve districts. None of them have any information on the guy. There's no record from Immigration that he's returned to Australia.'

Jack rested his head in his hands. 'Yeah. Sorry, Claudia. I'm worried we've got no one firming as a prime suspect and time's running out with that stupid deadline Batista imposed.'

'I sympathise with you, Jack I really do.'

'As if that wasn't bad enough, I completely ruined my date last night. I said something stupid and she left me sitting there like a stunned mullet.'

Taylor's eyebrows arched as she frowned and nodded. 'Again, I sympathise.'

Jack offered a lip curl of appreciation and flicked through the file on pastry chef Robert Gillon. He dialled the restaurant's number but got voice mail. Must be too early for the bistro to be open. He left a message for Gillon to call back and hung up. What to do next? Jack's mind was whirling, so many potential suspects, but there was nothing concrete to arrest any of them.

'How was your date?' Jack asked, looking through half-closed blinds at a flock of cockatoos commandeering a gum tree in the car park.

'Hmm?' said Taylor, eyes inches from her computer screen.

'Your date. With the non-married guy.'

'Better than yours, by the sound of it,' she said cryptically.

What could that mean? Did she sleep with him? Dammit,

he couldn't bear the thought, even though he'd leapt into bed with Marietta at the first opportunity. He was about to ask for more details, when she offered the sweet words herself. 'In other words, we said good-night at my door in an amicable fashion.'

'A third date on the horizon?'

She shook her head. 'I doubt it, the guy's very nice but, just between you and me, he's boring as bat shit.'

Jack smiled. 'That's a shame.'

Taylor moved her mouse around the pad and double clicked. 'Wanna know what isn't a shame?'

'Wot?'

'This email I just received from Margaret Proctor. Grab your jacket, the condom DNA results are in.'

———

PROCTOR BEAMED at the two detectives from behind her desk. 'This Rapid DNA technology is superb, don't you agree detectives?'

'It's bleedin' fantastic,' said Jack, mashing a wad of Extra gum. 'Best thing since sliced bread.' The rows of numbers and alien terms like sperm chromatin deprotamination, methylation and TUNEL assay made as much sense to the detectives as Mandarin. 'Can you please explain the results. I don't know why you just didn't summarise the findings in the email, would have saved valuable time.'

'I did.'

'What?' said Taylor.

'In an attachment.'

Jack exchanged a puzzled look with Taylor. The DC pulled out her mobile, logged onto her work email account. 'No, Margaret. Nothing there.'

'Show me!' Proctor took Taylor's phone and scrolled to

the end of the message. 'There it is, five lines from the bottom.' She frowned. 'OK, I can see where the confusion arose. It's a link to an external attachment sitting on a secure server. For some reason the link's not the usual blue, but black like the text. I can see how you missed it.'

'Thank God for that,' said Taylor, absently tugging her scrunchie. 'I thought I was going mad.'

'Come on Margaret.' Jack didn't feel the urge to be as forgiving as Taylor. A phone call from the forensics chief would have made more sense. She could have rattled off the salient details without he and Taylor having to traipse all the way over to the pathology lab.

'Come on what?'

'It's not like you to make a rookie error like that with a simple email message.' He wouldn't have been surprised if Proctor had camouflaged the link so she could regale the officers with her superior knowledge.

'Excuse me?' The hackles were up. 'Yes, I'm a genius when it comes to forensic science, but configuring IT settings and preferences for the entire QPS is beyond my remit.'

'It's OK, Margaret. He didn't mean it,' said Taylor.

'What she said.' Jack was glad Claudia was around to play good cop, because he never could. 'Enough chit-chat, ladies. Let's be hearing the results.'

'Sure. After running the polymerase chain reaction-based methods I described on your last visit, I was able to isolate the–'

'Stop!' Jack gripped the edge of the desk. 'Just tell us, whose penis was in the rubber, and whose vagina was it in?'

Proctor recoiled, quickly regathered her wits. 'The semen belongs to Snyder. No surprises there. And the analyses revealed it was indeed a female on the receiving end, so to speak. The long black hair we found in the bedsheets has the same DNA profile as the cells on the outside surface of the condom.'

'Who dammit?' Jack was standing now.

'Misty Roach.'

If a mule had kicked Jack in the testicles the shock would have been less intense. He would have bet money on it being Renee van der Klopp. He dropped back into the plastic chair. 'Say again.'

'Misty Roach, real name Michelle Roach. She's a sex worker.'

'I know who she is,' said Jack. 'I've cautioned her for soliciting on the Esplanade at least twice this year.'

'I heard she'd gone back to Mt Isa,' said Taylor. 'To relieve the copper miners of their hard-earned cash.' said Taylor.

'Apparently not.' Jack was already at the door gripping the handle. 'I know where her mum and sister live. Let's go.'

Chapter Twenty-Six

MICHELLE "MISTY" Roach was a prostitute of Aboriginal descent who had been relieving North Queensland men of their money for almost fifteen years. Thirty-seven years of age, tall and rangy and serene, Misty was much in demand by clients looking for experience, as well as a kind soul they could share their problems with. In many cases, problems their wives and girlfriends didn't want to know about. Since he'd been stationed at Yorkville station, Jack had dealt with Misty several times, all in his professional capacity as a cop. Never as a punter, despite the almost irresistible temptation. Once she provided Jack with confidential information that led to the arrest of a gang of bikers wanted for extortion. Apart from being a useful asset in the community, she was basically a good person. Jack liked her instinctively.

Detectives Lisbon and Taylor stood shoulder to shoulder on the porch of Betty-Lou Roach's house in the down-at-heel suburb of Thurston. Jack rapped hard three times on the door before Mrs Roach, frizzy haired and barefoot in a bright red-green-and-yellow sarong, opened up with a welcoming smile. Two small terriers scurried about under-foot, Jack nearly stepped on one. 'Get out of here, you two mongrels!' she growled at the scruffy creatures who yapped twice and obediently ran in the opposite direction. She looked up at the cops. 'I was talking to the dogs, in case you were wondering.'

'Betty-Lou,' said Jack. He and Taylor displayed their credentials like it was a synchronised move. 'Nice to see you again.'

'And you, Jack.' The smile, if anything, grew bigger and cheekier. In his peripherals he saw Taylor's eyes widen. God knew what she was thinking.

'We're looking for Misty. Is she here?'

'She's having a nap. She had rather a late night, watching movies into the wee hours. Don't stand there looking like a desperate pair of Jehovah's Witnesses. Come in.'

A ceiling fan in the wood-panelled interior rotated hypnotically overhead among a jumble of beams, dispersing the sweet, creamy fragrance of sandalwood incense.

'Wake her up please,' said Jack. 'We need to ask her some important questions.'

'She's not in any trouble is she?'

'No,' said Taylor. 'But she may know vital information that could help us crack the Cameron Snyder murder.'

Betty-Lou's smile vanished, her hand shot to her mouth. She took it away, shifted her gaze to Jack and said, 'I saw the Inspector and you on TV talking about this on the midday news. My, what a handsome man.'

'Him?' said Taylor, jerking a thumb at Jack.

'I meant Joe Batista. But yes, him too.' The smile was like a camera flash. 'Wait here while I fix us a pot of tea and some treats. I'll see if I can rouse Michelle.'

'Michelle, not Misty,' Taylor remarked as the swaying sarong disappeared down the corridor and made a left turn, dogs jumping at her heels. 'Perhaps we should call her that when we're talking to her?'

'Y'know, that's not a bad idea, sunshine.' Jack touched Taylor on the elbow. 'I reckon I will.'

Behind the wall a kettle whistled, a fridge door opened and closed, cups and saucers rattled. A yawning and stretching figure emerged from the dark of the hallway entrance into the living room. Like her mother, she wore a wraparound dress, white with a red hibiscus motif. Amber beads on a necklace, silver bracelets and anklets galore. Even with messy bed hair, Misty Roach was a mighty handsome woman. Jack understood why men paid top dollar for her company.

'Detective Lisbon.' She floated onto a vintage sofa like a leaf falling softly to the ground. She tucked her dress under her legs, reached for a packet of Winfield Blues. 'Haven't seen you for a while. How can I help?' She extracted and lit a cigarette, made her lips an o-shape and sent a jet of smoke to the ceiling. She pointed at a glass ashtray on the table beside Taylor. 'Could you pass that over, please, my dear?'

Taylor did as requested. 'I'm Detective Constable Claudia Taylor, by the way.' An extended hand was grasped limply. 'Keeping young Jack here in line.'

'G'day, love. Now, can you tell me what this is all about?'

Jack cleared his throat. 'It's a rather delicate matter, Mist…I mean Michelle.'

'Delicate and you don't go together, mate.' She burst out laughing and Jack felt his face flush.

Betty-Lou shuffled in with a tray laden with a steaming teapot wearing a woollen cosy, floral china crockery, and a frosted cherry Madeira cake. Jack asked her to leave the goodies and give them some privacy. Her features fell as she looked at her daughter. 'Sure you don't want me to sit with you, honey?'

A shake of the head and a flick of the black locks that said, *Off you go, mum I'll be fine.*

'Do you watch the news, Michelle?' said Taylor, slowly and deliberately.

'Yeah, sometimes.'

'Have you watched it in the last week? Like, since Monday night?' said Jack, pouring amber tea into a dainty cup. He was only just able to fit a finger and thumb in the handle.

Michelle's eyes darted about the room, her cool exterior heating up. 'Um, no as it happens.'

'Social media?'

'Only my Instagram. Bugger all news on that. I've been out of the loop for a few days. I felt I needed a rest, you know?'

Jack nodded. 'We could all do with a rest 'n all, right Claudia?'

'A-ha', Taylor confirmed.

'When was your last punter?' said Jack.

'Actually, Monday night. And why should I have watched the bloody news? I know there's some kind of big meeting going to be happening in Cairns. Is it something to do with that?'

'No, Michelle,' said Taylor. 'It was your last client, Cameron Snyder. He was murdered on the same night you had sex with him.'

'Oh my God, oh my God, oh my God.' Michelle made a rapid two-handed flutter gesture before her face, as if that would cool her down. 'No way, no way, no way!'

'Did you know the victim well?' Taylor again.

'What? Ah, yes. I mean no.'

'Be more precise, please,' said Jack.

'I mean we hooked up, let me think, four times since the start of the year. He was one of my new punters.'

'How did he become your customer?' said Taylor.

'Easily. I run a regular ad in the local newspaper. He rang the number, we met.'

'Why would he have picked you in particular? There are dozens of ads for escorts.'

'Yes, there are. Lots of the girls specify they're Thai, Chinese, Ukrainian or whatever. I decided, hey, why shouldn't I do the same? So my ad now mentions I'm Indigenous. And guess what?'

'What?' said Taylor.

'Business is through the roof. Just after New Year this Cameron guy contacted me, said I sounded just like what he was looking for. I always went to his house at night, which doesn't really suit me, I like to work during the day if I can. Anyway, I agreed because he offered me double the going rate.'

'Was he not open to the idea of meeting you during the day?'

'You know I got the impression he was terrified people might see me arrive during daylight hours. Didn't want people to see him with a hooker.'

'How would they know you're a sex worker?' said Jack.

'I like to dress the part. Crazy high heels, skimpy outfits, crimson lippy and a ton of eye makeup. Anyone would be able to figure it out.'

'If he was worried about being seen, why not simply meet at a hotel?'

'Maybe because you need ID to book a hotel room,' Misty shrugged.

Jack swallowed a piece of the cake, washed it down with tea. Not bad. He might have to find an excuse to visit the Roach household again. 'We have reason to believe the victim was abusive towards his ex-wife. How was he with you?'

'More physical than the average client, but he never actually hurt me. A lot of the time I just sat there in his kitchen, drinking gin and tonics and smoking cigarettes while he rambled on about his business, how he was going to build a huge empire.'

'Did he speak about his ex-wife?'

'He's got an ex-wife?'

'I'll take that as a no.'

'Did he ever rough you up?' said Taylor. 'Suggest doing anything you weren't comfortable with?'

'He liked to grab me around the neck, but it wasn't choking. I think he got off on the visual aspect. With Cameron it was all over pretty quickly, he wasn't a stayer.'

'It seems you were the last person to see Snyder alive.' Taylor locked eyes with her. 'Could he have overstepped the mark with his little strangling game? Got you mad enough to kill him?' The DC turned her palms upwards, inviting Misty to comment on the suggestion.

She raised a cup of tea with shaking hands, spilling some on the way to her mouth. It was too hard, she put the cup back down again. 'Look, I had nothing to do with it. Nothing at all. I didn't even know about it until five minutes ago!'

'Would you like to accompany us to the station?' said Taylor. 'Perhaps you'd like to discuss this in a more formal manner.'

'Oh, Jesus, do I need a lawyer?' Teardrops formed at the corner of her big brown eyes.

'Not unless you killed him,' said Jack. 'Did you kill Cameron Snyder, Michelle?'

'No! I didn't kill him. Why would I? Holy shit, what time did you say he was murdered?' As he watched her tears, Jack thought it a travesty Cam Snyder's last pleasurable episode was with the lovely Misty. The fact his end came in such a violent way served as a modicum of justice.

Jack said, 'According to our forensics experts, sometime between 10:00pm and midnight on Monday, 3rd of March.'

Misty's face brightened. 'I think I might have seen the killer.'

JACK BURNED rubber on the drive to Lydia's house. Literally. At the corner of Atkins and Smethurst Streets he floored the gas pedal, sent the Kia into a wicked spin. Tyres screeched inside a tornado plume of stinking smoke. The type of behaviour the DS would arrest young hooligans for. The type of behaviour to earn a rebuke from DC Taylor.

A quick call to the station on the drive to Lydia's house achieved mixed results. Yes, Trent Gillmeister had a car, and it matched Misty Roach's basic description. But it was still registered in NSW. Had been for a number of years. Legally, he was required to flip the rego over to obtain a Queensland plate, but for some reason hadn't done it. Which meant the address in the database from another state was totally useless. Moreover, Trent hadn't bothered to get himself on the voter roll. The school might divulge the address, but Jack had a feeling that, in the absence of a warrant, he'd be met with nervy gatekeepers hung up on privacy issues.

It was imperative to get Trent's address. And the only way to find out fast was to ask Lydia.

Two streets from their destination, Taylor launched a thought bubble. 'Maybe the car Misty saw wasn't even Trent's, but a similar one? Perhaps he'd hired or borrowed another car the night of Snyder's murder?'

'You're right.' Jack exhaled loudly, bunched his cheek muscles. 'But if Lydia confirms Gillmeister's still driving the car registered down south, that's enough for me to arrest him.'

Thought bubble number two was worse. 'Or maybe it was just a man who resembled the victim's brother-in-law and it wasn't Trent at all?'

'Dammit, Taylor. Stop sowing seeds of doubt. It's him and we both know it.'

She nodded. 'Looks like it. Here's the street, Jack. Make a hard left.'

THUMP THE DOOR. Wait a minute. Bash again. Call her name. *LYDIA!* Shuffling footsteps, door opens. Lydia's face looks like an unmade bed.

Inside the house, Lydia was barely coherent. There were more pills in her system than a pharmacy. 'What do you want? You know what time it is?'

'Ah, yeah,' said Taylor incredulously. 'It's three in the afternoon.'

'Really? I thought it was night time. Anyway, I gave the fucking swab like you asked, what else do you want? Go away and leave me alone, will ya.' She waved her hand dismissively, turned on wobbly feet, presumably to trudge back to bed.

'Not so fast.' Taylor forestalled her with a grab of the forearm. 'Can you please describe your brother's car for us?'

'His car? It's red, s'all I know. Normal size, not an SUV or anything like that.' Then a slight awakening, concern widening her eyes a fraction. 'Hey, why'd you ask that? Was he in an accident?'

'No. We just need to speak to him. But we have to make sure the car someone saw belongs to Trent.'

'Hmm.' She scratched her head. 'Oh, yeah. It's one of those European ones with a funny name.'

'Peugeot, Renault?' Jack hinted.

'No, not a French one…um…oh, yeah. Sounds like a soft drink…soda…'

'Skoda?'

'Yeah, that's it.'

'Superb?'

'It's OK, I guess.'

'That's the name of the model,' said Jack. His eye rolling attracted a death stare from Taylor.

'If you say so,' Lydia shrugged. 'You're lucky I even remembered Skoda.'

That was the clincher. A match with Misty Roach's basic description of the vehicle, an average-sized red sedan. Occupied by an average to large-framed man. Misty said the driver had tried to slink down into the seat as she'd walked past on the way to her own car. He wasn't quick enough. She'd had time to glimpse the blonde beard.

'Wonderful, Lydia,' said Jack. 'You've been a great help. Now if you could just let me know his home address, we'll be on our way. Oh, and his phone number. I somehow forgot to get it from him last time we spoke.'

BACK ON THE highway Jack flung the Ford Territory from lane to lane, zigzagged around slow-pokes who had the temerity to observe the speed limit. He turned on the blue flashing lights and sirens and a path magically opened up down the guts of the road. Taylor squinted and chugged a draught of water from a one-litre bottle, swallowed hard. She slowly opened her eyes, turned to Jack and said, 'How's about I put a call through to Cairns? Let's get a couple of uniforms over to Gillmeister's house, see if he's there. And if he is, make sure he doesn't leave.'

'No.'

'Why on Earth not?'

'I don't trust Cairns CIB.'

'Don't be obtuse, Jack.'

'No, I said. I want this collar. Jabba could have worded up the officers at Cairns station not to cooperate with me. He hates me now.'

'That's paranoia talking, mate.'

'Maybe so. Besides the matter of Hook, I don't want some plain-clothes dick stealing my…our…thunder.'

Taylor huffed, put the two-way receiver back in its holder. 'Your decision. If we arrive and he's not there…'

'Then we wait, we ask the neighbours, we track him down.'

'You've lost the plot.'

'Don't worry. He'll be there.'

'Spidey senses again?'

'Something like that.'

They drove in an uncomfortable silence for fifteen minutes before Jack spoke. 'I'm kind of in two minds about this arrest, Claudia.' He adjusted the radio to pick up an alternative indie music channel. He screwed up his face when the reception crackled then gave out, switched it off.

'Really? Nailing Gillmeister means you get to make your flight home.'

'Yeah. But he might've actually done the world a favour by ridding it of Snyder, know what I mean?'

'Jack. You can't be serious! Killing someone is never justified.'

He fixed his eyes on the Harley Davidson motorcycle in front. 'Yes, of course. Never justified.' *Like hell it wasn't.*

Chapter Twenty-Seven

TRENT GILLMEISTER RENTED a single-storied red-brick house. A soulless box, the perfect complement to all the other bland homes on the street. The front lawn needed a good mowing three weeks ago, now only slashing by a combine harvester would bring it under control. Junk mail jammed the mouth of the tin letterbox and spilled onto the pavement.

'There's the Skoda,' Taylor pointed to her left as the patrol car crawled past the house. The Czech-designed sedan was painted a colour the manufacturer called "corrida red". Named after the Spanish word for bullfight. Jack knew those weird details because Taylor couldn't help herself from researching the subject on the drive to Cairns.

Jack parked four doors down from Gillmeister's house, a row of vehicles and trees providing a degree of cover as they prepared to take down the suspect. He glanced at his watch. 5:03pm. He turned to Taylor and said, 'I want him in a holding cell before the sun goes down. Let's go.'

The detectives alighted from the vehicle, closed the doors gently. Both patted the Glock 22 service pistols concealed under their jackets and started walking. A light breeze was blowing inland from the Pacific Ocean, the sky was a blue so rich it felt like you could pluck a piece and rub it between your fingers.

They strode without speaking, footsteps falling into cadence, like soldiers. Then a right at the driveway of 17 Purcell Drive, along a cracked concrete path, still marching in sync. At the front entrance they exchanged a quick nod and a grim smile, what Jack called the "I've got your back" look. He rapped on the door with the back of his knuckles.

As agreed, Taylor called out. A female voice was less likely to arouse suspicion. Long and drawn out, a hint of pleading, like a helpless neighbour in need of assistance. *Tre-e-e-ent.* No answer. Jack turned the door handle. Locked. He pressed his ear to the door and heard nothing but the sound of blood pulsing inside his head.

'Keep trying, I'll go round the back,' he said.

A nod from Taylor and the DS took off.

The side of the house was a tangle of weeds. Rusty corrugated iron leaned against the perimeter fence, which left a gap barely wide enough to walk along. Jack high-stepped over rotting sleepers, ever mindful of poisonous beasties lying in wait for a careless English copper. He stopped at two sets of sash windows, curtains half drawn, and peered inside. An almost empty bathroom then another room, unfurnished except for a mirror and a pair of dumb-bells. At a guess there was 30kg of weight on each of those bad boys. Trent was no weakling. A dash up the other side of the house revealed three more sets of closed windows, this time with fully drawn curtains.

He made his way to the back door. The sounds of Taylor's insistent knocking and beseeching voice carried around the side of the building. Gillmeister should have answered the door by now. Jack was starting to think the man had flown the coop.

Both entrances covered, Jack was now in a position to force entry into the property. He cupped his hands to his mouth. 'Claudia! I'm going in. Stay there and stop him if he tries to escape.'

He turned the door knob. Locked like the front door. A quick step back to build momentum was followed by a violent kick to the middle of the wooden door. It rattled slightly in the frame, but Jack realised it was unlikely to yield to more kicks. He scanned the backyard. Ten metres from the clothesline was a copper-coloured metal bowl on legs. On closer inspection, a firepit. It contained plenty of ashes but also a small, half-burnt log of wood that had somehow escaped incineration. He grabbed it, returned to the back door and hurled the log at the bevelled glass panel. It shattered into tiny pieces on impact. A dog started barking in an adjacent backyard.

'Trent Gillmeister!' Jack roared into the empty space. 'Make your way to the back door with your hands up!' He stuck his head in the hole and listened. Silent as the grave. A glance down. The protruding key. He leaned over, turned it clockwise and pushed the door open.

It took less than a minute to determine Gillmeister was gone. Clothing yanked out of wardrobes in the bedroom and toiletries scattered around the bathroom floor told Jack their quarry had fled in a hurry. No laptops or other devices left lying around. What looked like his teaching timetable was scrawled on a whiteboard in the kitchen.

A series of impatient knocks reverberated through the house. *Shit, Claudia's still out there.* Taylor's hand-on-hip stance when he opened the door was worse than a slap in the face. 'I told you to ask Cairns CIB to secure the place. But no, Mr Wonderful can handle it all by himself.'

'Leave off, Claudia. I've got you here with me.'

'You know what I mean.'

'Sure.' She was right, but he felt no inclination to argue the point. 'Listen, interrogate the neighbours, see if they know anything. I'll call Lydia.'

'Does this look like the kind of neighbourhood where people even talk to each other, let alone know each other's business?' They both took in the surrounding houses, shut up tight and not a soul about. 'That's a rhetorical question by the way. And you'll be lucky to get any sense out of Lydia. Look at the time. She'll have dropped another Valium or Xanax by now.'

'Don't care.' Jack dialled the widow. He put his hand to his head, began pacing back and forth, looked up to see Taylor staring at him. 'You still here?' he barked. 'Go and talk to the neighbours.'

Taylor swore under her breath, made her way to the house to the immediate left. To Jack's astonishment, the widow Snyder answered on the fifth ring. 'Hello, who is it?' Still groggy, but hopefully more coherent than two hours ago.

'Hi, Lydia. Jack Lisbon here. We found your brother's house and his car, but he's not around.'

'Have you called his mobile?'

'Of course I have,' Jack lied. Ringing him would be a last resort if they couldn't track him by other means. An appeal to his conscience to do the right thing and hand himself in. But there was a risk Gillmeister would panic even more and disappear into the void. 'Perhaps you could be a love and call him for me, huh? He didn't answer when I rang. I think I might've said something to upset him.'

'What the hell's going on? This is all sounding very dodgy.'

Think, Lisbon, think. 'He's in terrible danger. I need to get hold of him before the bad guys do. Otherwise…'

'What bad guys?'

Taylor was back, standing close by Jack's side, arms folded across her chest and eyes ablaze.

'I can't say. But these people think Trent's going to finger them for murdering Cameron.'

'Wait, wait, wait. This makes no sense. Why has Trent told me none of this?'

'Because he doesn't want you in danger. He's very protective of you, am I right?'

'Yes.'

Jack resumed pacing, racking his brain. Taylor's eyes popped as his act became more and more bizarre. Jack stopped walking. *Bring it home, Lisbon.* 'We know Trent was watching Cameron's house the night he was killed.'

'What? No, I told you. He was here with me.'

'No, Lydia. He slipped out for a while when you fell asleep. He was on a stake out. He knows who killed your ex-husband. The culprit learned Trent saw what happened and wants to silence him. Forever.'

'Fuck!'

'Exactly.'

'What can I do?'

'Call him now, but do not, I repeat DO NOT let him think you know anything. If you do, he'll act erratically and be in even more danger. And so will you. Do you understand?'

'Yes.'

He took a deep breath. 'When I hang up, call him immediately. I need to know where he is, but you mustn't ask him directly. He might think the bad guys have got to you and he's being lured him into a trap.'

'OK.'

'Ask him if he's anywhere near the site of the gas leak in the city.'

'What gas leak?'

'There isn't one. I'm banking on him wanting to reassure you he's safe. He might say something like, *Don't worry, I'm at the shops* or wherever he happens to be.'

'Ah, I get it. You're a sneaky one, Detective.'

That was putting it mildly. 'Just a bit of Psychology 101. So, will you call him now please?'

'Sure. I don't want anything bad to happen to him.'

'I'll be waiting.' Jack disconnected the call, pocketed the phone. He ran a hand over his face, turned to Taylor. 'Any luck?'

'Yes, to my great surprise. But that performance with Lydia, wow. That was disgraceful. The lies!'

'Give me a break. What's worse, lies or murder?'

'I thought you said whoever murdered Snyder did the world a favour?'

'Never mind what I said. Tell me what you found out.'

Before she had a chance to speak, "London Calling" erupted in Jack's pocket. He jabbed at the green button to take the call. 'Lydia?'

'Put it on loud speaker this time,' said Taylor. 'I wanna hear what she says.'

Jack did as she requested, held the mobile out in his palm. 'Where is he?'

'He wouldn't tell me.' Lydia was on the verge of tears.

'What?' Jack thundered. 'He had to!'

'No need to yell at me, Detective.' She paused to sob and sniff. 'I did…exactly…what…you asked, but he… refused…to say anything. He must be really scared.' More sobs. 'Want me to…try again…later?'

'Yes. But be discreet.'

'Lydia,' said Taylor. 'I'm listening in on the call. Is that alright with you?'

'Of course.'

'Trent's neighbour Mrs Truelove said he left in a cab with a large suitcase about an hour ago. You know where he might be headed?'

Jack's eyes bulged. He held the phone against his thigh before Lydia could answer the question, said to Taylor, 'Call the airport, train station and bus terminals. Give 'em a description of our guy, ask their security to hold him till we get there. And…' through gritted teeth '…call Cairns Police, tell 'em to send all the squad cars they can spare to the transport hubs.'

'I thought you wanted the collar.'

'I do. But it'll be worse if he escapes, 'innit? Christ, it could already be too late.'

'Jack, you can't buy a ticket or go anywhere without handing over your ID, plus there's cameras everywhere. He can't get away. If he's flown to Sydney, we'll just ask NSW Police to grab him off the plane at the other end while we work the extradition procedures.'

Everything Taylor said made sense. As long as the suspect was heading for a major transport link. But

Gillmeister had already demonstrated he was no fool. Would he be so naïve?

'Just do as I ask, then call Batista, get everyone on the phones. Ring the airlines, Queensland Rail, the bus companies. You're right, he won't get away, but it'll save a shitload of mucking about if we apprehend him before he goes anywhere.'

Taylor said, 'Onto it,' headed to the Territory, hopped in and closed the door behind her. Jack remembered Lydia was on the line, waiting.

'I'm back,' Jack said apologetically. 'Where might he have gone in a taxi, leaving his car behind?'

'Ah, lemme think,' said Lydia, breathing heavily but the crying under control. 'Maybe he's thinking of flying back to Sydney to stay with mum for a bit. Hey, do you think he already found out the bad guys are looking for him?'

'I reckon he did,' said Jack. 'Apart from leaving the state, is there anywhere local he might have headed to? A bush retreat or somewhere like that where he could hole up?'

'He'd be useless out in the scrub. But if he was desperate. Geez, I'm so scared for him now…I…' Sobs returned, choked off her words.

'Friends, a girlfriend?'

'He mentioned he's been seeing a new woman. Name starts with B. Let me think…ah…'

The pause dragged on too long for Jack's liking. 'Do you know where she lives?'

'No idea. Like I said, she's new. He's only been dating her for about…a month. But from how he spoke about her, I reckon he was rather smitten.'

'Last name?' Jack looked over to the car, watched Taylor engage over the two-way, one hand waving about animatedly.

'Sorry, no. But I've remembered the first name, if that's helpful. Bronwyn. I've always like that name. Welsh isn't it?'

'Yeah, all the women in Wales are called Bronwyn. Anything else you can remember about her?'

'Nothing. I'm really sorry.'

'That's fine, Lydia. You've been a great help.' Jack prayed the Cairns cops would nab Gillmeister before he departed for wherever he was headed. He terminated the call and trotted back to the car. He ripped open the passenger door and shot Taylor a look of desperate expectation. 'Well?'

'There's only one major train out of Cairns per day and it leaves at 8:30am. Same with the bus, which goes an hour earlier at 7:30am. I can't imagine him sleeping on a bench until tomorrow morning to get the next one. Which leaves flights. There's plenty of them, heading in all directions, even overseas. My hunch is that's where he's gone.'

'Great.' Jack rubbed his forehead. 'He could be on his way to bloody Japan!'

'Unlikely. In any case, half a dozen officers have been dispatched to the airport. The Feds and airport security are also keeping any eye out for him in the international terminal.'

'OK, let's drive to the airport and see what's occurring.'

Taylor held up a hand. 'I think we deserve a ten-minute break first. You think there's any coffee in his house?'

How did she know exactly what he wanted? 'As it happens, there's one of those Delonghi espresso machines in the kitchen. Know how to operate one?'

'How hard can it be?'

Back inside, Taylor found two cups, figured out how the machine worked, poured two cups of steaming black coffee. Setting them on the table, she glanced up at the whiteboard, divided into days of the week, times and classes. 'What the hell is Bron, do you reckon?'

'What?'

'On the board. He's written. *Mon. 14:15. Gr.10. Self def. Bron. assist.* Could that be like a bronze medallion, you reckon? Like in surf lifesaving?'

'Like hell. It's Bronwyn!'

'Who?'

'I'll tell you in the car.'

Chapter Twenty-Eight

'YOU FIND any Bronwyns on the school's website?' said Jack.

'Just the one. Bronwyn Karlsson. Physical education teacher. A bit on the severe side, judging by the photo. Quite an attractive woman overall.'

'I don't care if she's a bleedin' super model. Where does she live?'

Within minutes Taylor had obtained the address the simplest way possible. White pages online. She dialled the number to make sure the B. Karlsson listed was the woman they were seeking. The chirpy voice mail message confirmed it was. *Hi, this is Bronwyn. Sorry I missed your call. Leave a message and I'll call you back. Bi-yee!*

'You're a marvel, Claudia. Sherlock Holmes, eat your heart out.' Jack grinned.

Taylor smiled back. 'When you've got it, you've got it, I guess.'

There was no time to savour the success of Taylor's

investigative bullseye. The two-way crackled to life. Jack snatched at the receiver.

'DS Lisbon.'

'Constable Smith here, sir.'

'Yes, Kylie. What've you got?'

'The Director of Yorkville General Hospital emailed me an extract from Lydia Snyder's medical record.'

'Well done, Smith,' said Taylor. 'How on Earth did you manage that without a warrant?'

'Narelle Plumpton, the Director, was very co-operative. When I mentioned there were strong suspicions Lydia had been a victim of abuse, she couldn't dig up the details fast enough.'

'What's in the record?'

'I've forwarded the file to both of you, and also to Batista.'

'We've no time to read it, Smith.' Jack failed to keep tetchiness out of his voice. 'Summarise it please.'

'Yes, sir. Lydia presented at the Outpatients Department on Australia Day, January 26, with a fractured cheek bone and bruising to the left side of her face. She claimed to have fallen against the side of a brick barbecue. She was intoxicated with a blood alcohol concentration of 0.15.'

'Thanks, Smith, well done,' said Taylor. 'We'll be sure to read it in more detail when we get a moment.'

'Oh, I'm not finished. I also asked if it would be possible to check Cameron Snyder's records.'

'And?'

'He had a broken hand set in plaster the next day.'

'Which means the falling-into-the-barbecue story was bullshit,' said Jack. 'Snyder's fucking well hit her.'

'I guess, so.'

Jack thanked Smith for her excellent work and promised to buy her a beer after they'd apprehended Gillmeister. Smith said his arrest would leave a hollow feeling in her stomach. Especially if he got a long sentence. Snyder's death was no tragedy.

'Perhaps,' said Taylor. 'But murdering Snyder wasn't the way to achieve justice.'

'Women are sick of waiting for justice, DC Taylor. If you ask me, Gillmeister deserves a medal.'

'I didn't ask you, Constable Smith. But I note your point of view.'

Jack said, 'Over and out,' and hung up the radio handset, turned to Taylor. 'I was sensing that wasn't going to end well.'

'No sweat. I wasn't keen on getting into a philosophical discussion with Kylie over the rights and wrongs of taking the law into your own hands.'

'Good. I'm never keen on that discussion.' Because I have done the same as Gillmeister, but you must never know, dear Claudia.

Updates poured in over the two-way. Police had their eyes peeled at Cairns airport. No sign of Gillmeister. He'd not booked any flights in his name, but no one could rule out attempts to travel on false identification, alterations to appearance such as losing the beard, shaving his head etc. Despite the long odds, officers were also posted at the Greyhound terminal and the city's only train station. Again, no sign of the suspect. Jack relayed to Batista his theory Gillmeister had gone to ground at Bronwyn Karlsson's rented property and that he and Taylor were on their way, ETA six minutes. Batista offered to contact Cairns station to secure reinforcements.

'Not necessary, sir. Taylor and I can handle it.'

'Overruled. Backup's non-negotiable. You saw what he did to Snyder, didn't you?'

Jack was formulating a riposte when Batista did to him what he did to Smith. 'Over and out.'

'IS THIS IT?' Jack searched for a letter box or a street number affixed to the lowset brick wall.

'Yep. GPS says it is. Looks like a half-acre block.'

'Lovely. Places to run and hide.'

The Territory bumped along a narrow, rutted driveway, branches slapping the sides of the vehicle as it bounced along. It took less than a minute before they saw the small homestead, a neat, white weatherboarder. The front lawn was modestly enhanced by potted red and orange geraniums, swans carved out of old tyres, a couple of avocado trees. Underneath a carport sat a lime-green Toyota Yaris and three bicycles. One was adult size, the other two clearly for small children. If anything looked less threatening, it was the picture of bucolic serenity before them. Jack wound down the window, cocked an ear. Nothing, save for chirping forest birds and insects.

'Sundown's in ten minutes. Ready for this?' said Jack.

'Of course.'

'Bring the taser. I'd rather not have to shoot him if at all possible.'

'You're thinking like Smith, aren't you? You see him as some kind of hero.'

'In a way, yes. But I'm worried about collateral damage. Look at those bikes. I reckon there's a couple of kiddies in there.'

'Fair enough. Still…'

'Still nothing. Check your weapon.' Both detectives inspected their Glocks. All in order. 'This time, you take the rear. Buzz me when you're in position by the back door. Got the taser?'

'Yes.'

In a crouching run, Taylor disappeared from view. In seconds, Jack's phone vibrated in his pocket. *She's in position.* Half a dozen strides onto the porch. No need to cup an ear to the door this time. The sounds of giggling children and the hum of a TV were clear. Not the ideal environment for taking down a desperate man. Three knocks packed with all the authority he could muster. 'Bronwyn Karlsson? Open up, please.'

The patter of small feet and the door swung open. A tiny hand gripped the doorknob. The snot-nosed kid in dirty jumpsuit beamed up at Jack.

'Is your mother at home?'

'Who is it, Oliver?' A squeaky male falsetto came from within the house. Then the voice's owner appeared next to the toddler. 'Waddaya want?' A skinny, bare chested teenager in camo shorts that struggled to stay up. Lucky to be seventeen, but already sporting a pierced eyebrow, a forearm tattoo and a no-fucks attitude.

Jack flashed his badge, made sure the teenager got a glimpse of his holstered pistol. 'I've come to collect Trent Gillmeister. Is he here?'

'He's down the back paddock with mum.' The sight of the gun had zero impact on the lad's demeanour. 'They're fixing a pump or somefin.'

'Are you Bronwyn Karlsson's son?'

'Yeah. Alex.'

'Reckon you could take us there, Alex?' said Jack.

'Too easy. Has he done somefin wrong?'

'We just need to ask him a couple of questions,' said Taylor.

The lad frowned and shrugged his scrawny shoulders. 'I don't give a rat's if youse are here to arrest Trent. I don't like him much, to be honest. Mum can do better.'

Jack and Taylor followed close behind the youth as he led them away from the house. They trod a worn pathway until it gave onto a wide open expanse. A hundred metres away Trent Gillmeister, with what appeared to be a wrench in one hand and a cloth in the other, was on his knees, craning his neck to inspect the base of a huge water tank. Bronwyn sat on her haunches a metre away from him.

Taylor touched the lad on the arm 'Go back to your brother and sister.'

'Can't I stay and watch?' The lad plucked a piece of grass and started chewing it.

'Go!' said Jack. 'I'll have you for abandoning small children.'

'Whatever.' Alex trudged back towards the house, kicking stones as he went.

'That's why I never want to have kids,' said Taylor.

'My Skye will never be like him.'

'Are you that naïve? Girls are even worse,' laughed Taylor. 'Come on, let's get him.'

Only twenty metres away now, their soft-footed approach had gone undetected. With his eyes glued on Gillmeister, Jack failed to see the bandicoot hole on the edge of the path. His foot dropped straight into it, twisted slightly to the right. Pain seared through his foot, but he managed to suppress a cry. Taylor instinctively grabbed Jack around the waist, he gasped softly under his breath. Leaning on her for support, he extracted his foot from the hole, wriggled it and winced. It hurt like the blazes. He made a tentative step. Yes, he'd manage to walk, albeit with a limp.

They edged closer, still undetected. Now a mere ten

metres away, they could hear the conversation between Gillmeister and his girlfriend. 'You'll have to pop down to the hardware store.' Gillmeister clambered to his feet and wiped his brow. 'Looks like the tap's completely buggered.'

'Are they still open?'

'No, it's…'

'It's what?'

'It's too late.'

'No need to sound so dejected, babe. We'll go tomorrow.'

'No,' interrupted Jack. 'He means it's too late for him.' Gillmeister stared blankly at Jack over Bronwyn's shoulder. She snapped her neck around, mouth hung open. Gillmeister dropped the wrench on the ground with a thud. Without being asked, he held his hands in the air above his head. Jack hadn't had a peaceful surrender like this in years.

'What the hell?' said Bronwyn. 'What's going on?'

'Trent Gillmeister,' said Jack. 'I'm arresting you on suspicion of the murder of your brother-in-law…'

'Ex!'

'…Cameron Snyder.' The rest of the rights spiel was conducted with Taylor aiming a taser squarely at the suspect's heaving chest. 'Do you understand what I've said, Trent?'

Gillmeister let out a deep breath, tears welled in the corners of his eyes. 'Yes, I understand. Let's get this over with.'

Jack extracted the steel cuffs. 'Hands behind your back, mate.' As he grabbed Gillmeister's left wrist on the way down, he heard a couple of loud yelps.

Taylor!

He swung his head to see Bronwyn, face down, resting on her fingertips like a Ninja. Taylor rocked back and forth on the ground, clutching her lower leg with interlocked fingers, the taser two metres away. Bronwyn must have executed a sweep kick on Taylor, caught her completely off guard, and the taser went flying.

The distraction was enough for Gillmeister to twist his body and break free from Jack's grasp. He turned and sprinted for a chain-link fence at the end of the property. Chasing him on a bung leg was pointless, and now Taylor was out of commission. He had to act fast, or Lucy Liu here would have Jack on the ground in no time, too.

There was only one option. He levelled his pistol, took careful aim at the legs of the retreating figure. Instructors always say to aim for the centre of the body, but that was when you were under threat. Hitting the legs was more diffi-cult, and Jack hadn't been as diligent in his shooting prac-tice as he might have. 'Trent!' he screamed. 'Stop or I'll shoot.'

The man kept running, the fence closer and closer.

Jack lined him up, squeezed the trigger.

BANG!

Trent ducked his head but kept running. Only ten or so steps and he'd vault the fence and disappear. He sensed Bronwyn approaching from the side.

'Jack!' Taylor yelled. Then a guttural roar as Bronwyn was struck by the taser. Taylor must have shrugged off the pain, crawled to retrieve it.

'Good girl, Claudia!'

Once more chance. He closed his left eye, steadied his grip, fired a second time.

This time, Trent went down and stayed down.

JACK HEARD another shriek from behind. He turned to see Taylor unceremoniously ram a knee, presumably the good one, into Bronwyn's back. She wielded the cuffs like a lasso before manacling the woman. 'Stop squirming, will you! You're only making things worse for yourself.'

'Get the fuck off me!' Bronwyn would not do as she was told, wriggled like a fish on a hook. From her position on the ground, she twisted her head, caught sight of her man lying prone by the fence. 'You've killed him, you bastards!'

'I don't think so.' *I bloody hope not.* Jack hobbled towards the body, sighed with relief when he saw the man's back rising and falling slowly.

Then, a new voice. 'Detective Lisbon?'

Jack spun around. Batista's promised backup. Two burly uniforms. Their ambling walk turned into a run when they clocked the two bodies on the ground and the limping detectives. 'Officers are back at the house with the three kids. They said they heard a couple of loud bangs,' said the taller of the two uniforms. 'Christ! What's happened here then?'

'One murder suspect shot in the back of the right thigh. He's in shock but not losing blood. Not enough to worry about, anyway. One aggressive female in handcuffs. What do you want to do with her, Claudia?'

Taylor scruffed Bronwyn by the collar, hauled her to her feet. 'I'm thinking of charging her with assaulting a police officer. That's in addition to aiding and abetting.' Bronwyn went still. 'But if she stops playing the fool, I could be persuaded to let her off with a caution. Are you going to behave?'

Bronwyn nodded slowly, staring at the ground. 'I've got kids and…'

'We understand,' said Jack. 'I'm sure DC Taylor won't

press charges. As long as Trent tells us you knew nothing about what he did.'

'I swear, I didn't know anything! I just acted instinctively to protect him just now. It's my army training kicking in.'

'I'm inclined to believe you,' said Jack.

Bronwyn silently mouthed the words *thank you*.

'You know, with sweet fighting moves like you demonstrated on my colleague here, you might like to consider a career change.'

Taylor flashed Jack a dagger stare as she undid the handcuffs. 'I'm sure she's needed at the school. If she teaches self-defence to those girls like she does the business, then that's the place for Bronwyn. Doing something useful. Not wasting her life in the force.'

Freed from her shackles, Bronwyn raced to Trent, dropped to her knees and let out a terrible wail. One of the uniforms pulled her aside. 'How is he doing?' Jack called out to the officers.

'He'll live,' said the shorter one. 'Ambulance is on its way.'

'Right.' Jack smiled at Taylor. 'Looks like I made my deadline.'

'Yep. With a day to spare. Just the paperwork and processing.'

'Couldn't you handle that for me?'

'No!'

Chapter Twenty-Nine

INTRODUCTIONS OVER, it was time for the interview. With luck, it would be a short one. Jack closely observed the lawyer as he pulled a manila folder from a shiny leather portfolio. He placed the case on the floor, addressed the detectives with a businesslike smile that was more flat line than upward curve. Errol Phelan was a natty little gentleman, slicked-down hair and round rimless spectacles. He'd been flown up in a hurry from Brisbane, paid for by Lydia from an emergency advance on the trust fund money she received yesterday morning. Because of the confidentiality clause, Garfield Walters couldn't reveal where the funds came from. Lydia didn't seem to care. To her it was manna from heaven.

The irony, Jack thought. *Money set aside by Hook for the victim being used to defend the accused.* As Phelan boasted prior to the interview, Lydia engaged him on the recommendation of Walters. Phelan had by far the best record of any defence lawyer in the state. Many of his clients walked even when it seemed their guilt had been proven beyond doubt. Her brother may have murdered the love of her life, Phelan explained, but she couldn't bear the thought of Gillmeister copping a long sentence for an act of protection. That sounded illogical to Jack, but then again, people's actions were often guided by feelings far removed from logic.

The evidence was in and it was conclusive. Gillmeister's dabs and DNA were now in the system forever. They were also all over the crime scene, from the trophy to the blood droplets trailing from the kitchen into the hallway. Only the knife was missing.

'Where did you hide the murder weapon?' said Taylor.

'I got rid of it. Tossed it off the end of the Yorkville Pier.'

Jack stopped the tape and suspended the interview. He called Constable Wilson to organise a team of divers to scour the sea floor for the weapon. On the resumption of questioning, Jack pointed out the evidence given by Misty Roach. Her testimony would place Gillmeister near the scene on the night.

'We don't intend to plead innocent in this matter,' Phelan explained. 'Mr Gillmeister will, however, be seeking a reduction in the charge of premeditated murder to manslaughter.' The brief looked confidently at Jack, switched his gaze to Taylor. 'There are genuine mitigating circumstances. Ones you may be aware of, others you may not.'

'If it were up to me, sunshine, I'd reduce the charges without blinking,' said Jack. 'But it's not up to me. In any event, we're fully aware Snyder abused his wife.'

'Ex-wife,' said Gillmeister, shackled hands resting on the table. He groaned softly as he shifted position in his chair. The bullet Jack fired yesterday had nicked the man in the fleshy part of the thigh and exited out the front. A quick visit to the hospital in the back of the ambulance, a couple of stitches and then back to the remand cell for an overnight stay. Strong painkillers, hot coffee and chocolate bars supplied by the night duty constable should have made the sleepover relatively comfortable.

'Uh-uh,' said Taylor. 'She was still his wife when this incident occurred. More than a year ago, when they were living together as man and wife.'

'Are you talking about when he punched her in the face last Australia Day?'

'Yes. We know about that incident.' Taylor leaned back in her chair. 'We've joined the dots.'

'Ha! His abuse of my sister went on for years. Ever since they were teenagers. And it continued after they separated.'

'And you resented that?'

'Of course I did. It all came to a head last Monday night. One thing led to another and I guess I snapped.'

Jack held up a finger. 'The problem's the way you went about it, Trent. That's what's going to see you locked away for a long time, mate.'

'My client asserts he was provoked,' said Phelan.

Jack shook his head. 'Perhaps. But the DPP's going to push for the maximum sentence because of the ferocity of the attack. Forensics has pieced it all together, mate. You belted him with the trophy, probably dazed him or knocked him out, then you've gone and got a knife, had a few practice attempts before plunging it deep into his neck.'

'Yeah, something like that.' Gillmeister glanced at the ceiling, took a deep breath, looked back at his interrogators. 'You know, in the end it wasn't his violence that made me... that enraged me.'

'No?' said Taylor.

'Nope. It was that prostitute walking out of his house with a big smile plastered all over her face.'

'Are you a racist, Mr Gillmeister?' Taylor again.

'Of course not! What kind of question is that?'

'The sex worker is an Indigenous woman,' said Jack. 'Perhaps that played a role in your behaviour.'

'It was night. All I saw was her short skirt and high heels. That's what wound me up. What she was, not who she was.' Phelan laid a hand on his client's forearm, but Trent wasn't shutting up. 'Lydia was still sleeping with the arsehole even though he was…well, you know what he was doing to her. To think he'd have sex with my sister when it suited him, and then other women, it made me sick to my stomach…Plus, I was already riled up.'

'Why were you riled up, Trent?' said Jack. 'You travel to spend the night with Lydia, she trots off to bed and you suddenly get the urge to visit Snyder? It's sounding more and more like premeditation.'

'Yes,' intervened Phelan. 'Perhaps you should stop answering questions now.'

'No, no. It's fine. I've always been honest. I tell my students to tell the truth. I'd be a hypocrite otherwise wouldn't I?'

Phelan nodded. 'Your prerogative, mate. Although I advise against speaking any further.'

'I don't care. What's done is done.' And then, out it poured. Lydia had fallen asleep while they were watching TV, stonkered by tranquilisers. Trent picked her up and carried her to bed. As he was tucking her in, her t-shirt slipped up and he saw welts and bruises on her hip. Whether or not it was the result of a beating by Snyder, didn't matter. He drove across town to Snyder's place, to have a stern word. Maybe slap him around a bit.

'I was mad as hell, but still more or less thinking rationally. I knocked softly, figured he'd think it was the hooker coming back. Maybe she'd left something behind, you know? It was all I could do not to smash the fucking door down.' He stopped for a moment, took a drink of water. 'I was right. There was a brief smile on his face. He thought it was her. The smile soon vanished when he saw it was me, let me tell you. Showed his true colours, the coward.'

Gillmeister described the confrontation in the kitchen, how he demanded a promise from Snyder that he'd cut all ties with Lydia. He vowed he would, but Gillmeister shoved him hard in the chest for good measure and he fell.

'Cameron banged his head on the way down. More words were exchanged. I tried to get the necklace.'

'The one with the charm locket with Lydia etched onto it?' said Taylor.

'Yeah. He didn't deserve to wear her name close to his heart.' Another sip of water. 'I curse myself for leaving it in his hands. Can I get it now?'

'No,' said Jack. 'It's evidence. What happened next?'

'We struggled some more. He must've known I was going to give him a serious arse kicking because he whacked me over the head with a coffee pot. I touched my head, saw blood, and that was it.'

'Keep going,' said Jack. He wanted all the details Trent could remember.

'Something snapped in my head. You know how people say you see red when you're angry? I reckon I did that night. It wasn't just the blood, everything was a red haze.'

'Go on.'

'I chased him down the stairs into the basement. I saw his fancy pool room, thought about his business growing while Lydia was stuck in that pokey flat.'

'That's not a reason to murder him.'

'No. But the bruises, the broken cheek bone, the lies. They were enough. I dunno, I grabbed something heavy, whacked him over the head. He passed out.' Tears formed, a stray one ran down his cheek. 'Then I raced to the kitchen, grabbed the biggest knife I could find, then back to where he was lying.'

'And?' Jack knew this part would play a crucial part in the sentence Gillmeister received.

'I propped him up, kind of poked him with the knife. Jesus.' He dragged his manacled wrists to his face, wiped sweat away from his chin with a forearm. 'I couldn't bring myself to do it.'

'What?'

'I lost my nerve.'

'But you...' said Taylor. She exchanged a perplexed look with Jack.

'I realised I'd made a big mistake, decided to go home and let him lick his wounds. I thought I'd frightened him enough that he'd do what I demanded. Stop seeing Lydia. And then...he came to. It was like a zombie waking up in a fucking horror film. His eyes snapped open, filled with evil. I couldn't help myself. I struck at him, drove the blade into his neck as far as I could. If he hadn't woken up at that moment, I would've turned around and walked out the door.'

The stabbing *was* instinctive. Almost. The fact Trent had gone back to the kitchen to get the knife wouldn't help the defence. Phelan might be able to get a reduction after all. He'd have to be in top form, though. The DPP in this region wasn't known for showing leniency.

'I'll have a word with the Prosecutor, sound them out on

the possibility of a plea bargain,' said Jack. 'What do you think, Claudia?'

She nodded. 'I agree. But only to spare Lydia the agony of a trial.'

'Excellent,' said Phelan. 'I'll gather my arguments and contact the Prosecutor's Office. I'll be pushing for a wholly suspended sentence. Trent's got no priors.'

As Taylor exited Interview Room 1, Jack hung back to close up after Phelan and Gillmeister vacated. 'Come on, guys. Let's go. You've got a ride waiting for you.' Trent, now formally charged with murder, would be held in remand at Copperhead Jail until his case came to trial.

Phelan rested a hand on Gillmeister's shoulder, offered a last word of encouragement. 'Stay strong. We'll get through this.'

The prisoner's face fell as the reality of his situation finally hit home. 'You think so?'

'I'm sure of it.' Phelan then embraced Gillmeister, tears cascading down his face, pulled him close for a hug.

Jack wasn't as confident as the lawyer. But it didn't matter what Jack thought. He'd done his part, what was expected of him, caught the perpetrator and charged him appropriately.

As the escorts took Gillmeister to the waiting armoured van, Jack stood with hands on hips. *Good luck, Trent. You're going to need it.*

Chapter Thirty

THE DESK TIDY UP. A widespread ritual performed by people preparing to go on holidays. A paper placed in a tray here, bulldog clips in that container there, pens in a holder, done. The real work of the tidy up – sorting the files – would be handled capably in Jack's absence by Constable Ben Wilson.

A glance at the bottom right corner of the computer screen told Jack the good news. Shift was over in ten minutes. He logged off all systems and shut the computer down. He stood, scooped the three essential items from his desktop and delivered them to their allotted pockets: wallet – pants back, keys – pants front, phone – jacket inside.

Not many colleagues to farewell, the office was almost empty. All available uniforms were attending a serious accident involving a petrol tanker and a telegraph pole. No injuries but lots of directing traffic required. Jack could imagine the fumes, the horn honking by frustrated commuters. Sucks to be those cops, especially with a late afternoon storm forecast. Only Claudia and Batista were left on deck.

'See you in a month, Claudia.' Jack said, barely believing the words as they left his mouth.

'What? You're leaving already? There's still...nine minutes to go.'

'If I don't hustle, Batista will have me down at the crash site hosing petrol off the bleedin' road.'

Taylor rocked back in her swivel chair, looked up at him with a faint smile. What was that in her eye? Sadness? She leapt to her feet, threw her arms around his neck. Her breath was hot on his skin. 'I never thought I'd say this, but I'm going to miss you, Jack.'

'Steady on, DC Taylor,' Jack whispered an inch from her right ear. 'You weren't like this last time I went on holidays.'

She let go, took a step back. 'Your last break was a one-week fishing trip to the Great Barrier Reef. This time it's a whole month. And with this murder case coming up...'

'Relax. I checked. The Gillmeister trial doesn't come up in the court's schedule until after I get back. I'll be there to support you when it's time for us to give evidence.'

'I could've handled it without you.'

'Of course, I didn't mean...'

They stood staring into each other's eyes for a moment, unable to look away. Jack blinked first. 'Right, I'll be off then.'

'See you, Jack. Say hi to that kid of yours for me.'

'Will do.' He tipped her a salute, turned and headed for the car park.

———

STUCK IN PEAK-HOUR TRAFFIC, Jack cursed himself for taking Oliphant Avenue, busy at the best of times. In his haste to escape, he'd forgotten about the oil tanker spill. Cars were banked up for four blocks, funnelling three lanes into one like treacle through a colander. All was not lost, he had his music for company. With thoughts of London flooding through his mind, he pressed the forward button on his music compilation USB. The numbers ticked along until he reached the treasured folder. The one containing MP3 files of every Clash song ever recorded. It played in alphabetical order, but Jack liked to mix it up with shuffle. Thumping the steering wheel and shouting the lyrics to "Rock the Casbah", he attracted goggle-eyed stares from other motorists, finger pointing from children. He didn't care. He was going home.

As the song faded away, the next one launched without a pause. Only it wasn't the USB, it was his phone. He'd left it in the pocket of his jacket lying crumpled on the passenger seat. The Bluetooth connection between the mobile and the Hilux's speakers brought the details up on his dash monitor. *Holy mother of God.* What's this all about? He switched off the music, took the call.

'Assistant Commissioner, what a surprise. I thought you were still in intensive care with tubes up your honker.'

'They discharged me, thank Christ. Juanita's promised the doctors she'll put me on a strict diet so I can get this operation happening.'

'I'm pleased to hear it.'

'Listen. I heard the news this morning.' Hook's breathing came in rasps that echoed inside the car. 'You've made an arrest. Congratulations.'

'Thanks.'

'Only one problem. You've obviously got the wrong man.'

'The man you suspected, Randall Sowell, had nothing to do with the murder.'

'Bullshit.' *Cough, wheeze, cough.* 'It had to be Sowell. You've fucked up somewhere.'

'No, Ray. It's you who's fucked up. We've got over-whelming circumstantial, medical and physical evidence, and if that wasn't enough, Trent's bleedin' confessed.'

'What? I don't understand. Lydia's brother?'

'I know all about your dalliance with your wife's sister and the kid she popped out. The one you've kept hidden. What a violent prick he turned out to be, hey? There were plenty who wanted him dead. Including Trent Gillmeister.'

'I've no idea what you're talking about.'

'Yes, you do. Why deny it? Of course, you'll be called upon to give evidence, too.'

'What's in my past has nothing to do with this matter.'

'Are you referring to how you threatened four lads when they were about to testify against Snyder?'

'Hearsay.'

'You were aware Snyder systematically abused Lydia, right?'

A long pause. 'No. That's bullshit, too.'

'We'll see about that. And I'm confident the Financial and Cyber Crime Group are going to take a very keen interest in where you got the $250,000 from.'

Choking and gasping from Hook's end of the line.

'But, hey. I'm reasonable. I could be tempted to say nothing about it.'

'What?'

'Lydia's using some of that cash to pay for Trent's defence. If I spill the beans, well, the money would be confiscated, leaving poor old Trent high and dry. And that's something I don't want to happen.'

'Poor old Trent? You must be joking. He killed my son!'

'So now you're saying it *was* Trent, not Sowell?'

'I…ah…no!'

The sky darkened as low thunder rumbled and the blanket of slate-coloured clouds lowered. The forecast storm was coming early. Droplets appeared on the car's windscreen, activating the automatic wipers.

'Dear oh dear. You're in quite a pickle now, aren't you, Ray? Nothing you can do about it though.' Jack drew up next to the accident scene. He smiled and waved at Constable Trevarthen, who was directing traffic around a series of orange cones. Trevarthen flashed a big grin and gave a thumbs-up. 'I haven't decided which way I'll run with this. I guess we'll have to wait till the trial. A month in the Old Dart and it'll be clearer in my head which way to proceed.'

'Fuck you, Lisbon.'

'Everyone at Yorkville CIB wishes you a speedy recovery, sir!'

Jack disconnected the call, turned up the music and burst into song.

Chapter Thirty-One

THE FIRST-CLASS WINDOW seat offered a perfect view of London as the Qantas 777 circled in a holding pattern. Or it would have, if the fog hadn't blocked out everything except the tips of the tallest buildings. Heavy air traffic had pushed back arrival time by 45 minutes. Sarah would be pissed off with the delay, but Skye would be jumping out of her skin. It wasn't everyday she got to visit the busiest airport in Europe.

'Another drink, sir?' The flight attendant, polite to the point of annoying, tilted her head to the side and beamed through a face packed with make-up thicker than a slice of bread.

Jack blinked, tired from a lack of sleep over the 18-hour flight with only a short stopover in Singapore. Waiting to reboard at Changi Airport he'd checked his email. He nearly fainted when he read the message from Taylor. *Hook had another heart attack. Didn't pull through.* 'Any chance of a coffee?'

'Certainly.'

Jack fired up his mobile, connected to the onboard Wi-Fi and re-read the press-release attached to Taylor's email. Raymond Ogden Hook was described as a role model for every officer in the Queensland Police. An unblemished record of service stretching over 35 years. He left behind a wife and two children. *Would have been three if Trent hadn't offed the secret son.* Jack was in two minds about exposing Hook now he was dead. Seemed in poor taste.

The attendant brought the coffee and asked if Jack wouldn't mind drinking it fast. She'd had word they were about to commence descent. As she picked up another passenger's tray, the pilot announced it was time to buckle up, he'd received clearance to land. Jack's heart thumped as the wheels dropped from the undercarriage and the engines roared. After five years away from home, he was finally going to see his beautiful daughter.

The formalities were a blur. He'd never flown first class, so the expedited clearance of security and customs came as a pleasant surprise. Walk-through metal detector, a going over with the buzzy wand thing, retina scan, a glance at his passport, all over with a minimum of fuss.

And then, it was time to face the audience. His heart galloped, he felt like a teenager on a first date.

Carousel. Suitcase full of gifts. Green lane. The automatic door slid open, he rushed through, almost tripping over his drag-along bag.

And there she was. Skye. Dressed in the Yorkville Scorpions basketball uniform he'd mailed her for Christmas, hopping up and down. Untamed curly hair and a smile brighter than North Queensland sunshine. Twice as big as he remembered her. The suitcase castors clacked on the concrete floor. Jack was sprinting now. Her arms were outstretched, her eyes gleaming. Jack grabbed her under the armpits, she squealed as he hoisted her into the air.

And then, the old familiar voice, the Jamaican accent. In his fixated state, he'd somehow failed to see Sarah, his ex-wife, standing next to Skye. 'You be damn careful, Jack Lisbon. Don't you hurt that child, or there'll be hell to pay.'

Jack pulled Skye's head tight against his cheek. 'She's in the safest hands she could possibly be.'

'If you say so. C'mon. There'll be a long queue at the taxi rank if we don't hurry.'

'I've pre-ordered a limo.' Thanks, Jabba. First class perks supplied from beyond the grave.

'How on Earth can you afford that?'

'Because,' said Skye. 'My Daddy's the best detective in the whole wide world!'

'What she said.' Jack laughed, put Skye back on the ground.

Then, something dawned on him. His adoring daughter might be delighted with the return of Jack Lisbon, but there were many in London who wouldn't be. He'd made a ton of enemies when he worked for the London Metropolitan Police, criminals with long memories and short fuses. Coming home could have put not only his life in danger, but Skye's. If anything happened to her he'd never forgive himself. He gripped her hand tight. 'You ready? Let's go.'

Next in The Fighting Detective Series

vinci-books.com/shot-heart

When detective Jack Lisbon's daughter is kidnapped, he assembles an unlikely team to track down the culprits.

Keep turning the pages for a free preview…

A free prequel novella...

vinci-books.com/takedown-free

**Get the explosive prequel to The Fighting
Detective series, absolutely free.**

Shot to the Heart: Prologue

MCNAIR'S BOXING Club lay in wait at the end of the alley like a vengeful enemy. It was the club where Jack Lisbon trained and fought as a young man. It still bore the name of its original owner and founder, Angus McNair, a light-heavyweight who abandoned the tough shipyards of Glasgow to pursue a boxing career in London.

The tale of the rise and fall of Angus McNair was the stuff of urban folklore. Jack had heard the story a hundred times, often with different endings, depending on who was telling it. Some elements were undeniable truths. Others were shrouded in speculation.

As Jack and his daughter Skye strode down the alley, hands gripped together, his mind harked back to the colourful history of the gym and its eponymous owner.

Angus McNair, apprentice welder with a guaranteed future of drudgery had he remained on the docks, had a special ability. He could fight like a tiger. After moving to London, he rapidly climbed to the top of the light-heavyweight rankings. A rare talent, he defeated every opponent who stood in his way. McNair claimed the title of British Southern Area Champion in 1968 by conquering the legendary West Indian pugilist, Clive Anderson. Killer Clive, loved and respected as a hard-but-fair boxer, had made the fateful error of not retiring in time. Cocky to the point of arrogance, 41-year-old Anderson agreed to defend his title by taking on the younger, fitter, hungrier Angus McNair. By the accounts of those who attended, it was a classic duel, a dog fight that went the full fifteen rounds. The canvas became so slippery with blood, sweat and spit that the boxers, slipping and sliding, had to expend massive energy reserves just to keep their feet. The champ Anderson fought bravely, with every fibre of his being, taking innumerable blows to the head and body. He hit the canvas twice, clambered to his feet and shaped up to resume the battle both times. As the surviving footage shows, he dished out as good as he got, also sending McNair to the deck two times. At the final bell, the referee raised the Scotsman's hand, new champion by a split decision.

Over the next two years, Angus McNair grew in skill and mental toughness, defeating every contender who dared step into the ring, the majority by knockout. He scraped together enough money to put a deposit down on a loan to buy the derelict R.J. Grace boot factory in Peckham, South London. Over the next year he converted it into a rudimentary gym, setting up a future for himself and his young family.

He hired a manager to run the gym and concentrated on his boxing career, dreaming of making the big time in America, his name in lights at Caesar's Palace. But, just like Anderson and a thousand fighters before him, McNair came to believe in his own invincibility, fought one fight too many when he should have hung up the gloves. That was one version of the story of the fall of Angus McNair, and a plausible one at that.

According to the second version, McNair's trainer, renowned disciplinarian "Sugar" Richard Higgins, pushed his charge into the bout when he hadn't fully recovered from a bad shoulder injury. Again, it wasn't too hard to agree with that.

And then there was the third version, the one aired in bars and lounge rooms around London to this day. The one Jack believed.

The man who took down McNair was a dirty southpaw from the East End, Alexander Gallagher. One balmy summer's night in 1973, in a crowded, smoky auditorium in central London, Alex Gallagher shattered Angus McNair's dream of retaining his title for a record sixth time. He also shattered the plucky Scot's jaw, nose and cheekbone. Gallagher sat McNair on his backside ten seconds into round eight with a savage combination of head shots. Fifteen minutes later, the Scotsman was in the back of an ambulance, struggling to breathe through a smashed nose, a mouth turned to pulp, blocked with twisted cartilage, broken teeth, swollen lips and tongue. Two days later Angus McNair died on a hospital bed. Internal bleeding leading to heart failure.

How had the fight taken such a lethal turn?

According to the story Jack believed, between the seventh and eight rounds of the fight, Alex Gallagher cheated. He'd run out of ideas, McNair was dominating, closing in for the kill. Surrounded by his trainer, cornerman and cutman, who obscured the view of the referee and any cameras that happened to be filming, underneath his padded boxing mitts Gallagher slipped on a pair of weighted gloves. They were made of light material and had pockets filled with flat bits of steel. These made his punches three times harder and heavier. The assertions could never be proven, especially with the passage of time, yet Jack had no doubt about its veracity. Why? Because in his formative years Jack had come to know Alex Gallagher well, after the man had become Jack's own mentor in the junior ranks. And he'd learned the boxer-turned-trainer was an unethical, unscrupulous, contemptible bastard.

A decade after the deadly bout, Alex Gallagher secretly purchased the gym from McNair's widow. Where he got the money from was a mystery then, and a mystery today. In a gesture of magnanimity, Gallagher bestowed upon it the name of the man whose life he'd taken in the ring. Gallagher successfully maintained the pretence he was only the manager of the gym, that it was owned by a secret syndicate. But after his death five years ago, it was revealed the deeds to the boxing club were in Gallagher's name. Why he chose to hide his ownership remained a mystery, one Jack, despite his natural curiosity, was in no way keen to unravel. *Let buried dogs lie, sunshine.*

Shot to the Heart: Chapter One

ON A COOL AND CLOUDY AFTERNOON, Jack stood in a cobblestoned back alley in South London, clutching a tiny hand, contemplating his next move. A paraphrased Clash tune came to mind. *Should they stay or should they go?* Should he lead his daughter away from this place of bad memories, or should he let her learn about the reality of his past? The smart thing would be to leave – take her to the zoo, to the London Eye for a spin, maybe Madam Tussauds or a cruise up the Thames. Something fun that a girl her age would enjoy.

Then again, why shelter her? She was a tough kid. She deserved to know more about her own father, about his roots. And for that to happen, a visit to McNair's Boxing Club was mandatory. Besides, Skye herself said she was dead keen to check the place out. She'd seen most of the famous attractions the capital had to offer, but never the inside of a grimy South London gym. And Jack would protect her. What could go wrong?

The blinking neon sign out the front had been fixed

since Jack's last bloody visit five years ago. And a new door had been installed, solid steel with a security number pad. Back in the day, anyone could simply walk in off the street, pay the entry fee, do a spot of training and be on their way. The gym was a democratic facility, accessible to all. Gallagher was happy to take anyone's money. But lately things in the old town were changing, and not for the better. Jack had read a newspaper story about a spike in street crime in recent months, even a random terrorist attack less than a mile from where they stood. An extremist of some faith or other hacked a grandmother to death with a machete in broad daylight. Now it seemed even a gym full of tough geezers was scared. Which went some way to explain the new security arrangements.

Jack cupped an ear to the door. Faint sounds of activity inside. A humming blended with intermittent clanks. The new door must be inches thick, he couldn't tell if there was one person inside training or a hundred. He knocked hard and waited for half a minute. No response. He gazed down to his left. 'You sure you want to go in there, love? It's nothing special, you know. Just a gym.'

'Yes, I'm sure. I want to see where you learned how to be a boxer so you could collar all the villains and toe-rags.'

Jack raised an eyebrow. 'Where did you learn to speak like that?'

'Watching cop shows on television.' He'd have to have a word with his ex Sarah about the girl's viewing habits.

He knocked two more times. No luck.

Maybe it's not meant to be after all. With an apologetic shrug, he tugged Skye's hand and turned to head back to the other end of the alley, when a track-suited youth with a spring in his step stopped, removed his headphones and smiled at Jack, then Skye. Garbled rap music escaped the cans. 'You need help?'

'We'd like to go inside for a look.'

'Why?'

'I used to box out of this gym when I was a lad. My name's Jack Lisbon.'

The lad's eyes widened, as if the name meant something. 'One second.' He turned, tapped a combination of eight numbers, which Jack discretely observed and memorised. The door made a beeping sound and the teenager shouldered it, held it open with his back and waved the visitors in. 'After you, Mr Lisbon and guest.'

Then, a hesitation. The question repeated in Jack's head. *Should they go in or not?* Surely what happened five years ago was fading in people's memories. Alex Gallagher's murder made national headlines at the time. Jack prayed that half a decade later the matter was no longer a topic of conversation.

'You two comin' in or what?' said the lad, tapping a foot.

Jack clapped his hands and exhaled heavily. 'Yeah, why not!'

The wiry youth disappeared behind a rack of disc weights and Jack and Skye stood blinking in the dimly lit open space. Besides the refurbished entrance via the alleyway, not much had changed since Jack was last here, when he'd emptied the safe of tens of thousands of pounds and legged it from the scene of the gruesome crime he'd committed. He took in the same old boxing ring with its tattered turnbuckles, the same old concrete floor, cracked paint on the walls, ancient body building equipment. Off to one side, the small administration area, home to filing cabinets full of personal records, and also the place where Jack had killed Gallagher with a sharp letter opener to the jugular. How he itched to get in there, see if there were any blood stains left behind after all this time. Overarching everything tangible was that characteristic smell, almost a taste, caressing the palate of his mouth. A blend of chalk, liniment and stale sweat. To Jack that aroma was like the finest perfume.

'As I live and breathe.' A voice came from behind his left shoulder. Jack turned to see a familiar face, a man roughly his own height and build, lighter coloured hair and features that were much less battered. He dabbed sweat from his underarms with a fluffy white towel. 'It's Jack Lisbon, back from Oz. And who's this?' The man looked down at the beaming young girl gripping Jack's hand.

'All right, Bruiser.' He could hear his own London accent, softened after years in Australia, thicken as he spoke to another born-and-bred Cockney, Lex "Bruiser" Buskin. Jack gazed down at his daughter, his chest swelling with pride. 'This is my girl, Skye. I thought I'd show her around the old stomping ground.'

'Not a nice place for a young lady, though, is it?' Bruiser shook his head. As Jack recalled, the man was a stock market trader who liked to spar with semi-professional boxers. He was almost good enough to have a crack at competitive boxing himself, but the man treasured his good looks too much to risk it.

Grab your copy…
vinci-books.com/shot-heart

About the Author

Blair Denholm is a born-and-bred Australian crime fiction writer whose previous jobs have been as varied as translator, debt collector, technology researcher, banking and insurance consultant, and even car-wash attendant. Over the years he has lived and worked in New York, Moscow, Munich, Abu Dhabi and Australia. His life-long love of sports is reflected in the plots of The Fighting Detective series.

Denholm's flagship series, The Fighting Detective, stars ex-boxer Detective Sergeant Jack Lisbon and is set in the steamy tropics of North Queensland, Australia. The series features heavy doses of noir crime with a vigilante justice twist. So far there are eight novels and one prequel novella in the series, with more in the pipeline.

Denholm's debut novel, *SOLD*, is the first in a noir trilogy featuring the detestable yet lovable one-man wrecking ball Gary Braswell. The book was long-listed for movie adaptation by Screen Queensland in 2019. The other books in this series are *Sold to the Devil* and *Sold Dirt Cheap*.

Denholm has also written two thriller novels set in Russia. Captain Viktor Voloshin is a hard-boiled investigator who has to fight the establishment in order for justice to be served in his own special way. The first in this series, *Revolution Day*, was published in 2021, with the follow-up, *The Defector*, released in 2024. One more book will round off this series.

In 2024, Denholm signed on with UK-based publisher Vinci Books.

Blair Denholm grew up in suburban Brisbane, Queensland. After two lengthy stints in Tasmania, he now resides in the relatively cooler climes of the Southern Downs region of Queensland with his partner, Sandra, and faithful dog, Bruno.

Acknowledgments

A huge thanks to everyone who helped me produce this novel, the third in The Fighting Detective series. Props to all my advance readers, Don and Jiver for spotting the typos that elude me, and my growing band of Jack Lisbon fans. And always, to Sandra.